ACHARYA CHATURSEN

Acharya Chatursen (1891–1960) was one of Hindi's most prolific writers. He studied at Jaipur Sanskrit College, where he obtained Shastri and Acharya degrees in Literature and Medicine. He started his professional career as a physician before devoting himself to writing. Over a writing career spanning four decades, he published more than eighty works spanning the genres of Fiction, Drama, Politics, Literary Criticism, Poetry and Medicine. *Vaishali Ki Nagarvadhu* (literally, *The Bride of the City of Vaishali*, of which this book is a translation), *Somnath*, *Goli* and *Vayam Rakshamah* are among his famous novels. His novel *Dharamputra* was adapted into a Bollywood film and won the National Film Award for the Best Feature Film in Hindi in 1961.

PRATIBHA VINOD KUMAR

Pratibha Vinod Kumar (1941–2020) obtained a BA in English Literature, Philosophy and Sanskrit from Maharani College (Jaipur), MA in English Literature from Rajasthan University and BEd from Annamalai University. She won gold medals at the intermediate (senior school) and BA levels. She taught English at Banasthali Vidyapeeth (Rajasthan, 1961–1963), St. Michael's School (Durgapur, 1963–1985) and Rotary Public School (Gurgaon, 1985–1991). Her previous published work includes translations of two classics of Hindi literature – Jaishankar Prasad's *Kamayani* and Bhagwati Charan Verma's *Chitralekha* – and an anthology of new writing, *Hindi Tales of Mystery and Imagination* Vol. I into English. A.K. Kulshreshth is her son's pen name.

BALWANT KAUR

Balwant Kaur has BA and MA degrees in Hindi Language and Literature from Miranda House, Delhi University. Her area of research in her PhD was the comparative study of Hindi and Urdu women writers. Apart from four languages (Hindi, English, Urdu and Punjabi), she also has a deep interest in Indian classical music. She has taught at Miranda House for the past fifteen years. Her areas of focus are modern fiction, gender studies and the partition of India. She was a member of the editorial team of the prestigious Hindi Literary Magazine *Hans* for ten years. She has had many essays and translations published in literary journals. She has also edited some important literary works, including an anthology of women's autobiographical fiction, two collections of Rajendra Yadav's editorials, a fifteen-volume collection of Rajendra Yadav's complete works, and the re-issue of a rare 1931 Hindi collection of poetry by women.

BRIDE OF THE CITY

VOLUME 2

First published in Hindi in two volumes in 1948–1949

This translation © 2021 Ashish Kumar

Published by Cernunnos Books Pte. Ltd., Singapore, 2021
www.cernunnosbooks.com

Literary editors: Balwant Kaur (Hindi) and N. Henaff (English)
Hindi advisors: Archana Verma and Balwant Kaur

Interior design and composition: 52 Novels
Cover illustration and design by Zoya Chaudhury

ISBN: 978-981-14-9553-3

BRIDE OF THE CITY

VOLUME 2

'VAISHALI KI NAGARVADHU'
वैशाली की नगरवधू

ACHARYA CHATURSEN

With an Afterword by
Balwant Kaur

Translated by
Pratibha Vinod Kumar and
A.K. Kulshreshth

Cernunnos
BOOKS

Dedicated to the memory of
Archana Verma

INTRODUCTORY NOTE

The original text uses ancient Indian units of time, such as mahurt. For the sake of simplicity, these have been converted in this translation into their modern equivalent. A 'watch' equals three hours.

The traditional units of distance used in the original text such as dhanush and kos have been converted into miles and feet. Ten feet are equal to one metre and one mile is equal to 1.6 kilometres.

Some names and descriptions of places have been shortened in this translation for readability. The cities of Vaishali, Rajgrih and Champa are in the present-day Indian State of Bihar, while the Kingdom of Kosala is in eastern Uttar Pradesh, to the west of Bihar.

Names are spelt in a simplified way. Generally, an 'a' at the end of a name should be pronounced as 'aa', as in the end of Africa.

The book contains several references to the distant University of Takshila, the world's first university established 2,700 years ago in the Kingdom of Gandhar. Takshila is in the Punjab province of Pakistan.

Northern India
c. 500 BCE

CAST OF PRINCIPAL CHARACTERS

VAJJI REPUBLIC

Ambapali, Bride of the City.
Mahanaman, her father.
Madlekha, her maidservant.
Lallbhatt, her guard.
Harshdev, her first lover.
Sunand, the chief minister.
Singh, a leader in war.
Kapyak, his principal aide.
Jayaraj, a soldier.
Balbhadra, a bandit.
Bhadranandini, a courtesan.
Prabhanjan, a barber.
Kritpunya, a merchant.
Gautam, the Buddha – the Shakya Sage, sometimes referred to as Tathagat.
Mahavir, the founder of Jainism, born in Vaishali.

KINGDOM OF MAGADHA

Bimbisar, the emperor.
Acharya Varshkar, the chief minister.
Chandrabhadrik, a senior general.
Somprabh, a soldier and a scholar.
Kundani, his sister.
Shambh, his follower and assistant.

KINGDOM OF ANGA

Chandrabhadra, the princess.
Dadhivahana, the king.

KINGDOM OF KOSALA

Prasenjit, the king.
Vidudhab, his son.
Kalingasena, a princess.
Bandhul Malla, a general.
Karayan, a general.
Ajit Keskambali, a priest.

PREFACE

I had dreams of making bags of money when I started out on the writer's life. I was young. This was in 1909. In the four decades since then, I have written eighty-four books of various lengths and on diverse subjects. My articles in magazines would run into, perhaps, ten thousand pages. I did not gain anything in material terms from my writing journey. I did lose a lot. I could even say that I lost everything – wealth, peace of mind and rest. My youth and my reputation wilted away.

Today, I gladly declare that my previous literary output over the last forty years of my life – this body of work that cost me all that I had – is worthless. I humbly gift this book to my readers as my first work.

It is true that this is a novel. But it is even more true that this is a serious enquiry seeking to peer through the haze of two millennia that has shrouded the ebb and tide of religion, literature, politics and culture and that historians have chosen to ignore.

That I have declared my past work to be worthless and this to be my first work is an outcome of my belief. However, I have no right to take pride in my work. I request you, dear reader, to see if you can discern a latent meaning that is separate from the narrative. You may find the fundamental truth that drove me to research the Aryan, Buddhist, Jain and Hindu literature for ten years as I wrote this book.

Chatursen

1 January 1949
Gyaandhaam
Shahadara
Delhi

CHAPTER 91

A FINE MORNING

The flames of the scented lamps had dwindled and disappeared into the soft light of dawn. The mellow light peered through the windows and peeped into the corners of the rooms. A singer's melodious voice sang to a skilful lute player's strumming, adding exuberance to the fresh morning air.

Ambapali stretched on her luxuriant, milky white bed. She pulled her disarrayed robes to cover her body. Her eyes were still bleary as she looked at the bright rays of the sun streaming through the large windows of her room. She enjoyed the rise and fall of the song. 'Ah, Madlekha', she murmured. It was such a divine pleasure to wake up in this soft bed, after a good night's sleep, caressed by the morning breeze and nourished by Madlekha's song. She reached out and struck a copper gong next to her bed.

A young woman appeared. 'Good morning, Lady!' she said with a shy smile. 'It is the first morning of the Spring Festival.'

A dreamy smile played on Ambapali's face. Languidly, she rolled towards a chest next to the head of her bed and picked up a pearl necklace. She tossed it to the young woman with a smile. She caught it, bowed and put it on, her dimples showing as she suppressed her laughter by pressing her lips.

'Bless you, girl', Ambapali said. 'Go get the dressing room ready.' The young woman hopped away.

Ambapali sank back into bed and closed her eyes again, lost in the song and soaking in the morning's joy. Through her closed eyes, she could make out the usual movements in the room. A maid came in to light incense sticks in each corner of the room. Another brought in flower garlands and started stringing them together. A third opened the smaller windows. Soon, the room was full of light and scent.

Shortly after the song stopped, Madlekha knocked on the open door and smiled at Ambapali. She bowed and said, 'The dressing room awaits you, Lady Ambapali. Your admirers have been lining up since the crack of dawn to express their greetings on this festival day.' Her eyes twinkled. 'I wonder if they have bothered to wish their own families yet!'

Ambapali laughed and stretched her arms again. She rolled to the edge of the bed and got out of it. She looked into a large mirror with her intoxicated eyes. The mirror never ceased to flatter her, its eloquence so subtle compared with that of her admirers. 'Sister, tell them Lady Ambapali will grant them an audience in a while', she said.

Madlekha grinned, bowed and left. When she looked over her shoulder from the door, Ambapali was still smiling at the mirror.

CHAPTER 92

SPRING FESTIVAL

The outermost courtyard of the Palace of Seven Worlds was full of every means of transport available to the civilised world. There were chariots, elephants, horses and palanquins. In the inner yard, the rich and the powerful rubbed shoulders in all their finery. Uniformed guards scurried about, directing a web of activity.

A wide, sweeping path went through to the inner buildings of the Palace of Seven Worlds. At the end of this path stood Ambapali's chariot, which had the status of a national emblem. Eight horses were harnessed to it, each of them a fine specimen of the Indus breed, with straight ear lobes, long muzzle and flaring nostrils. The carriage had golden urns at the corners and white silk draping and flaming orange flowers decorations. Its flag, bearing the symbol of a fish, fluttered energetically in the breeze. The chariot stood in front of a large wooden door painted a dull red.

The door was flung open, and the strident sounds of conches filled the air, drowning out the hubbub of the waiting crowd.

At the centre of the doorway stood Ambapali, dressed in a shimmering yellow dress flowing from her shoulders to her toes. She wore a diadem topped by a rare yellow topaz. Her earrings were of blue sapphires, and her necklace dotted with emeralds. Twenty-one jewels weighed the waistband, stressing her figure. The morning breeze played with her thick tresses and made her robes hug her body and outline her firm, shapely breasts. The light smile playing on her lips would have struck any man whom she favoured with a look like a bolt of lightning. But she gazed into the distance, regal and confident, aware of the effect of her appearance on the crowd.

A deathly silence fell on those closest to the doorway, spreading in an instant over the entire crowd. Ambapali took handfuls of marigold petals from the large baskets her maids held and scattered them in the breeze, and dozens of maids followed suit. The wall of the large compound became a canvas of yellow dots.

The crowd exploded in a spontaneous, primal chorus. 'Victory to Lady Ambapali! Victory to the queen of the Spring Festival! Victory to the Benefactress of the City!' The shouts echoed in the skies as they blended into a systematic, ordered chanting led by the most enthusiastic men. Ambapali laughed with childlike joy and joined her palms to acknowledge the fervour of her admirers. Pulsating drumbeats lent a cadence to the chants, and an invisible group of musicians struck up a lively tune on their lutes.

The head of security, a giant named Lallbhatt, walked up the steps to Ambapali. 'Victory to Lady Ambapali!' he said, with his gaze lowered to the ground as if he was addressing a goddess. 'The chariot is ready, and the Sun god signals his approval for the procession to start.'

Ambapali turned back to take in the sight of the Palace of Seven Worlds on this very special day. Then she nodded and walked down the steps with her graceful gait, following Lallbhatt who raised his thick golden staff to signal that the waiting men must make way for the Bride of the City. Her ardent admirers showered flower petals on her, even as they kept a respectful distance. The ground turned into a bed of roses and marigolds.

The music reached a crescendo as Ambapali climbed on to the chariot and raised her hands, turning in each direction to greet the delirious crowd. Two maids applied red paint to the edges of her soles and then sat at her feet. Two other maids took their positions behind her, fanning her with feather brushes. A troop of cavalry from Kamboj formed a rectangle around the carriage. As their horses started trotting, the charioteer cracked his whip in the air, and the chariot lurched forward, its bells tinkling.

The cheering subsided a bit as the crowd manoeuvred itself to align with the stately procession. Many men abandoned their horses to run along with the chariot, holding on to it. The road ahead was full of festive revellers. The windows of the houses lining the path seemed to overflow with women and children calling out to Ambapali, showering flower petals on her, and waving flags. Ambapali was a consummate public figure by then. She bowed to the crowds, raised her hands, touched her heart and joined her palms. Her smile did not lose its radiance for even an instant. The bright bunting and flags, the riot of colours, the city people exuberance, their obvious efforts to wear their best new clothes and jewellery and their loud cheering made her feel giddy with pleasure.

The chief of the army joined the procession at a large junction, raising his sword to his head in salute. Ambapali greeted him with joined palms. Four of his personal guards followed him. He carried a silver trumpet that he blew every few feet, as he called out to the crowd, 'Citizens! Make way for Lady Ambapali, the queen of the Spring Festival! Make way!' He showed no resentment at the joyous chaos ahead of him. The procession inched forward, with Ambapali being feted at every turn of the chariot's wheels. The earlier chanting had decomposed into a boisterous general commotion.

The sun was high and bright when the chariot reached its destination, a mango grove. Ambapali allowed her maids to help her down. Despite the infectious energy of the crowd, she was a little tired. Beads of sweat glittered on her forehead like small precious gems. The maids led her to a milky white canopy covering a large white seat lined with cushions. Ambapali sank into the chair and rested her shoulder on a thick bolster. She closed her eyes and took in the mango leaves' scent. The air was cold, and the dense trees filtered the tumult.

'Sister Madlekha, bring me some Madhvik wine', Ambapali said. Madlekha poured the red wine into a small green emerald bowl. Ambapali smiled at her and drained the wine, swirling it in her mouth to relish the sensation.

Soon, beds and cushions dotted the grove and nearby forest clearing, found occupants, and the wines flowed freely. Groups of musicians and dancers performed for the assembled citizens, many of whom joined in the dances before returning to seats to rest and drink. Some young men preferred to prance about with their friends and companions on tree branches.

The more energetic of the men rode out hunting. An area had been set aside for the spoils of the hunt, and men were at work to skin and cook the animals. The trickle of hunted animals grew into a large set of piles. There were deer, rabbits, boars, skylarks, pheasants and even a few bison. Ambapali praised the skills of the hunters, and every word of praise from her energised them to go back for more trophies.

CHAPTER 93

THE HUNT

The third watch of the day had passed. The sun's fierce rays pierced the canopy of the trees with less ferocity. The sunlight had mellowed. Some young nobles who had had their fill of wine asked Ambapali to join the hunt. Ambapali was rested and felt content with the wine and light food she had consumed. Troupes of musicians and dancers had regaled her with their performances. She accepted the invitation with alacrity, as she was itching for a change.

The hunting party undertook their activity with mock seriousness. They arranged a hunting outfit for Ambapali. She wore a white silk turban topped by a diamond and a loose brown jacket over her dress, trousers and knee-length leather shoes. She transformed herself into a handsome, if effeminate, hunter from a noble family. When her maids showed her a mirror, she burst out laughing and rolled on the mattress until tears came to her eyes. Then she proudly stepped out of the canopy. Stunned, the young men around remained silent for a few moments and then burst into loud applause.

Prince Swarnasen jostled to the front of the crowd, leading his horse, and bowed theatrically. He said, 'May I request you, good sir, to do me the honour of being my partner in the hunt?'

Ambapali replied with a straight face, 'I will be delighted to accompany the honourable prince, if only I may have a horse, a bow and arrows.'

'Ah, that is easy to arrange, Sir!' Swarnasen said. He leapt off his snow-white horse, bowed again and gave his own bow and quiver to Ambapali.

Ambapali fastened the bow and quiver full of arrows to her shoulders. She struggled so hard to contain her laughter that she seemed to frown. 'Will the prince not help his guest on to the horse?'

'Not only on to the horse, but I shall also be available to get you off the horse, Sir!' Swarnasen said.

Ambapali burst out laughing and gave her hand to the prince. She was an expert at horse-riding, and the prince had little effort to make to help her. The prince snapped his fingers, and another horse was brought for him.

As they readied to gallop into the forest, Lallbhatt, the head of security, motioned for her to stop.

'Oh, don't worry!' Ambapali said. 'Stay here with Madlekha and the others.' Before Lallbhatt could protest, the horses' hoofs were kicking up dust. Swarnasen and Ambapali disappeared into the forest.

After a few minutes of riding, Swarnasen slowed his horse, and Ambapali's followed suit. Swarnasen said, 'It is so peaceful here!'

'Indeed', Ambapali said. 'If only man's heart could be like this.'

'That would be the end of interesting times.'

'Why?'

'Only the disquieted heart can dream of courage.'

Ambapali smiled.

'Have you thought about it, Sir – I mean, Lady Ambapali?'

'About what?'

'The grave aspect of love, where a man loses himself and gets the fruit of life?'

Ambapali smiled. 'No, I cannot say that I have had the chance to think of such heavy matters.'

'So, you consider this heavy?'

'If a man loses himself and gets the fruit of life…that sounds like a heavy matter to me.' Ambapali looked askance at Swarnasen.

'Are you still joking, Lady?'

'Oh no, Sir, I am very serious now.' Ambapali put on a severe mask. They had let the horses slow down to a canter. They had been riding uphill, and the climb was now steeper, the forest thicker. A golden light played on the two riders' faces.

'What are you thinking, Prince?' Ambapali asked after Swarnasen seemed to lose himself in a train of thought that made him frown.

'Shall I tell you the truth?'

'If it is not unpleasant.'

'I dare not.'

'I thought you were renowned as a brave prince!' Ambapali said.

'Now you must joke, Lady. Well, I wanted to say that I love you. More than my own life.'

'Only that much?' Ambapali laughed.

'Is that too little?'

'Why would it be too little?' Ambapali's eyes twinkled.

'Then, you accept my love?'

'But I am bound to, am I not, Prince? I may love every man in Vaishali, may I not?'

Swarnasen's face fell. 'But my love is unlike that of the others.'

'I see.' Ambapali suppressed a smile. 'So, does it have a singularity?'

'It is pure. It comes from my heart, Lady Ambapali! And the day you accept my love for what it is will be the day I consider my life blessed.'

'Well, well! That is a strong statement to make, Prince. On the one hand, you can consider your life blessed today. On the other, I need more than a declaration of love at this moment. I need…water. I am completely parched after all that wine!'

'In that case, we are at the perfect spot. Do you see the pond there? It has clear, blue water. Let us stop, drink our fill, and cool ourselves in the fresh shade next to it.'

'That is just what I needed. But I have to say that my stomach is rumbling as well!'

'I have something that will help, Lady. In my pouch, I am carrying roasted nuts and pork. The meat is still hot. In fact, my Greek slave is without parallel when it comes to roasted pork.'

'Perhaps you love her, Prince?'

'Oh, no, no, Lady. There are flowers that are meant to be offered to the gods, and those that are meant to be…'

'I see. But the pond is here, and you were right, it is inviting!'

The prince stopped his horse, jumped down and offered his hand to Ambapali to help her dismount. Ambapali thanked him with a smile. She went straight to the pond, lay on the ground and drank her fill. She enjoyed the mixed scents of the moist grass and mud. It had been long since she last experienced them. Then she sat and gazed at the water and the sky reflection in it. The prince said something which interrupted her trance. She stood up, walked to the thick shade of a tree, and lay on the carpet of grass.

As the prince walked to her after drinking his fill, she said, 'Now is the time – perhaps I should verify your slave's skills?'

Swarnasen took his pouch to her and brought out the packets of nuts and pork. Ambapali tasted them in small bites, closed her eyes and purred with happiness. 'Ah, Prince, these are delightful! You must try them as well!' She looked askance at him. 'Your Greek slave appears to have put her heart into her cooking.'

Swarnasen laughed. 'Perhaps she has, but are you jealous, Lady Ambapali?'

'Of a slave's love? No, friend, I am not keen on competing with such intense love. I should congratulate you, though, Prince.'

'You are too hard, Lady Ambapali!'

'And the woman is perhaps as soft as butter, Prince?'

'But why compare at all, Lady?'

'Now that you mention comparison, if there were no comparison, why would this lowly prostitute Ambapali be envious of her?'

The answer perplexed the prince. 'Forgive me, Lady Ambapali. Perhaps we did not intend the conversation to go there.'

Ambapali chuckled, and her eyes danced. 'Let us leave grave matters for grave times. Here, enjoy this.' She placed a choice piece of meat in the prince's mouth.

Swarnasen closed his eyes and sighed as he basked in the warm sensation of being fed by Ambapali. When he opened his eyes, he saw that Ambapali was pale and trembling. A loud roar made the ground and the air shiver. The horses, startled, stopped grazing and whinnied in fear. The birdsong around them stopped.

Swarnasen sprang to his feet. The pall of fear that had cast a shadow on his face only lasted for an instant. He listened for more signals and then beckoned the horses that came straight to him and stood with their ears erect.

'It is a lion. We must hurry, Lady!' he said. He did not need to urge Ambapali. In an instant, the two were on their horses, and Swarnasen's eyes darted around, his arrow ready to fly.

'Is it close?' Ambapali asked, keeping her voice steady with some effort.

Before Swarnasen could reply, a large blurred shape of brown broke through the forest ahead of them. In an instant, Ambapali's horse had been clawed down, taking Ambapali with it. Swarnasen's horse bolted at lightning speed.

CHAPTER 94

DISASTER STRIKES

Prince Swarnasen's attempts to control his horse were useless in the animal's panicked state. When Prince Swarnasen burst into the festival spot alone at sunset, panic and chaos ensued. The merrymaking had continued unrelenting through the day. Food and drink were still flowing aplenty, and the song and dance had become more energetic and joyous. All this stopped when the first screams greeted the sight of the bedraggled prince hanging on to the wild-eyed horse.

Suryamall helped the prince off the horse and gave him a cup of water. The prince splashed the water on his face, and as he wiped his face and stood there slumped, the gathering knew something had gone very wrong.

'Friends, a catastrophe has fallen on us. A lion attacked Ambapali. I fear she may be no more', the prince said. In a few moments, stunned silence had swallowed up the sounds of revelry. The prince recounted the story to the gathering. 'I have failed in my duty to protect the benefactress of the republic', he said. He hung his head.

Suryamall and Lallbhatt sprang into action, ordering more torches to be lit, and search and rescue parties to be formed. They talked to Prince Swarnasen about the location of the lion's attack and then set off in groups of horsemen and foot soldiers, all heavily armed.

They searched every foot of land around the pond. They discovered the dead horse, with its ribs brutally clawed out of its chest. Of Ambapali, they found no trace. They expanded the search frantically, calling out to Ambapali, going into caves and thickets, without luck.

In the dim light of dawn, the tired, dispirited soldiers trooped back to the festival grounds. Wails of despair greeted their arrival. On Ambapali's ceremonial chariot, Madlekha wept like a little girl, and no one stepped forward to console her. Before sunrise, the news had spread through the city of the Bride. The shops closed in mourning, and the assembly meeting was adjourned to mark national mourning.

CHAPTER 95

THE ARTIST-SOLDIER

Ambapali awoke from unconsciousness. She raised herself to a sitting position, and the aches in her shoulder and the side of her thigh brought tears to her eyes. Her blurred vision perceived thick trees surrounding her, and a pond in the distance. Her mind was a blank. Then she saw the lion and screamed.

Footsteps thudded as someone ran to her. 'Do not be afraid, friend!' a calm, matter-of-fact voice called out to her. A man's voice. 'The lion is dead.'

Ambapali squinted up to see the silhouette of a lanky youth towering over her. He stood on a rocky slab, with the golden sun behind him. He came closer, and she realised with relief his mouth was smiling, and so were his eyes. They had a kind look. 'Friend, are you hurt? That was a nasty fall. Shall I help you up? I can hold you around your chest.'

Ambapali's reeling mind was functioning again, but her breath was still shallow. She remembered the events leading to her fall and the man's dress, which added to her discomfort.

'No…no thank you, Sir. It hurts, but I think nothing is broken.' Ambapali tried to order her garb.

The young man came closer. 'But your voice is like a woman's! Are you a merchant's son? Were you out deer hunting?'

Ambapali nodded her assent.

'I see. You are still very young. Was it your first time, then?'

'Yes', Ambapali said in a deeper voice.

The man laughed at her obvious attempt to break her voice. 'Your companion was the one on the other horse?'

'Yes. Where is he?'

'Oh, the horse bolted, and there was nothing he could have done to stop it. It will have galloped back to the camp you stared from.'

Ambapali's face fell at the thought of being alone and hurt in the forest. She wondered if Swarnasen was alive and well.

The youth saw her stiffen and reached out to place an arm on her shoulder, before stopping himself. 'Do not worry, young man', he said. 'He will be all right, and so will you. The mud is soft here, and you were thrown clear of the horse. I was painting the sunset from that hidden corner of the pond.'

He pointed to a bend in the shore. 'This is a very special spot, venerated by the tribals. You will know why when you take time to just sit and watch the sunset, instead of dashing about hunting.

'Anyway, I chose not to disturb you and your friend, as you seemed busy talking, and I preferred not to be disturbed either. When I heard the roar and saw what happened to you both, I picked up my spear and ran here. The lion had fastened itself on your horse, which never stood a chance. I pierced the lion's heart with my spear. I am sorry for your beautiful horse.'

Ambapali looked around her and digested the young man's story. He had told of his killing the lion as if he had swatted a fly. She could not help comparing him to the vain men with whom she had spent that day, and all her other days and nights. She sighed. 'Thank you, my friend, a thousand thanks', she said. 'But how can I get to Madhuban, the site of the Spring Festival, now? I am being missed there, surely. It is dark already. Can you take me there?'

'Oh no, that will be impossible. The dark here is not like that of the city.' The man smiled. 'Nor do you have a horse. I think the spot you have in mind is a mile away. You cannot go anywhere now. But that is all right. You can sleep with me tonight.'

'What! That is impossible!' Ambapali said. 'Do you –' She checked herself as she realised she would be very rude and arrogant to ask if the man knew who he was talking to. She was not yet sure that it was safe for her to disclose her identity.

Her saviour looked at her, almost in shock. He peered closely at her and then nodded. 'I see. You are not used to the idea of living in a hut. I understand. It is not the right type of abode for you, but believe me, you cannot go anywhere else now. I will do what I can to make your stay tolerable.'

Ambapali felt a pang of remorse at her unbridled reaction. Her famed poise and exquisite manners had deserted her in these strange circumstances.

She asked, 'Friend, do you live close by?'

'Yes', the man laughed. 'Else I would not have here. See that hill and the hut on its top?' He pointed out to a distant spot.

'Yes, I see it', Ambapali said, taking care to use the male gender for herself. 'But, friend, what do you do here? In this ghostly forest, and next to this pond that must be a watering hole for the fiercest animals?'

'I paint.' He laughed. 'For the last few days, I have painted the sunset. I fell in love with this place when I came upon it as a wanderer.'

'So you are…an artist? A painter?' Ambapali could not keep the disbelief from her voice.

'Yes, as you can make out from my canvas, and the brushes and colours there.'

'And your spear? Your undoubted skill with it? And your bravery? Are those useful in your work?'

He laughed. 'You are a funny man, friend. Do not mind my saying this, but it's not only your voice. Your manner of praise is feminine. They are useful to stay alive, and that is one of my objectives. The sun will sink below the horizon very, very fast now. Come, let us go. Shall I help you?'

Ambapali got to her feet and limped around for a few moments. She was hurt but relieved to find out she had not been seriously maimed. 'I will walk on my own', she said. 'I will feel better that way. Why don't you lead, and I will follow you?'

He shrugged to show his acceptance, led the way to the place where he kept his tools and arms and wrapped them with care. Then he showed Ambapali the way to the almost-hidden opening of a forest trail that climbed steeply. He measured his footsteps and walked like someone knowing every spot of the landscape.

They were only halfway there when darkness descended, and Ambapali had only the starlight to help her stay a couple of steps behind him. She noticed he kept his paces slow to help her. The dark curtained her from this brave young man, and that was a relief to her. The night she would spend here, unplanned and unforeseen, would be like none of the thousands of nights at the Palace of Seven Worlds. They reached flat land, and Ambapali discerned the outline of the unprepossessing hut.

He pointed to a stone and said, 'Friend, wait there while I get a light. Welcome to my palace.' He turned and chuckled. Ambapali thanked him and sat down. Her aching feet and joints had been screaming for relief.

He was back in a few moments, carrying flint stones that he used deftly to light a small fire. He brought a lamp from inside, lit it and put it back. When he came back, he said, 'Do you see that box there? It has extra clothing. And the pot next to the door has water for anyone that strays here. Which is to say, you will be the second man to share it.' He laughed. 'The shelf inside has some venison and fruits. Help yourself to them. Do not hesitate to take as much as you like. The forest has enough for us. I am running short on fuel. I will come back soon with firewood. I would have asked you to join me, but I see that you need to rest.'

Ambapali felt a surge of emotion at the stranger's kindness. She joined her palms and nodded.

He smiled, picked up an axe and took long strides to merge into the darkness.

CHAPTER 96

THE MAGIC LUTE

The hut had little by way of provisions. That did not surprise Ambapali, but what did was an extraordinary lute that dominated the bare interior. She was struck dumb by its magnificence. She had, of course, seen supreme musicians performing with the best lutes in the world, but never seen one like this. It was longer than usual, but the thing that struck her most was the extreme intricacy of its ivory inlay work, which seemed as if superhuman fingers had crafted it. The hollowed body was exquisitely shaped, and its wood gleamed with the look that could only come from having been lovingly cared for by a passionate musician. Ambapali looked at it for a long time, and then her eyes moistened as she realised that she was, in fact, wrong. She had seen this lute earlier.

But what was it doing here? And who was this man who had felled a lion with a spear and not bragged about it?

She lifted the lamp and examined the hut. The far wall had been shaped by slapping mud around a straight line of tree trunks. Against it rested three spears, a massive bow, four quivers full of arrows and a sword. A lion skin covered a rocky slab which served as a bed large enough for a single person to sleep well. In the corner stood a wooden box and a shelf with the food helpings her saviour had promised her. She looked at the lute again, with longing. It brought back memories of her time with King Udayan.

A loud clatter sounded outside as he threw a bundle of firewood to the ground. The young man's footsteps came closer. He stood in the doorway, crossed his arms and looked askance at Ambapali.

'I see you have not found the time to change yet', he sneered. He bore no anger. 'Nor have you eaten. Could it be because you were busy admiring the lute, my friend?'

'Where did you get it?' Ambapali asked, not bothering to disguise her voice.

'So, you recognise it, Sir?'

'I do. This is the Manjughosha veena, the sublime lute King Udayan received after the gods, and the Gandharvs blessed him.'

He tensed. 'That is so', he said. His eyebrows were knit, and his forehead wrinkled. 'That is true. But how do you know its history? Are you a city boy from Vaishali?'

'I have heard it played.'

'Impossible!'

'I have.'

'No, you can't have…Where?'

'At the Palace of Seven Worlds.'

'Lady Ambapali's palace? And who played it there? Did you dream the episode? Or are you dreaming now?'

'I might be dreaming. Who knows? How else could I come upon this lute here, of all places?'

'I don't understand this. Who played it in the Palace of Seven Worlds, friend?'

'The only one who can.'

'King Udayan?'

'Yes.'

'And he went to Lady Ambapali's palace?'

'Yes, last spring. He played the lute, and she danced…'

'And you – you say you watched her dancing? I know that even seeing her slaves dance is a privilege for the mighty and the rich.'

'But I did.' Ambapali fought back a blush.

The youth stared at her. After a while, he asked in a softer tone, 'You seem to be truthful. Tell me, do you know Lady Ambapali?'

'I know her well enough.'

'Well, well! Well enough, you say? And so casually? Then you must do me a favour.'

'To pay you back?' Ambapali asked.

'No, no. That is not what I meant. But I have – I have a dream.'

'May I know what it is?'

'I did not mean to keep it a secret. I would like Ambapali to dance before me.'

'In front of you? You do have high hopes, friend!' Ambapali could not restrain herself and burst out laughing.

The man's face clouded, and his gaze turned hard. 'Why is it so funny?' he said, an edge in his voice.

Ambapali was still laughing. The day's events had perhaps been too much for her. Relief and the comic nature of the situation now overwhelmed her.

Laughing, she said, 'Do you even know how difficult it is for an ordinary mortal to see her dance? Legend has it that even the gods vie for that favour!'

He stood there wondering how someone to whom he had shown such kindness could scorn him so. 'I have told you what I want', he said.

'Yes, you have. And perhaps you will play this lute like King Udayan had?'

'Yes, I will.' A light shone in his eyes now.

Ambapali repeated herself. 'So you will play this lute?'

'Yes, I will.'

'And can you play three melodies in harmony?'

'Yes, yes!'

'And who gave you that gift?'

'King Udayan. Only two humans can play this veena in that manner. King Udayan and I.'

Ambapali stood still for a long time. She sensed the man wondering if she was all right. She said, longing in her eyes, 'Say what you want from me.'

'It is very simple. All I ask is that she dances for me, to my music, as she did for King Udayan.'

'And where will she do this?'

'Here! In my hut!'

'In this hut! Friend, are you mad? Forgive me for saying this – you have saved my life – but I am sure you don't expect me to take that message to her?'

'I do, friend! Look around you when you wake up in the morning. This is a pure, sacred spot. It is cleaner than the Palace of Seven Worlds! Money does not buy entry here!'

Ambapali's heart broke as she heard this, but she had learnt to mask heartbreak. 'What will you do if I make your dream come true?'

'Anything you ask, except the gift of this lute.'

'Of course.' Ambapali smiled. 'I will not ask for that, but will you let me watch her dance as well?'

'That's not possible. The king told me human eyes cannot see her.'

'Then, I cannot help you.'

'I see.' The man gazed her at without rancour before turning his eyes away. 'Thus it will be, then. I shall find another way of achieving my dream. We have discussed this matter enough. Let us turn to more pressing matters. I will go out and get more food. Meantime, you can change and eat a little.' He picked up a spear and strode out.

Ambapali said, 'Wait!' She wanted to reach out and squeeze his shoulder, to talk more to him. 'Why… Where will you go at this unearthly hour, friend?'

'There is nothing unearthly about it. It is a chore for me. This is a good time to hunt.' He turned his back on her without a word, leaving her speechless.

CHAPTER 97

IN THE LONESOME FOREST

Ambapali felt her aches acting up, and her heart was heavy with the thought that she had perhaps offended her saviour. She sat on the lion skin covered slab and looked at the lute, mystical in the flickering light of the lamp. She only had to close her eyes to bring back memories of the magical moments when the lute's three melodies had touched her soul and given her the inner energy that propelled her to dance with her heart and made her feel as if no higher pleasure was worth pursuing.

King Udayan of Kaushambhi had appeared a year earlier in a Palace of Seven Worlds' garden, at the spot where she least expected an intruder, as if by magic. His divine body, dignified conduct and ability to touch her heart with his music had shown Ambapali a form of maleness unknown to her. She recalled she had no intention to dance to his music, but he had established such a connection with her being that dance became an awakening for her.

As her feet and limbs had moved faster, her movements had gained fluidity, and the air had become sweeter and invigorating. The pleasure she experienced at the end was multidimensional and infinitely greater than any sensual pleasure that she, the Bride of the City, had ever known. She had felt together intense cold and heat as her seven chakras – the life force centres – were lit up one after the other by an energy that made her feel united with the entire cosmos, at peace with humanity, and wanting nothing more than just that moment. How King Udayan had appeared and vanished still intrigued her, but she accepted the experience as a celestial reward she was fortunate to receive.

These thoughts danced in Ambapali's mind as she sat alone in the hut. When her mind wandered back to the present, she thought of the pink pearl necklace that King Udayan had gifted her. It now pressed against her breasts, under the man's dress that she wore. She smiled wistfully as she dwelt on how often she had relived those moments of union between two souls.

The sight of the divine lute in this simple hut in a hidden corner of the forest and the circumstances in which she saw it confused her. On the one hand, she had already been transported back in time her meeting with King Udayan. On the other hand, her saviour, a man who lived in this solitude, an artist of sensitivity, a simple and generous host, a gallant warrior and a gentleman, could also play this very lute – or so he said. But, she thought, how foolhardy he was to demand that she dance for him here and to refuse to go to the Palace of Seven Worlds! King Udayan himself had no such delusions of grandeur, and he had presented himself before Ambapali to request her to dance for him.

So who was this forest-dwelling artist-soldier? Who was this paradoxical mix of iron will and gentle manners, altogether ordinary and humble, extraordinary and arrogant? By what magic was he slowly captivating her heart?

She looked again at the lute, and this time she got goosebumps. The man's face stared back at hers. She closed her eyes for a moment, and when she looked again, he was still there, grave although smiling with confidence. Her hands flew to her cheeks, and her heart thudded against her ribs. The face multiplied into a hundred instances, each of them mouthing the words, 'Dance, Ambapali! This time will not come again! Dance, and it will be like the only other time!'

A fierce heat engulfed her, and she shivered with cold at the same time. She trembled as she cast off her man's clothes and stood erect, a goddess possessed of inexhaustible energy. The melody of the lute played in her mind, and she took the first few graceful steps to the music that poured forth from thin air and controlled her.

CHAPTER 98

THE DIVINE DANCE

When he entered his hut, carrying a coarse sack of freshly roasted meat, he stood transfixed. It was as if night-flowering jasmine had blossomed in a desert. He had left behind a callow, effeminate youth in a drab hut. Now, he dropped his sack and gaped at a dancing woman surpassing in beauty the nymphs of his fertile imagination. Her form was exquisite, her movements graceful and fluid. She was in a trance, uncaring for her surroundings.

As she swayed like a she-serpent, her long, curly hair traced magical patterns in the air. Her slender arms and shapely feet called him to the lute. Each of his senses screamed she performed the divine dance in a vacuum he must fill with music to do justice to it. Did he imagine it, or did the dancer's footfalls create vibrations that strummed his lute and produced the exact melodies he would have played?

Before he knew it, the strings pressed against the hardened tips of his fingers. Instead of the usual cold sensation, he felt as if he had been playing for many hours. The dancer's and his eyes met and conveyed a sense of bliss to the vortex of their two beings.

It was like an erupting volcano. Lost in their worlds, the musician and the dancer were aware of each other's instincts and intent. They took and ceded the lead by turns, their minds and bodies working in harmony, their beings united.

As their awareness of inner consciousness heightened, they lost control and receded from the physical and biological world. The dancer who had been a broken and wounded wreck, and the repulsed musician who had walked away in a fit of rage for a pointless hunt to appease his hurt pride, now had supreme reserves of energy. They inspired each other, improvised and challenged themselves, surpassed all they had so far achieved in their lives. Every atom of their joint being focused on their instantaneous harmony. Then they reached an inter-section of space and time without earth, sky, bondage, birth, death, with nothing and everything.

CHAPTER 99

AN AGONISING BLISS

Ambapali returned to consciousness with a sense of loss. Thick shafts of dense light pierced the darkness of the hut, lighting up thousands of floating flecks that would have otherwise been invisible. The sun's heat had penetrated through to the cool floor. Ambapali had woken from a deep sleep when the warmth crossed a threshold. She realised that she lay in a sprawl on the floor.

She jerked herself to sit upright and looked around. She was alone. She opened a window on the eastern side. A blast of fresh, warm, invigorating air greeted her. She could see jagged hills at the far horizon. In front of the hut, a million shades of green dotted the trees. The forest and the slopes echoed with birdsong.

The memory of dancing in a trance came back to her. She turned to look over her shoulder. The lute was on the sandalwood cot where she had first seen it. Was it all a dream that she had been in? Or had she really danced? The glow she still sensed in her heart, the sight of the young man united with his lute, her body's awakening – all of it was too real for her to have imagined it. Did anyone exist who could equal King Udayan in his mastery of music? Who was this young man? Was he a divine being, cursed to eke out a lonely existence by a more powerful god? Was he a Gandharv, a spirit, who had taken human form? She could not drag her train of thought away from her saviour. Had she spent the night in the hut with him? Where was he now? Where?

She realised she was aching for him. Her intense, overriding need to see him seemed to make her cry out into the forest and say, 'Where are you? You have made a slave out of me! Come back to me!' This man, delicate as a flower and hard like a rock, made her feel like she never had before. She, who had vowed revenge on all men, because men had robbed her of her innocence. How many men had she reduced to drivelling, bankrupt fools as they floundered in the maze of desire that was her Palace? How many had become objects of her pity? Had she considered even one of them a man? No, she had trounced them. She considered her purity inviolable, her spirit unbroken, her integrity higher than that of all of those grovelling weaklings. And now, a man had conquered her! She had lost her completeness. She had become a woman yearning for a man. And where had he disappeared? Why had he taken over her soul, but not her body? Every part of her tingled with a burning wish to be touched and loved. Each instant was full of agony. 'Come to me!' her heart cried. 'This body – this lowly woman's body yearns for you! Take it with your manhood, merge me with you! Become one with me! Leave no trace of my single existence!'

Ambapali hugged her heaving chest. Her body burned as if with a fever. The room seemed to whirl as she swayed with her arms outstretched, and her eyes half-closed.

The young man pushed the door open to see Ambapali in a delirium, her hail dishevelled, her face pale, her limbs trembling, and her eyes closed.

He sprang at her and gathered her in his arms. His lips were on hers, and as he pressed her heaving breasts against his chest, he felt the fluttering of the heart that no woman could ever simulate. He sensed her fevered being calm down. He saw her eyes close as a deep sense of peace and relief descended on her. Beads of sweat glistened on her forehead and nose, and she moaned like a woman possessed. He lost all control. He laid her down in his lap as he sat on the rock that was his bed. He kissed her lips, her forehead, her eyes, her cheeks, her neck, her breasts. Her lips sought his, she pressed herself to him and pulled him to her.

Ambapali opened her eyes slowly. The man closed his and shuddered as tremors coursed through his body. He carefully laid her on the lion skin. She sat up, and they looked at each other. Her eyes were moist and downcast. A flush appeared on her cheeks.

'Lady Ambapali, I do not know what to say. I could not control myself', he said.

Ambapali smiled at him. 'So you recognise me?'

'Yes, I do. I knew the moment I saw you.'

'And did you like the dance?'

'In this world, only you can reach the heights you do, Lady.'

'And your music? What do you think of it?' she asked.

'I get by, Lady. I still have some way to go. Your dance spurred me beyond my limits.'

Ambapali's heart ached at these modest words. He was different in every way from all the men who slobbered around her. 'Even King Udayan cannot play like you', she said. She reflected that he knew of her identity now, but she still had no clue of his. How should she ask him who she was? She felt unusually inhibited. 'What now?' she asked.

'What now?' he replied mechanically.

'I will have to return…Will you not tell me your name?'

'Of course. I am Subhadra.'

'Very well, Subhadra. Now I must go.'

'Not now!'

She looked askance at him.

'You must dance one more time', he said.

'Dance?'

'Yes. And it will be difficult for you.'

Ambapali laughed. 'Difficult, Subhadra?'

'Yes', he said. 'I will not play the lute this time.'

'But…'

'I will paint you.'

'But how will I dance?' she asked.

'You will act', he said.

She smiled. 'Very well.'

'Oh, and you will have to act many times. I want to capture you in many forms.'

'But…' Ambapali frowned.

'What is it, Lady?' he asked.

'My return…'

'It will have to wait', he said.

'Why do you not come to the Palace of Seven Worlds? You can paint there.'

'At that Palace!' A tremor entered Subhadra's voice and his face clouded. 'I am not a Licchavi, and I hate the idea of the law that made you the bride of the city. I detest that your unparalleled beauty became a public good.'

'And would it have been better to have it as one man's personal good?'

'It should have belonged to you, and only to you!'

She leant forward. 'What do you mean, dear one?'

'Each one of us has the right to self-actualisation. You should have fulfilled your needs in meeting those of your chosen one. In a grammar class, the second person follows the first person. I know what the cursed law of the Licchavis inflicted on you has scarred you.'

This man's unconventional logic spoke straight to Ambapali's heart and startled her. A teardrop formed in her eye. She was overwhelmed with gratitude that the creator had planted one man on the earth who did not see her as common property. She was fortunate to have given her heart to him, and she would have been twice blessed if she had given her body to him. But she had already sold it many times, although at terms making her the victor of each transaction. She thought about how he had kissed her in a frenzy, then gently laying her aside with love coming from his heart.

'Where are you, Lady?' Subhadra chuckled.

She smiled at him. 'How can I ever refuse you, who saved my life?'

•

Subhadra took his time to prepare his paints and canvases. He trooped around the clearing to select a spot to work. Ambapali watched his every movement, leaning against the wall of the hut. She was at peace with herself and with the world, secure with this man who had saved her, content in this space and time intersection where routine and ritual were meaningless.

He worked with intense concentration, aware of her gaze. Sometimes, he looked up at her, as if to chide her for her unblinking gaze. Then he smiled, shook his head, and returned to his work. When he had mixed his small pots of paint and settled down, he called Ambapali. In a few moments, their roles absorbed both of them.

Subhadra directed Ambapali with quick and polite instructions, which Ambapali followed. They lost track of time. By noon, they were tired, and Ambapali was sweaty.

She straightened herself, stretched, and said, 'My stomach rumbles. My intestines are dancing. Are you going to paint them?'

Subhadra's frown gave way to a childish grin. 'That was well-timed', he said. 'I am almost finished, and I will complete this without troubling you to pose.'

Ambapali walked into the hut and sat on the bed. He stretched and followed her. Ambapali felt a shiver of delight as he sat next to her and their sides brushed.

He turned pensive. 'Ambapali, will we remember these moments forever? Will we have a measure of them? Will we count them?'

'There will be countless moments to cherish them', Ambapali said. 'And I shall. Will you?'

'Do you think I have power? Energy?' he said.

'Well, I have evidence you killed the lion, and I know from experience that you conquered this hardened woman's heart with relative ease.' Ambapali smiled, and her eyes twinkled. 'Are you considering any more demonstrations of your might?'

'I still lack the power to value these moments.' He lowered his head and gulped.

Ambapali recalled a moment in her wanderings in the Palace of Seven worlds when she had stood to watch a banyan tree leaves fluttering on a quiet spring afternoon. She trembled like those leaves. A few strands of her hair were matted on her pale forehead. Even inside the hut, the warm forest breeze, heavy with the scent of wildflowers, caressed and aroused her, and made her more aware of his presence.

He took her hand in both of his. 'Ambapali, if I say I love you, that does not do justice to how I feel. What I may do with my body would not express a fraction of the intensity of my feelings. All I can say, in my clumsy way, is this: Remember now, and forever, that I am your worshipper. You attract me, of course, and I worship your body, your beauty, your youth…but I also love you for your soul. In the Palace of Seven Worlds, mounds of gold and gems will surround you, and emperors and merchants will kiss the ground before you. Spare a thought then for this insignificant worshipper of yours and his far superior love. Whenever you do, it will reach me, and my love for you will have remained unchanged.'

Sliding down to the floor, Subhadra hugged Ambapali's legs. Ambapali fought back her tears of love and leant over him. Her heart was pounding.

Much later, as she nuzzled her head against his chest, she said, 'You are a bad man, Subhadra. You took away all I had – my possession of myself. How will I live now? Tell me!' Something came over her – a feeling she had never known – and she broke into sobs, the way she had only done before her anointment. 'Who are you? Are you a man, a Gandharv, a king, a demon? You have consumed me! What shall I do now? Take me to the edge of the world, where you drove me yesterday when I danced to your music! And let us live there as one.'

'We have become one, dear', he said. 'In those magical moments of the evening, we fused into one being without touching each other. We won't part until the sun and moon remain, in this life and the next. Our bodies will live their lives, my love. And if we try to mould those lives into our love, it will end badly for us. I am nothing, and I have nothing to lose, but your magnificence and splendour will end. However cursed that law may be, we cannot change the past, and your future beckons you.'

He gently pushed her head up and kissed her on her lips and eyes. 'You must remember me, and you must not let your path being greater than mine dishearten you. This world has not seen a woman like you. You must continue on your path and reach the acme of your way of life. You have my wishes, for I cannot give you much more.'

Ambapali closed her eyes. No words came to her.

After they had eaten, Subhadra told Ambapali to rest while he went out. He said that she would be safe inside the hut. He promised to be back by sunset.

He kept his promise. At sunset, the two lovers sat on the edge of the slab in the opening, watching a pale sun sink below the wooded hills in the distance.

CHAPTER 100

UNITED HEARTS

On a slab outside the hut, under a deep indigo sky dotted with stars, the lovers lay entwined, wishing that dreamlike chapter of their lives would never end. Subhadra rested his back on a slope of rock. Ambapali lay with her head in his lap.

'Isn't enjoyment the reward of love?' Ambapali asked, her voice husky.

'I don't know. I would say it is perhaps the reward of desire', Subhadra said.

'Do you mean lust? And is that not a flower of love?' she said.

'I think it is a base instinct more than anything else', he said.

'But lust and enjoyment drive this world!' she said.

'And when lust and enjoyment drive the world, what does that leave for love?' he said.

'Bliss! Pure bliss!' she said.

'What bliss?'

'Bliss beyond the realm of senses and the attainment of a climax. Bliss without expectations or attempts to achieve things. A bliss that does not flag and shrivel after it is attained.'

'And that is why the body is lost to the senses when love is in its infancy. It has no time to get the true taste of love!'

'Then...'

'Yes, Ambapali, this is man's misfortune. Man and woman are the only creatures who have the gift of love. Animals and birds have the mating instinct. But think about it – do humans really go much beyond those lower life forms?'

'If the desire is nothing, does it not mean beauty and youth are worth nothing?'

'Why should it mean that? The human heart is the source of the arts. All the arts of the world have sprung from it. One who is strong enough to save one's love from the leaping flames of lust can know the taste of love. And that person is blessed.'

'I am blessed. I have tasted love', Ambapali said. She put her arms around Subhadra's neck. Her cheeks were wet.

'Are you?' Subhadra smiled and wiped her cheeks tenderly.

'Oh, yes, I am.' Ambapali sighed. 'I do not know how to express it to you.'

'Do you not know that you do not need to? The sensations flowing in your mind and body do not differ from those flowing in mine. We are one. No explanation is needed.' He bent to place his lips on hers. They kissed with languid ardour.

She placed her head on his chest. They lay still and tranquil for a long time.

He said, 'Why are you quiet?'

She said, 'What is there to say?'

'So you know everything there is to know?'

'Everything.'

'Really?'

'Really.'

'You are fortunate, Ambapali!'

He freed her from his arms. He said, 'Then farewell, Ambapali! Till the morning.'

She sank her head between her knees. She spoke in a subdued voice. 'And where will you sleep?'

'There are many caves around. Look, there is one right here. I only need one.' He smiled. 'You will be safe here, with the fire.' Ambapali wanted to smother him with her kisses, but even more to just look at him.

He gave her a chaste kiss on her forehead, picked up a heavy spear, adjusted his simple clothes and strode away.

Ambapali placed her bosom on the spot he had lain on.

CHAPTER 101

FAREWELL

Seven days of work had passed. The portrait was ready. Ambapali had steadfastly fought back her craving to see the artist's work-in-progress. When, after his intense labours were done, and he declared that he had achieved his mission, she stepped across to the other side of the canvas with trepidation. What she saw brought tears to her eyes. She was both inflamed with pride and overwhelmed with humility. She knew that she was especially endowed with physical beauty – that was the gift that had propelled her to the path her life had taken. Subhadra's portrait imbued her with dignity and a soulfulness that made her feel that in that portrayal, she epitomised all a woman could aspire to be. Subhadra watched her as she drank in the sight of her image. They said nothing. Words were redundant.

That evening, when Subhadra stood up after their rudimentary dinner, he said, 'Dear, this is your last night in this bare hut. We will go to the city at the crack of dawn tomorrow. I do not want to go to the city in broad daylight. We must restore you to your rightful surroundings of luxury and ease. I will bring a horse.' He smiled, but Ambapali saw that his eyes were dull.

'Not tomorrow!' Ambapali wanted to scream. 'Let me stay! Let me stay forever!' She said nothing.

Subhadra saw her swallow. His face fell. 'Do you want to say something, dear?'

'There is so much to say…I do not know how to say it.'

'Please speak your mind, dear!'

'You are a mysterious and complex man. You do not reveal yourself to me. Will you not tell me about yourself? Share your secrets with me?'

Subhadra chuckled. 'But do you need any further introduction now, dear? I am yours – you know that well. Perhaps you will know more of me later – why the anxiety?'

Ambapali sighed as she looked at his smiling face. 'Where have you acquired your skills, Sir? They are not ordinary, by any means.'

The young man nodded as if he understood her sense of wonder. 'Well, formally, I have studied at Takshila. But I have also inherited many gifts. And the university of life took me to every part of India and to the eastern islands across the ocean.'

Ambapali bowed and touched his feet. It was a spontaneous gesture that she had never foreseen she would perform to honour a man. 'I am your disciple', she said.

Subhadra hastened to pull her up and embrace her. 'And my guru!' he said.

'How so?'

'We shall discuss that later, but I really must leave now', Subhadra said. 'Remember we have to leave early. Farewell!'

'Good night!'

Subhadra was lost in the darkness and Ambapali in her thoughts. She trudged to the bed in the hut where she spent the night longing for the touch of the man who had so possessed her mind and body.

.

It seemed that sleep had just descended on her when a knock sounded on the door. It was Subhadra.

'Are you ready?' he asked.

'I will be soon', she said.

When she stepped out, the air was cold, and the sky only tinged with light.

'Did you not sleep well, dear?' Subhadra asked.

'It was a strange night, my love', she said.

He sighed and lowered his head as if mulling over what to say next. When he looked up, he only said, 'The horse is ready. Will you go now?'

'Yes', she said.

He pointed to a lion skin that lay spread on the rock slab near them. 'That is the lion that almost killed you. May I keep the skin in remembrance?'

'It is yours', Ambapali said. 'And so is my body – skin, flesh, soul and all.' Tears streaked down her eyes.

They walked out to the edge of the clearing, where a horse stood waiting.

'Why only one horse, dear?'

'Because you only need one.'

'And you?'

'I move on foot. I am your follower. You are the guru.'

'That cannot be!'

'Oh, it can. Very well. Come, let me help you up.'

'But why will you walk, dear?'

He placed his hands on her shoulders and looked into her eyes. 'Because you are above this world. I cannot ride with Lady Ambapali.'

He helped her up, and when she had taken the reins, he asked her to wait. He picked up a roll of canvas that lay next to the lion skin. She took it with trembling hands and pressed lips.

They started their journey. The eastern sky was now pale, but the outlines of the trees and the hills were still dark. The footman led the rider at a slow, but sure pace. They were both silent. A cuckoo's call pierced the song of the cicadas and the other birds. A soft glow lit up the path, but the breaking light did nothing to lift Ambapali's spirits.

The sun was a pale ball behind them when they reached the city gates. It was closed. Subhadra pulled at the bell rope.

'Who is it?' a sleepy guard asked.

'Chitrabhu', Subhadra replied confidently.

A creaking sound started before the doors moved. A chink opened, and then the opening widened. Every degree the doors rotated, every screech of the door's metal and wood, drove Ambapali to a new height of despair.

'Farewell, my dear. This is where I must go.' Subhadra's voice was hoarse. His face was stony, but when she bent to lay a hand on his shoulder, she felt him trembling like a leaf.

A teardrop formed in her eye. She nodded, unable to speak. He turned and strode away.

CHAPTER 102

BACK IN VAISHALI

Just as the news of Ambapali's death had spread like wildfire, so too did the news of her miraculous return. In the Palace of Seven Worlds, colourful flags with the fish symbol fluttered in the hundreds. Within a few moments of the first sighting of the benefactress of the republic, drumbeats sounded. The crowds that gathered at the Palace gates, drawn by the drumming, became ecstatic when they heard the news from the mouths of the guards. By Ambapali's orders, the Palace of Seven Worlds abandoned its desolate look and became, within an hour, a riot of colour. Trumpeters rent the skies with their jubilant bursts.

Soon, a sea of humanity collected at the outer wall and the main gate. The crowd buzzed in every corner of the Palace of Seven Worlds. The stories were told and retold and passed into legend. It seemed that Ambapali had been invited to the land of the Gandharvs, where the Gandharv King Chitraratha had himself played the Manjughosha Veena, his magical lute. And Ambapali had danced her celestial dance to his music. King Chitraratha had himself taken the easel to paint a portrait of the dancing Ambapali, and gifted it to her as a token of his admiration.

All day, Ambapali lay on her familiar soft bed, gazing vacantly at the ceiling. She had forbidden any visitors before evening. Many of her ardent admirers – princes, merchants, ambassadors – had waited in vain in the palace corridors for a glimpse of their beloved Lady Ambapali. Madlekha had bowed, smiled in her most ingratiating manner and sent them packing with a clear message. They should not expect to see Lady Ambapali before the evening. They made no fuss over their peremptory ejection, sensing Ambapali was exhausted and needed rest. They took heart from the preparations for the evening, harbingers of the return of the good times.

By evening, the Palace of Seven Worlds exuded joy and vibrant energy. Hundreds of perfumed oil lamps had been lit, and flowers, garlands, and bunting festooned the whole complex. As usual, couches, cushions and bolsters had been placed in every clearing. Aromatic wines had been stocked up, and pitchers of wine and tumblers awaited the thirsty revellers. Hosts of beautiful slave girls adorned in all their finery had gathered in the gardens. Armies of servants scurried to prepare for an evening to remember.

The sun turned mellow, and then a deep red. As the sky darkened, the lights in the Palace of Seven Worlds brightened. Light from inside the main building filtered through coloured windows to play magically on the Blue Lotus Pond. Vehicles of all types occupied the outer courtyard, and their passengers – the elite of the land – were already in the inner courtyards of the Palace of Seven Worlds.

Soon, the wine started flowing, and so did the music and dancing. However, it was clear the young men of the city were only slaking their appetites as a formality. They were eagerly waiting for their goddess to appear.

One and a half watches of the night had already passed. A hush fell in the innermost courtyard when Ambapali stepped into the public space for the first time after her disappearance. Not a word, not a single exclamation came from the gathered crowd at first. They took in the sight of the benefactress of the republic. Her clothes were austere by her standards – she wore a flowing white robe that did not accentuate her figure. Her face was pale, and her eyes bore a sorrowful look that gave her a certain grace. She joined her palms to greet the gathering.

At once, all the men, slaves and servants let loose a thunderous round of applause. Wild cheers filled the skies and echoed over the city.

Ambapali seemed to have gained an even more heavenly stature after her rumoured stay as an honoured guest of the Gandharvs. She smiled and waited for the commotion to die down. 'Friends, welcome to the Palace of Seven Worlds. May you live long.'

'Victory to Ambapali! May you live long!' This time, the enormous crowd shouted in unison, bringing a shine to Ambapali's face. She stepped forward and sat on a crystal pod. She saw that one of those in the forefront was Prince Swarnasen.

She said, 'Prince Swarnasen, come forward! See how we were parted and how we meet again. Does not life work in mysterious ways?'

Swarnasen lowered his head. 'Lady, I am ashamed of myself. I did not – I could not – protect you. I am responsible for your misfortune.'

'What misfortune, Prince?'

'I still tremble when I think of it. What a beast that was. I wonder...'

'That was perhaps a blow the gods inflicted on us, on you and me. But what happened after that was unearthly.'

'Is it true then, Lady Ambapali', another man came forward, 'that you saw the king of the Gandharvs?' The man who had spoken was handsome, tall and well-built. His hair was long, curly and blond, and his eyes had a blue tinge.

'May I ask who you are, Sir?' Ambapali said with a smile. 'I do not recognise you.'

Swarnasen spoke before the man could. 'This is my close friend, Manibhadra from Gandhar. He is a member of the delegation coming to us with Singh. Manibhadra has studied the eight branches of medicine under Professor Agnideva. He is here to work with Acharya Gaurpad in the field of chemical experiments.'

'I see. Welcome to Vaishali, Sir', Ambapali said. 'Your good-looking friend Singh is, it seems, opposed to the pleasures of the Palace of Seven Worlds. How did he allow you to visit us? And what experiments are you working on?' She smiled at Manibhadra.

'The experiments are concerned with iron and with the human body, Lady Ambapali', Manibhadra said.

'I see', Ambapali said. 'Well, I, for one, am terrified of Acharya Gaurpad and his experiments.'

'And why is that, Lady?' Manibhadra asked.

'Oh, just his fierce looks', Ambapali said. She laughed, and Manibhadra joined in her laughter. Ambapali held out her hand, and Manibhadra bent and kissed it.

Manibhadra said, 'Is it true, Lady Ambapali, that –'

Ambapali said, 'Yes, as true as your experiments.'

Swarnasen said, 'What about the lion's attack? I wonder if that was a punishment from the gods?'

'Perhaps it was. Have you not seen the portrait in the hall?'

'I have, Lady Ambapali, and I congratulate you on being its subject!' Swarnasen said.

'And I echo his congratulations. You are most fortunate.'

'Thank you, my friends!' Ambapali said. 'Please continue to enjoy yourselves tonight. Today, I am complete, I am grateful, I am blessed. I have been united with the gods.'

The men cheered loudly. It seemed as if Ambapali had breathed life into the celebrations. The evening took on a familiar hue.

CHAPTER 103

TWO TRAVELLERS

Asthik was a small village. Its claim to fame was that it stood at the junction from where three roads branched out to Champa, Rajgrih and Vaishali. Because of its strategic location, it had a floating population of merchants and other travellers. Several inns catered to travellers who stopped there. An elderly man of the Vratya community owned one of these inns. The lodgings tended to be well occupied.

The sun was a fiery orb low in the sky. A Brahman traveller was saying his evening prayers under the shade of a thick banyan tree, by a small pond. The place, next to the Vratya's inn, was lonely. The middle-aged Brahman dressed like a villager. It seemed he had left the throng inside the inn to seek solitude here. He had an aura about him that belied the rusticity of his clothes.

Another traveller trudged to that lonely spot, looked around and settled under the tree without talking to the Brahman. The lines on the newcomer's face eased as he lay himself down to rest. He looked tired in both mind and body. After a while, he took off his clothes and stepped into the pond, muttering inaudible words. After he came out, dried himself and changed, he looked utterly energised. He took out a parcel of food and laid it out.

Only then did he look at the Brahman and join his hands in greeting. He asked, 'Where are you from, Brahman?'

'From Magadha', the Brahman replied.

'Very well. Sir, I have food. Will you not join me?'

'That is very kind of you. May I know who you are?'

'A merchant.'

'Where from?'

'Vitibhaya.'

'Very well.'

The Brahman joined the merchant, and they said no more. The merchant pushed the parcel of food – bread and two large sweets – closer to the Brahman, divided the food into halves and gave the Brahman a portion. They turned away from each other so that they could eat separately.

The Brahman was tired and hungry. He took the big sweet ball into his hands and hastily crushed it so he could consume it. He gaped at what he saw. The sweet crumbled to shower dozens of radiant gems. The Brahman's mind reeled. He gathered the gems into a neat pile and looked from them to his weary, bedraggled companion and back. After dwelling on the incongruity of what had just happened, he set aside the gems with care and ate the meal, which was more than welcome to his grumbling stomach.

When they had eaten, the Brahman swept the gems into a fold of his clothing. He looked at his benefactor, and asked, 'What is your name, good sir?'

The man hesitated before speaking firmly. 'I am Kritpunya, son of Dhanavah, of Vitibhaya.'

'Merchant Dhanavah! What a coincidence! He has been my patron, and I have been a priest to him! Indeed it is a small world…But, bless you, young man, where are you headed? And may I presume to ask how you ended up in this state?'

'I am going to Champa, Arya', Kritpunya said.

'Champa! You will walk there? With no means? I…' The Brahman frowned. 'Why?'

'I must, Arya. It is the only path open to me.'

'Tell me more, young man. I have been a priest to your father, and I am a true Brahman.'

'Well, Sir, my evil mother has turned me out of the house. My middle wife was kind enough to give me a way to survive. She said I should head for her father's place and find shelter there.'

'But why in this manner, the manner of a vagrant?'

'I do not know what other manner I could adopt. I have no means.'

'Who provided your meal, the one you so kindly shared with me?'

'The same wife gave it to me. She did it secretly.'

The Brahman nodded. He frowned, lost in thought, and then his face cleared, and he chuckled.

Kritpunya stared at him with a stony gaze. 'Is something funny, Sir?' he said.

'Just that you are not good at lying.'

'What do you mean, Sir?'

'Tell me the truth, young man. Trust me! Who are you?'

'Have I not told you, Sir?'

'You have, but you lied.'

The young man met the Brahman's gaze, but could not hold it. He lowered his head. 'How did you know, Arya?'

'I just knew. You are a courtier, not a merchant.' The Brahman did not mention that he had noticed the outline of a sword under his companion's clothes.

The young man seemed deeply moved. He bowed and said, 'You are a true Brahman, Sir. I am a courtier's son, as you say. That evil woman chose me to be a husband to her daughters-in-law, to give her male heirs. Now that she has achieved her goal, she no longer needs me. Luckily, my middle wife loves me and will join me in Champa.'

'But you have not answered my question. Who are you? Maybe I can be of help to you.'

'Well, Arya, I am a Licchavi, but one who has been trampled by Vaishali, and one who lives with the aim of destroying Vaishali in return.'

The Brahman's eyes widened before he controlled his facial muscles to present a neutral mask. 'A Licchavi, and yet you wish to destroy Vaishali? Why so, young man?'

'I loved Ambapali, and she loved me before she became the Bride of the city.'

The Brahman sighed and nodded. His silence conveyed his grave sympathy for the young man. After a while, he said, 'Young man, are you staying true to the burning desire of your heart? Are you not trapped in a mundane existence that does not take you towards your higher goal?'

Harshdev sank his head between his knees. When he looked up, he said, 'What should I do, Sir?'

'Keep your promise to yourself. Destroy Vaishali.'

'How?'

'Follow me!'

A light appeared in Harshdev's eyes. 'I am your follower, Sir.'

'Very well. Take this.' The Brahman took Harshdev's hand and put the handful of gems into it.

Harshdev exclaimed as he opened his hand to see what the Brahman had given him. 'These jewels – what… What should I do with them?'

'Bring them to Pawapuri, about twenty miles from here. Go meet my friend and classmate Indrabhuti. Here, take this.' The Brahman fished out a gleaming yellow ring from somewhere in the folds of his clothing. 'Give it to him. Tell him I have sent you. He will help you use these stones to equip yourself as a prosperous merchant. Go to Champa as Kritpunya, not Harshdev, with pomp and be an honoured guest at your father-in-law's house. Do not waste your time pining for your middle wife.

'Engage in trade. Carry gifts for your father-in-law and take a loan from him to ply your trade onwards to the east – to Banga and down the coast, all the way to the southernmost tip of the land. Tell Indrabhuti of this plan. He will give you a list of influential men in each city you will visit. Show this ring to those men and take contributions from them. Do not be timid when you ask for them. This ring will be influential. When it is done, return to Vaishali and stay there under your new identity. Wait for me to reach out to you.' The Brahman paused after this long monologue.

Harshdev looked at the jewels in his hand, wondering at the vagaries of life. He sensed the Brahman, like him, had assumed an identity and was no ordinary man. Something prevented him from questioning his newfound guide. 'As you command, Sir. But how shall I know when you send for me?' he asked.

'Good question, young man. There is a market run by one Nandan Sahu in Vaishali inner city. You can reach me if you ask for the travelling Brahman there, but that will not be necessary. Just settle there in an office doing justice to your position. I will hear of your arrival. Just wait for my signal.'

Harshdev bowed and joined his hands in a namaste.

'Go, Son, and complete your mission', the Brahman said.

When Harshdev had left for Pawapuri, the Brahman slung his bag on his shoulder, picked up his walking stick, and stepped out in the other direction.

CHAPTER 104

BALBHADRA, THE BANDIT

A fearful spectre loomed over Vaishali. In the streets, market squares and inside the walls of houses, the rumours spread like wildfire. Tales of Balbhadra's daring robberies and acts of terror circulated in whispers inflamed the citizens, and placed the council under pressure. The senior leaders were strangely subdued.

Balbhadra and his band continued to evade the security forces. They robbed the rich with impunity. The locus of their deeds seemed to widen, spiral and shrink at their will. One day, the gang stole a tax payment convoyed under armed escort from a village to the treasury. A few days later, they mounted a daylight raid on the treasury in the main market and escaped with a huge catch. A trickle of people started migrating away from Vaishali. The common people took to burying their valuables deep in the ground and became less carefree in displaying their jewellery.

The courtiers flocking to the Palace of Seven Worlds remained apathetic in the face of all this. They spent their days languidly waiting for the sun to set. The mellowing sun was the signal for them to stretch, bathe, bedeck themselves, stuff their purses with gold and silver and make their dashes towards the giddy pleasures of the evening. They were addicts of the mix of young beauty, wine, gambling and music. The bright lights of the Palace of Seven Worlds drew them like moths to a flame. They returned drained in every way, often lolling as their attendants helped them onto their chariots as the skies were lightening. They spent the day recuperating from the excesses of the night. The deity of their dazed existence was the shining, ever-smiling Ambapali. Their heaven was the paradise she had set up on earth – the brilliant, scented Palace of Seven Worlds with its unending throng of young beauties.

CHAPTER 105

SWARNASEN, THE HEIR APPARENT

warnasen guzzled down the red wine and thrust the empty cup at the slave girl. 'More!' he snarled, looking at her with half-closed eyes.

The girl took the cup and remained bowed, making no move to refill his bowl.

'Give me more, girl!' Swarnasen said.

'No more', she whispered.

The prince forced his eyes open. 'Why no more?' he asked huskily. 'Slave, give me more.'

'But it will be too much', the girl said, trembling.

Swarnasen staggered to his feet. 'Give me more wine. More', he mumbled as he raised his hand in a gesture that lacked vigour but was still threatening enough to cow down a slave girl.

She gulped, hastily filled the cup from a pitcher beside her, splashing wine, and handed it to the prince. As Swarnasen greedily took it, he heard footsteps thudding from the corridor leading to the room. A guard burst in, panting. Chief Security Officer Suryamall was on his way and wanted an urgent audience, he announced. Swarnasen registered no emotion. Suryamall was a close friend of his and was free to come and go as he liked. Swarnasen's head was swimming, though, and from that point of view, it was not a good time for a meeting.

When he forced his bleary eyes open with an effort, Suryamall stood before him, grim, lips taut. Swarnasen raised an eyebrow. Suryamall looked at the girl, and she and the guard left the room at once, shutting the door behind them.

Suryamall said, 'Have you heard, Swarn, that the market treasury was robbed today?'

Swarnasen's lips still touched the cup. His eyelids were drooping again.

'I bring a message from the supreme commander of the army!' Suryamall could not hold back his disgust and anger.

'And what message has that good man sent at this untimely hour?' Swarnasen spoke in an unsteady voice.

'That we are taking a division of ten thousand to Madhuban. Right away.'

The empty cup slipped and fell from Swarnasen's hand. 'Why now?' he asked. 'Why not some other time?'

'Because we know Balbhadra is there!'

'Are you scared of that bandit, Suryamall? Shame on you.'

'I repeat. The supreme commander has ordered us to attack with a division, right away.'

'Why tell me? Why do you not just do it? Are you…'?

'I will be with you!'

'Well, well.' Swarnasen sighed. 'Help me up, friend.'

Suryamall's face was a mask of stone as he helped the prince. The prince swayed, and for a few moments, it seemed it might be touch and go. He managed to straighten himself and slurred, 'Let us go.'

'Are you sure?' Suryamall asked. 'You will ride to Madhuban?'

'Madhuban? No, I meant, let us go to Ambapali.'

Suryamall recoiled as if someone had slapped him. 'And the order?'

'We shall carry it out…yes, we shall. But tomorrow morning.'

'But Balbhadra…'

'Yes, him. Hmm…Let that unfortunate man spend a day in the forest. Let him. And tomorrow, I will splay him with this sword…Ah, I don't have it now. But I will.'

Suryamall's biceps bulged, and a vein in his forehead throbbed. 'This cannot be! We have an order!'

'Yes, we have. No denying it.' Swarnasen's speech remained slurred. 'But listen. Listen to me. I am the prince. Here is what I have to say: come to the Palace of Seven Worlds. Think of the release awaiting you there.'

'I shall go alone to Madhuban', Suryamall said, choking.

'Ah, friend, you are emotionless. Look outside! The moon is out! Does it not make you feel romantic? Think, when you step out, think of the cool breeze that will caress you as you indulge in the pleasures of the Palace of Seven Worlds. Come with me. That is an order!' Swarnasen slumped onto his friend's shoulder, exhausted by his long speech. Suryamall stood silent, head bowed, eyes closed.

Then he slowly helped his friend the prince towards the spot where his chariot was waiting.

CHAPTER 106

THE RETURN OF THE WANDERER

The markets of Vaishali were buzzing with the news of the arrival of Kritpunya, a legendary merchant who had travelled to the southern tip of India and back, and amassed a fortune in money and – more uniquely – experience and insight. The merchant's guild showered him with honours, and its head invited him home to host him for a special dinner. The merchants of Vaishali, accustomed as they were to the rich and the powerful of the world, were still impressed by Kritpunya's hoard of goods, his regal and quiet demeanour and his generosity. A huge retinue of employees, servants and slaves accompanied merchant Kritpunya. His inventory of possessions was massive, and many modes of transport were available to him, each one of them embellished with the finest material. Word had it that Kritpunya had amassed the hidden wealth of Champa after its sacking and multiplied it in his peregrinations across the land. Now, he wanted to live a stable life with his base in Vaishali.

Rumours spread about the extent and the origin of his fabulous fortune. One story said he had returned from an island with a ship full of the gold of a mine he had discovered. His gold was not on display, but his eight statuesque white Arab horses were highly visible and were the talk of Vaishali. Kritpunya's rode out onto Royal Avenue every evening on his favourite stallion, and the daily event never failed to create hushed awe even in that most cosmopolitan of cities. With his platoon of very well-dressed servants, the cherubic boy confidently riding a magnificent horse drew open admiration and greetings from all those he passed. He acknowledged them with good grace.

The seeds for Kritpunya's triumphant entry into Vaishali were sown when Harshdev followed his Brahman advisor's instruction and went to Pawapuri. There, Indrabhuti treated him as an honoured guest. He helped him to acquire an impressive wardrobe and ornaments and introduced him to the elite of the city as the wealthy scion of an old trading house. Harshdev used the seed money he had to buy enough valuable stock to start a trading mission. Equipped with the necessary papers and lists from Indrabhuti, Harshdev travelled with a convoy of fifty mules, an armed escort and a group of slaves to Champa.

At Champa, instead of being at his father-in-law Sagardutta's mercy, he went as a wealthy peer and a successful member of the family. Champa was recovering from the pillage of war, but Sagardutta had invested his wealth in a vast trading network stretching to the Eastern Islands. He had not heard the news from his daughter yet and seeing Kritpunya overjoyed him. He helped Kritpunya to sell his goods at a handsome profit, and to invest the earnings in goods that would be valuable along the route he planned. Sagardutta arranged for his daughter and Harshdev's wife Mrigvati, and her son Pundrik, to join him at Champa. Mother and son travelled non-stop on the fastest horses in Sagardutta's possession, and Kritpunya once again united with those who had loved him in his darkest hour. He enjoyed married life and the privileged status of a son-in-law for a while.

Soon Harshdev's sense of duty asserted itself. He set out on a sea voyage, taking Mrigvati and Pundrik with him. His entourage comprised three laden ships with guards, assistants, servants and slaves. They travelled along the busy sea lanes, selling and buying goods at each harbour, relying on the trading networks of Sagardutta and the political networks of Indrabhuti. At each port of call, Harshdev ensured he carried out his political instructions to the letter. They travelled through the kingdoms of Banga, Kalinga, Bhoj, Andhra, Mahishmati, Bhrigukach and Prathisthan. Harshdev delivered top-secret letters to the designated contacts and carried back sealed messages. His newfound acquaintances guided him on the best means of travel. For parts of the journey, when travelling by land was more convenient, the ships sailed separately with Harshdev's trusted assistants.

Towards the end of his voyage, Harshdev travelled to the Eastern Islands. At the isle of Hastisheersh, he met a group of other intrepid merchants and they formed a larger convoy. As luck would have it, they had only sailed for two days when a furious storm hit them. Most ships were lost, and there was no hope of finding survivors. Harshdev hugged his dear wife, and together they embraced and calmed their son, preparing for death. Fortune smiled on them, as theirs was the only ship that survived the tempest. The wrecked boat ran ashore on a small island.

To their ship's crew, the islet, called Kalika, was of no interest to traders and had no inhabitants. The survivors prayed for their departed fellow voyagers and thanked the gods for their lives. Within a few hours, they discovered the island had fruit trees and fresh water. Considering themselves twice blessed, they planned the repair of the boat and to wait for the next favourable wind.

At one point, as Harshdev stood discussing matters with the captain, a sailor came running and spoke to the captain in a high-pitched tone, in his strange tongue. The captain listened to the man thoughtfully, stroked his long, unkempt beard and closed his eyes as if lost in thought. Another sailor stepped forward and made suggestions.

The matter became clear to Harshdev after a few rounds of heated discussion between the crew members. It helped that Harshdev had given the crew a fair and generous treatment. The crew members also respected Mrigvati, who had tended to many of the recovering men, and loved the precocious Pundrik.

The matter was that the gods had not only spared them but had chosen them for a fairy tale event. On Kalika was a gold mine requiring only the simplest steps to sift the gold. And there was so much gold there was no need to fight. The travellers decided amicably how they would distribute the ship's capacity among themselves. Thus was Harshdev's fortune transformed again through a dizzying cycle of unanticipated misfortune and blessing. Having more than he needed, and with the support of the crew, he turned back to Bhrigukach, from where he travelled on land.

By this time, his possessions had swollen to enormous proportions – but his head had not. He remained a grounded, methodical man with a mission. A small contingent of armed men – infantry, cavalry, archers and elite body-guards – now protected his entourage. He had appointed skilled horse keepers. The finery and the discipline of his procession evoked wonder and awe wherever he went. His blend of trading and martial skills, and his acuity and humility, won him respect everywhere he went.

The Harshdev who had left Vaishali as a bedraggled, contemptible man re-turned to the city as a triumphant man lacking neither wealth nor status. The wheel of time had taken a full seven years to turn such that the former beggar established himself as the renowned 'Kritpunya' in a resplendent, tasteful white marble palace.

CHAPTER 107

A CHIEF MINISTER IN EXILE

Vaishali was shaken. It was as if an earthquake had hit it. On its majestic Royal Avenue, a tall Brahman with a heavy-set body trod slowly towards the assembly hall. He had the gait of a man unused to walking long distances on foot. Mud caked his bare feet, and he wore a simple loincloth tied around his waist and a threadbare upper garment that did not hide his sacred thread. His tattered clothes were at odds with his regal looks. His eyes had a shine, and sandalwood paste lined his forehead. His face had the equanimity coming from having wielded tremendous power. His bearing was grave, and his shoulders erect, but his eyes were downcast.

He was not alone, though he walked by himself. It seemed as if a thousand others, mostly Brahmans, were walking in his shadow. They maintained a distance as if scared to go too close to him. They were similarly attired. Behind this first contingent was a more mixed crowd of curious onlookers. It was clear that all the strata of society were represented in the throng. From the barred and ornamented windows of the mansions that lined the avenue, many pairs of eyes peered at the tall Brahman who walked alone in the middle of thousands. All conversation took place in hushed whispers, as if the raising of one's voice was an insult to such a great soul.

That great soul was the world-famous scholar and practitioner of political science, the redoubtable man who had been chief minister of Magadha, Varshkar. The astounding news he had been stripped of his powers and banished from Magadha had preceded his appearance in the city.

The representatives of the eight clans were waiting for him in the courtyard of the assembly hall. They had gathered in haste as breathless guards conveyed word of his arrival to each of them. They had not donned their finest clothes but displayed in their manner the importance they attached to the event. Jayaram, the chief policy planner and foreign minister, stepped forward and welcomed him on behalf of the leaders and the assembly. He guided Acharya Varshkar to the council hall, while the others followed them.

In the hall, Jayaram asked Acharya Varshkar to take one of the high seats. The acharya ignored the request and walked two more steps to stand in front of the chairman's seat. He turned and looked at his hosts. For a few moments, he stood silent and expressionless. There was pin-drop silence in the hall. When the acharya spoke, his voice was low but deep. The others strained to hear every word he pronounced.

'Enough. That is enough courtesy', he said. 'The eight clans must not be deluded. I am a poor Brahman. I do not have any office. I have nothing. In the time-honoured tradition, I have come to ask for food to fill my stomach. If my scant knowledge may be of use to you all, perhaps the eight clans will consider providing me with a livelihood. In return, I shall serve you.'

The reception committee had taken their seats after guiding Acharya Varshkar into the hall. Now Jayaram sprang to his feet. 'Arya Varshkar is a legend. It is Magadha's misfortune it no longer has your services. We do not claim any right to your services either, Arya. We are honoured to have you here as our guest. Your presence blesses this land.'

'That is very assuring. May the powers that be bless the eight clans. I shall not accept charity. I do not ask for it. If this Vajji Union gives me food and sustenance for my work, I will gladly live off it. Not otherwise.'

An aide transmitted a message from the Foreign Secretary to Jayaram. He nodded and said, 'Acharya Varshkar is a great man, indeed. As the acharya is aware, Vaishali is a republic. Only the elected representatives of the eight clans may actively administer matters of state. The caste-based systems of other states do not apply here. This is our ancient tradition.'

'I am not aware of such a constraint, as a matter of fact', Arya Varshkar said. 'You need to be cautious and alert, I agree. But I do not offer my services in administering your state. I only wish to earn the livelihood I am given.'

'But do you command us so, excellency?' the Foreign Secretary, Nagasen, interjected. 'We wish to treat you as an honoured guest.'

'I see what you mean. But other norms apply here. I am needy and in search of a livelihood. I only ask you to grant me this wish in a manner that preserves my dignity.'

'Arya, it is enough that you bless this Union of ours, the Vajji Union', Jayaram said. 'That itself is a service we value very highly.'

'Gentlemen, I am a career diplomat and politician. I have no experience in dispensing blessings, and I do not see why my blessings should carry weight.'

There was some shuffling in the panel of the men of the eight clans. Chief Minister Sunand passed a piece of parchment to Jayaram. He read it with a frown and composed himself before speaking. 'If Acharya Varshkar wishes to press charges of ingratitude and misdemeanour officially towards the emperor of Magadha, the Vajji Union is prepared to consider such a proposal.'

Acharya Varshkar received this proposal without any display of emotion. 'The emperor of Magadha is not a subject of this union. Hence the Vajji Union's resources are perhaps not best utilised for such an end. I think it bears repetition that I only need a means of making my ends meet. I do not bear rancour towards the emperor.'

'And if you hold an official appointment and we mount a campaign against Magadha, will you not be in difficulty in the ensuing war that ensues?'

'What difficulty?'

'A dilemma, perhaps?'

'Perhaps. But why will the Vajji Union give up its values and adopt an expansionist policy?'

'True. How about the other scenario? It is true, is it not, that Magadha may attack us? What will the Arya do then?'

'I shall do what is appropriate.'

'And what will guide appropriateness? Discretion, justice or diplomacy?'

'Diplomacy.'

'Whose diplomacy?' Jayaram smiled for the first time.

Varshkar trembled with passion. 'My diplomacy, young man!' he said.

'Then, by your logic, the future of the Vajji Union in such an eventuality will be driven by your diplomacy?'

'If the leaders of the Vajji Union deem it fit, yes.'

'Arya, this goes against the values of our republic. Such an approach may fit into an imperial establishment, such as that of Magadha. A republic may only govern by the clauses of its constitution, without being made susceptible to the personal preferences of an outsider with a conflict of interest, however learned he may be.'

'Then the Vajji Union will not provide support to this Brahman?'

Sunand spoke up for the first time. 'Arya, you know well that our decisions are governed by consensus and precedent. We will need some time to discuss this matter. We do not have an adequate mechanism to take an immediate decision. We request that you be our guest till such time as we consider the best way forward.'

'Chief Minister, I do understand the situation. Very well, it must be so', Varshkar said. 'May I spend this time as a guest of Somil, the scholar, in the southern part of your Union?'

Relief showed on Jayaram's face. He said, 'As it pleases his Excellency. We will arrange payment of a thousand gold coins daily and appoint slaves for the arya's comfort.'

Varshkar bowed deeply and left the hall. He cast a lengthening shadow as he receded from the council members.

CHAPTER 108

BHADRANANDINI

Vaishali had seen many staid days. Now there was excitement in the air. The dramatic entry of the dishonoured Chief Minister Acharya Varshkar and the settling in the city of a creature quite different from the tattered Brahman caused the excitement. The new migrant was the exquisitely beautiful prostitute Bhadranandini of Vidisha. Just as Acharya Varshkar was a world-renowned pundit in his sphere, Bhadranandini was a celebrity in hers. Within no time, all Vaishali grovelled before her, and her glamour even threatened to rival Ambapali's.

It became common knowledge that Bhadranandini had been the mistress of Vidisha's crown prince and had left the city in a huff after a misdemeanour that the prince committed. Like her peers in those times, she was a wealthy, powerful and accomplished woman. She was beautiful, of course, but she was also a graceful dancer and an accomplished singer who had mastered the theory of music. She had mastered fourteen fields of study and excelled in visual art. She was highly conversant with the scriptures and could intellectually stimulate the greatest of scholars. Her visitors had to pay a hundred gold coins to see her dance. She declared herself a snake woman, and she allowed no man to touch her body. She had become the toast of the rich and mighty in Vaishali. They flocked to see her, because of her beauty, her idiosyncratic personality and her mystique. Those who saw her dance grew besotted with her, and the fact they could not enjoy her did nothing to loosen her spell on them. The rumour grew that the prince of Vidisha was a snake god who had sent Bhadranandini to get even with Ambapali after she had spurned him.

The door to Bhadranandini's mansion was always closed and guarded by a large contingent of soldiers heavily armed. A big drum stood in the middle of the square the guards occupied. Whoever wanted to see Bhadranandini perform had to beat the drum and hand over the fee of a hundred gold coins. The chief of staff led him through a small opening in the door into a world of enjoyment. Women surrounded the visitor, gave him wine and invited him on a luxurious mattress garnished with silk cushions and bolsters. Bhadranandini's rule was to allow only one man into the pleasure house at a time.

It was a cold new moon night in January. The sky was clear and starlit. One and a half watches had passed, and the streets had fallen silent. A young man rode his horse at a leisurely trot along the deserted lanes. He stopped at Bhadranandini's mansion, where a caretaker, recognising him, came forward to take the horse's reins as the rider dismounted. The chief of staff stepped forward and asked, 'Sir General, what do you want?' He seemed to think the visitor may not be willing to pay the fee.

The rider appeared none-too-flattered by the use of the honorific title. He fished out a bag of coins, tossed them to the man and casually beat the drum twice. The sound pierced the chilly, still night and must have made many people, ensconced in the warmth of their homes, start. The visitor strolled to the opening in the door.

The guard standing by the opening gulped, unable to bring himself to question the man. He looked at the chief of staff, and asked the visitor, in a small voice, 'Sir, is it a full hundred coins? We have to –'

'It should be. Should be more, not less. You men can keep the extras.' The young man smiled affably.

'May the gods bless you, Sir!' the guard said, his teeth glinting, and he ushered the visitor inside.

Inside, the chief of staff led the visitor through a corridor decorated with paintings and flowers and lit with rows of earthen lamps with scented oil. At the end of the gallery, the young man walked alone through curtains of beads and entered a room where day and night lost meaning. He rounded a pillar to move into a small lounge where Bhadranandini and her maids stood waiting for him.

The composed young man wilted for a moment at the sudden sight of the famed beauty. She smiled, and her dimples drew his attention. She stepped up to him and took his hand to lead him to a plush seat. He sank into it. Not a word had passed between them. Bhadranandini was aware of the effect she had on him. She bowed and asked, 'How does the gentleman wish to be entertained? Drink, dance, song, a game of dice, a comedy? Anything is possible here.'

Bhadranandini's expert touch had its impact. Her visitor had recovered his poise. He looked into her eyes and said, 'No, dear lady, I only want your company in private, and I wish to converse with you.'

'Since the gentleman seems aware that his pleasure must be limited to conversation, I shall be honoured.' Bhadranandini bowed again and nodded curtly to her servants, who vanished in an instant. She waited while their footsteps receded, and the sounds of doors being shut were heard. She poured wine into two crystal cups and served pieces of meat on a silver dish. She laid the liquor and the food in front of her guest. 'How may I serve you, Sir?' she asked coyly.

'Come and sit next to me, Lady!'

His tone was devoid of lasciviousness, and she did as he bade her. She smiled sweetly and looked into his eyes. 'You do know I that am a snake woman', she said, 'that I am not touchable?'

'I do, dear. This intimacy is intoxicating enough for me. I am fortunate to be here.'

Bhadranandini placed a cup of wine in the young man's hands and raised her own. 'May I ask with whom I have the great privilege of spending this hour?' she asked.

'Oh, I am just a citizen of Vaishali', he said. 'An insignificant one.'

'Come now, Sir, you are too modest. You do not have the bearing of an insignificant man. The number of men who cross the door to this hall is not too great.' Bhadranandini's eyes twinkled.

The man chuckled. 'No, it is not, given the barriers', he said.

'Well, may I know your name, Sir?'

'Ah, let us just say that you can call me what you like. Having the most beautiful woman in Vaishali name me will honour me.' He laughed.

'And will that name become your official name?' She smiled at him.

'That is immaterial. It is enough that you will use that name in this hall.'

Bhadranandini's eyes danced as she sipped her wine. 'I see that you are a stubborn man and that you wish to remain anonymous. May I ask why, at least?'

The man was visibly enjoying himself. 'Surely someone assuming a false name knows what the reason may be?' he said. He took a swig of the wine. It looked like it agreed with him.

'You seem to be an exceptional debater!'

'Perhaps I am an extraordinary lover?' He drained his cup and handed it over to her.

Bhadranandini laughter was musical. She filled the cup in a fluid motion and pressed it to his hands. 'Maybe you are. Your eyes hold deep secrets, and you chose your words carefully. That is an interesting paradox.'

He raised the cup and surveyed the glimmering red wine. 'And do you think plying me with liquor will resolve the paradox?'

'No, I had no such designs. I am only surprised that here, where I have seen men completely lose themselves, you are so guarded. I have not met such a cautious man in Vaishali!'

'And not in Magadha either?' He lifted his cup and gulped down the wine. He looked at her askance, a slight smile on his lips.

For the first time, she appeared ill at ease. She looked hard at him but did not detect any signs of hostility or malice.

His grin broadened as if to show he had no intent to threaten her. 'Did I make you uncomfortable? I think I can blame the wine if I was rude.'

'No, not at all. But I never went to Magadha.'

'Ah, I see. Then I must be mistaken. I thought your guards' headgear was popular among Magadha's Vratyas. But perhaps my mind works too much.' He still smiled as he probed her eyes.

She could not hide the gulping movement in her throat, though she kept smiling. 'I never paid much attention to that. Yes, in fact, I believe a couple of my guards are from Magadha.'

'Yes, yes. And maybe your earrings are gifts from them, or from an ardent admirer with a connection to Rajgrih. I know the jeweller who makes them.'

Bhadranandini's smile vanished. She traced the outline of her right earring thoughtfully, clearly wondering where this discussion was headed.

The youth laughed, stood up and stretched. He walked over to the wine pitcher and filled both their cups. He handed the full cup to her and said, 'Drink up, dear woman. Drink to this insignificant citizen.'

A light smile played on her lips. 'You are an artful man!' she said as she sipped her wine.

'I am satisfied!'

'To be called names?'

'No – to see you drink from the cup I filled.' He drank up, still standing.

She stood up as well and moved near him. She took the cup from his hand, filled it and handed it back to him, holding it in both hands and bowing. 'Now, be more content.'

'Bhadranandini's wish is my command!' he said, tilting his head at her. 'I shall take your leave after this drink.'

'Can I not do anything else for you?'

'Oh, you can! You can remember this slave of yours.' He bowed to her.

She gave him betel from an ornate gold box and sprinkled perfume on him. Then, in a clear departure from tradition, she held his hand and said, 'You are an interesting man indeed. When can I expect to see you again?'

'Any time. Very soon. I am smitten by you, Snake woman who cannot be possessed!' He laughed, waved and turned away.

Bhadranandini stood there for a long time after he had left.

When he came out, tossed a gold coin to the usher and strode on in purposeful steps. When he rode out, he knew Bhadranandini was looking out of the window, and her eyes were on his back.

When he had turned the corner, she looked at a mirror in a corner and nodded. A maid appeared. Bhadranandini said, 'Send for merchant Nandan.'

The maid gaped at her for a while. 'But it is late night!' she said. 'If we wake him up, people will talk about it.'

'No. Just do it. Go to the pool and sing the song you have practised. Make sure you are loud enough. That is all you have to do. He will come.'

'Are you certain? At this time…' She trailed off as Bhadranandini glared at her, bowed and pressed a panel in the wall. A shelf moved to open a secret door.

Bhadranandini went to her room and wrote out a few lines on a parchment, choosing her words with care and frowning with concentration.

CHAPTER 109

MERCHANT NANDAN

erchant Nandan's shop was a landmark in Vaishali's main market, the place where one could buy all they needed for their daily life, from spices to slaves to enrich their harems. The establishment opened at sunrise and closed only two watches into the night. Regulars knew they could strike the best deals during the second night watch when the shop was about to close. To a newcomer, the store aisles seemed to stretch without end, and the non-living objects to form haphazard heaps. Overall, the atmosphere inside was not cheerful. Nandan was popular for his inventory and his sense of trading, not for his bonhomie. If anything, there was a pall of gloom in the place. But that did not prevent it from teeming with customers.

The shop had four principal staff members: merchant Nandan, his wife Bhadra, his daughter Shobha and his son Daamak. At the age of sixty, only three insistent strands of hair graced the merchant's bald pate. People said of him he had never had a stomach full of food in his life. His skeletal appearance gave credence to the rumour. He typically donned a dirty loincloth and spent most of waking hours seated on a wooden chair, getting commodities measured. No one had ever seen him fall ill. While he was not friendly with his customers, he was matter-of-fact and gave them no palpable reason to dislike him. He was economical with his words and quick to count money. He was a man of his word.

Nandan was something of a legend in the city. But he had a well-kept secret.

CHAPTER 110

THE EXILE

Vaishali was a massive city. It had three major districts – the Upper District, the Middle District and the Lower District. The Upper District had seven thousand palaces in a setting that sparked the myths prevalent in distant villages that Vaishali's streets were paved with gold. The nobles and the richest merchants and traders lived here. The palaces ritually had urns of gold. In the Middle District were about fourteen thousand houses of the well-to-do. These houses had silver urns. The common citizens and the servant classes lived in the Lower District. By convention, their houses had copper urns.

There were also two suburbs in the North-East of Vaishali. One was called the Northern Brahman-Kshatriya District and housed particular clans of Brahmans and Kshatriyas. A famed garden with an abbey stood at its edge. The other was the Southern Brahman-Kundpur District. This was a place earmarked by tradition for a class of Brahmans called the Shrotriya Brahmans.

On the western edge of the city lay a village of commerce. The area was home to the Vaishya Caste of skilled artisans and farmers. The three districts, two suburbs and the trading village together made up the greater city of Vaishali.

In the Southern Brahman-Kundpur District lived a master of the Vedas, the logic, and the ritual, the rich and learnt Brahman Somil. Many powerful nobles and wealthy merchants as his clients, and many scholars from abroad travelled to spend time with him, learning at his feet. To the less educated, he was the one in whose house parrots recited the Vedas and corrected the students. Legend had it that Somil's father, the seer of his era, Rishibhadra, was such a luminary that the Goddess Sarasvati herself would appear to wipe the sweat from his brow as he performed yagyas. Somil's house usually had a yagya fire burning at any time. Somil would start a yagya at the crack of dawn and only be done with it by midday. Then, red-eyed and sweating, he would sit on a straw mat to commence his teaching duties.

This Somil was the one appointed to host the exiled former chief minister of Magadha, Acharya Varshkar, according to the agreement reached in the council. Acharya Varshkar received a handsome salary and a daily supply of goods that did justice to a very important person's needs. Besides, unsolicited gifts from those who had heard he stayed in Vaishali flooded him. The energetic Brahman did not touch any of the presents. He gave them out to beggars. Throngs of beggars and poor Brahmans visited Somil's house once word of Acharya Varshkar's generosity got out.

It did not take long for the story of the austere scholar-statesman Varshkar's banishment and his daily donations to spread far and wide. Many well-to-do people joined the crowd outside Somil's house just to see the great Acharya Varshkar. He received them sitting, calm, and mostly silent, on a cushion of Kush grass, dressed in two pieces of simple cloth and no other adornment but his sacred thread. His modest wooden cot, placed in a corner of his bare room, was visible to the visitors. He turned away the best cooks sent from the State's guest houses. He ate the leftovers from the daily yagya, mostly dishes cooked carefully at home by Somil's wife, Bhadra. For his meals, his only companion was Somil. He rarely left his room and the ritual hall, except to visit the outhouse. He refused the services of the slaves the assembly arranged for him. He only interacted with Somil, discussing philosophy and logic. Somil told many of his disciples, family and friends of the Magadhan's intellectual keenness and of his ability to span quickly from very distant perspectives to minute details.

Soon, well-off visitors and other citizens of Vaishali started adding their own donations to Varshkar's, and the lines of beggars and donors extended. Those who received the alms, and those who added to offerings, all went away singing Varshkar's praises. The stories of the great man in exile multiplied and grew more lyrical. His piety, frugality and generosity, his rejection of the slaves sent to him, and his calm acceptance of his fall from the dizzying heights of power gave people much to discuss.

CHAPTER 111

HARIKESHIBAL

et another character had arrived newly in Vaishali. This one had been an itinerant all his life. He was tall, not pleasing to behold and blind in one eye. He was visibly quite aged and thin as a reed, but his vision was sharp, his speech firm and his body wiry and muscular. An observer could be forgiven for speculating that he was perhaps not in the habit of bathing and that he may have saved on the expense of buying clothes by putting on those that were discarded in the cremation grounds. Needless to say, such an observer may also have concluded that this character had not wasted time and effort on washing the rags that he wore.

This character was a man who was free from all worries. He wandered as he liked – at the doors of houses, in the alleys of the main market, along Royal Avenue. He had no fixed shelter where he would regularly sleep or rest. He carried no essentials with him. His emancipated, untroubled attitude to the world was not reciprocated by those he encountered. He was abused, shouted at, and shooed him away from the places he wandered to, as his presence made them less pleasant. This ignominy did not seem to affect him in the least.

He spoke calmly when he asked for alms. 'I am Harikeshibal, the Chandal. I am a self-restrained celibate who had renounced all material possessions. I do not cook with my own hands. Give me something to live on.'

Sadly, many of those whom he addressed gave him abuse, threatening gestures and sometimes even beatings. He bore all of those and turned away to go to the next available source of alms. He had only survived because generous and kind people outnumbered those scared by his sight. He remained hungry very often when he lay under a tree for a rest, but hunger did not seem to demoralise him.

One day, he reached Somil's neighbourhood and watched with interest the beggars and donors lines, which started at the doorway and grew longer each moment. He joined the beggars' queue, where he was not for once made to feel unwelcome. As he drew closer to the meeting point of the two lines, he saw Acharya Varshkar seated on a cane chair covered by a plain thatched umbrella. Varshkar sat overseeing the distribution of gold coins and other presents to the mendicants, acknowledging their greetings with meekness. A group of scholars chanted the holy mantras as they did the work of parcelling out alms, receiving gifts, and controlling the snaking queues of men and women.

When Harikeshibal drew near the great man's seat, the assistants shrank back in horror. One of them lifted his long wooden staff, ready to hit the filthy man at the slightest provocation. Another shouted at him, 'Who are you? Do you not see that they are all Brahmans in this line? Run away!'

'I am Harikeshibal, the Chandal', he said. 'You are right, I am no Brahman. I am a celibate, however, and I have renounced all possessions. I do not cook with my own hands, and I live off alms. Please give me some food.'

The Brahmans looked at one another, and their panic multiplied. 'Go now! Go away!' another one shouted in a high-pitched voice.

He did not flinch. He said in his humble tone, 'I only ask for leftovers to eat. I do not need gold or clothes. I have no use for them. I am hungry, and you have much food. I need little, I need less than most men. I observe austerity. Just give me half of what you would give another.'

A rising chorus of warnings to go away and reminders of his low caste greeted him.

'The farmer sows his seeds whether rain is too little or too much. He sows seeds on high ground and on low. Give me food like the good farmer plants his seeds. Your act of kindness towards this low caste ascetic will stand you in good stead.'

The Brahmans had been restrained in their behaviour in the presence of the great ex-chief minister. The dirty Chandal beggar's words now inflamed them. 'Fool, scoundrel! You dare to call yourself an ascetic! Do you know what the word means? Do you not know that only Brahmans can receive alms and only alms given to a Brahman bring credit to the giver?'

'He who is devoid of anger, pride, violence, falsehood, stealing and greed is suitable to receive charity. Caste does not bind such suitability. He who has memorised the Vedas and does not understand this is no sage. He who keeps his equanimity and believes in the equality of humans, on the other hand, is more fit to get alms.'

'You, One-eyed Chandal, you dare to preach to us about false learning!' The Brahmans were now aghast, and several of them were visibly itching to get their hands on this peace-breaker. 'We will let our food rot rather than give it to one as haughty as you.'

'Then I must say that you will never earn virtue in your life.' Harikeshibal made this statement in a firm voice, without rancour.

It was as if a dam had burst. At this last insult, three Brahmans leapt forward. One had a stick with which he rained blows on Harikeshibal. The two others pushed him away, wrinkling their noses as they came into contact with him. 'Push him away!' the others shouted.

A sixteen-year-old girl came running and inserted herself between the three Brahmans and their victim. She raised her hands, and the Brahmans froze. They looked at her in wonder. She was a beauty dressed in the finest crème-coloured silk clothes. Her long hair was tied in a bun and adorned with diamond pins. Her neck and waist glittered with pearls and gems.

'Stop!' she shouted. The Brahmans gaped at her.

'Stop, you men! You do not know what you do!' she said, gasping. 'Do you know who I am?' She glared at Harikeshibal's attackers, and they hesitated and then moved back. 'I am Jayanti, princess of Pundarikini in Eastern Videha. My father, King Mahapadma, gave me in marriage to this man. And he refused to accept me. He has taken a vow to remain a celibate ascetic. He is a master of his senses, a remarkable sage and a man with divine powers. He has conquered his anger, but you must not provoke him beyond a point, because you do not wish to see what happens when he loses his great patience.'

Her words quietened the mob of Brahmans. The one who had the stick in his hand gulped and shrank back. They stared at the Chandal, wondering what to do next. One of them was still muttering, but he made sure he was inaudible.

At that very moment, merchant Nandan reached the spot with a cart-full of food and groceries. He had become a regular at the daily almsgiving. He took one look at Harikeshibal, rubbed his eyes as if in disbelief and then prostrated himself before the ragged man. Now the Brahmans who had just attacked Harikeshibal let out exclamations of shock. Little had they imagined the recipient of their blows and abuse would first have a princess come to his rescue, and then merchant Nandan lie prostrate before him.

Nandan rose and looked at Harikeshibal's fresh bruises. He sighed and turned to the cowering Brahmans. 'Gentlemen! This man standing before you is no ordinary human. Do not let his attire mislead you, listen to his voice and bask in the warmth of his inner light!' he said. 'Sage Harikeshibal has performed the hardest penances, and mediated with the greatest devotion, to attain high spiritual prowess. Do you not know of Kantar's abode spirits, to our north, where none of you dares to venture at night? This man has spent many seasons there and made the spirits of the place his slaves. If you failed to recognise his greatness, as many do, you made a terrible mistake. May I suggest you ask his forgiveness?'

The Brahman's stood rooted to their spots. They were perplexed and stunned. Some looked at one another, waiting for someone to take the first step.

Nandan sighed again and bent to touch Harikeshibal's feet. 'Great sage! Forgive these Brahmans. They did not know what they did. Please accept my alms and bless me and my future generations. Come with me, let me take care of you, my lord.' He bowed and asked Harikeshibal to follow him. The Brahmans watched the receding pair, followed by Nandan's servants.

Acharya Varshkar had sat silently through the whole episode. No one turned to him for advice, and he did not volunteer it.

CHAPTER 112

THE CHANDAL SAGE'S FURY

Princess Jayanti berated the Brahmans. 'Oh Brahmans, what you did was inglorious. At the hour when alms were being given out, in the presence of such a great man, you refused him leftovers! You abused him! You even attacked him… All I can say is this – if you value your lives, run after him now. Go to Merchant Nandan's place. Prostrate yourselves before him. Remind him that he considers anger a sin. Beg for forgiveness!'

The Brahmans listened to her. Some of them seemed half-convinced by her, but the doubters prevailed. One of them said, 'Shall we allow ourselves to be taken in by this passionate beauty? We know who we are, and we know there is a sanction for what we did.' He turned to Somil and Varshkar for support, but they sat silent as if they had not heard him. He frowned, but raised his fist and shouted, 'We will not rub our noses in the ground before a Chandal!'

Jayanti nodded grimly and left. More of the Brahmans joined the discussion. They criticised her for overstepping her limits. What right did a young princess have to command them? It was time for their meal, and they sat in lines, as was their custom, to start eating. After they had eaten, their gifts were brought for them. But before they could thank their benefactors and leave, a ghastly tragedy unfolded. The Brahmans seemed to first get drunk, though, of course, they had not touched a drop of wine. They swayed, rose to their feet and danced. They threw away their clothes and acted obscenely. Many vomited blood and fainted.

Varshkar and Somil had served the food themselves, as was their wont, and then retired. They came out on hearing the noises and stood watching the horrible spectacle. Varshkar was stoic, but Somil was teary, and his breath became shallow. 'Dear God! Arya, what… what is this? What can we do?' He was wringing his hands and would have collapsed if Varshkar had not steadied him.

'This is a tragedy', Varshkar said. 'I am sure it is Harikeshibal's wrath at work. How he has worked it, we can only guess.'

'What – what shall we do now?'

'Somil, the Brahman's treatment of Harikeshibal was abominable. I have no role to play here, and I did not think it proper to exert my authority. I do not have any. The princess was right. Take survivors to wherever the sage is and ask them to plead for forgiveness.'

Varshkar spoke with quiet authority. Somil needed no urging and took a large group of Brahmans to Nandan's mansion. They saw Harikeshibal seated on a high chair, the table in front of him, heavy with delicacies. The other Brahmans cowered behind Somil, who had not said a single word to Harikeshibal. Now when he spoke, he was grave and humble.

'Great Sage, forgive me. Forgive us. Treat us as ignorant youth, for that is what we are, compared with you. We prostrate ourselves in all humility.' He saluted Harikeshibal by lying on the ground in a seven-point position. The other Brahmans followed him with alacrity.

'We shall never make the same mistake again, with you, Arya or with anyone else. We ask for forgiveness and magnanimity!'

Harikeshibal looked askance at the Brahmans. 'Proud Brahmans! Do you really repent?' he said. 'If you do, you must go to Sankoshtak Abbey, and pray before the spirit Shulpani. You must please the spirit; your scriptures and yagyas are no use any more. That is the only way for you to survive! Accept it or die!'

The Brahmans took his words to heart. They bowed and left at once for the abbey he had designated to them. They were hungry, thirsty and exhausted when they reached the sanctuary. They begged a monk to guide them to the statue of the spirit, and prostrated themselves before it, chanting, 'Forgive us! Protect us!'

A light flickered behind the sculpture, and a beautiful woman stepped out, dressed in red and carrying a trident. 'Fools!' she screamed. 'I shall eat you all! I am the spirit's wife! You, who insulted the greatest of souls in your pride, have no right to live. Your craven apologies are not heartfelt!

'Does your reading blind you to the facts of life? Do you not know that Brahmans and Chandals are born in the same way? That they have the same life energy, sleep alike, have the same desires, jealousies, sorrows?'

The Brahmans trembled at the scorn and fury of the warrior woman.

'You said food could go to waste, but you would not feed the great Harikeshibal! No. You must all die.'

'Goddess! Forgive us!' the Brahmans wept. 'We thought…we made a mistake! Forgive us!' one of them wailed.

'Fools! You clean your outer bodies with water and feel holy. But you know nothing about the purity of the soul! Your artifices of yagya, incense, sacrifices – what are they good for? Have you given up falsehood? Greed? Desire? Your desires know no bounds! Look at your stomachs! You do not even know the true yagya, the true meaning of sacrifice!'

The Brahmans wilted in the face of her righteous anger. 'Show us the way, goddess! We shall follow you!'

'Fools! Start with austerity! Endure hardship, hunger, thirst! That is yagya! The life force that will possess you when you conquer anger, desire, lust – will stoke the fire of the true yagya. Unity of mind, speech and action will scent your lives more than incense! Understand the meaning of karma. Self-contentment is the final offering in the true yagya. Experience the unity of self and attain equanimity. The ideal to aspire to is Harikeshibal's state of mind!'

'May you be blessed!' Somil said. 'I accept every word of yours from the bottom of my heart. I take responsibility for the heinous behaviour of the Brahmans in my house. I ask for forgiveness. Your words will become our creed, and we shall spread it.'

They prostrated themselves again. Jayanti touched Somil's head with her trident.

'You speak the truth', she said. 'We will spare you. Go now!' She disappeared behind a rock.

CHAPTER 113

WAR DRUMS

The fields had been harvested, and the skies rumbled as if they were about to burst with rain. A different storm was also brewing. There was talk of war in Vaishali. Spies had brought news that Emperor Bimbisar had launched large-scale preparations for a campaign. The members of the assembly of Vaishali had invoked a clause calling for an emergency meeting. The representatives of the eight clans of the Vajjis, the nine Malla Unions and eighteen guests representing the Kosi-Kolon Republics were in the forefront, but the entire assembly was present.

Chief Minister Sunand cut a sombre figure as he inaugurated the proceedings. 'Gentlemen, may I have your ears', he said. 'I wish to describe the critical developments that led us to convene this special joint session, in which we welcome our Malla and Kosi-Kolon friends. You know that the emperor of Magadha has always been keen to destroy the eight clans. We discuss these grave matters together today because our fate is linked to that of our guests. Our Head of Planning, Arya Jayaraj, will explain how Magadha schemed to thrust war on us. We had hoped his crushing defeat at Prasenjit's hands would douse Magadha's militarism, but that was not to be. Despite our disinterest in expansion, we maintain facilities through which we gather accurate information on what our neighbours are planning. We heard of Emperor Bimbisar's war preparations as soon as they started. Gentlemen, not to put a fine point on it, war is likely, and Vaishali needs to prepare for it.' He took his seat.

Foreign Secretary Nagasen rose to speak next. 'Gentlemen, your attention, please. I shall explain the political context of this situation. As you know, until recent times, Champa was a thorn in Magadha's flesh. As long as Champa was independent, Magadha could not dominate the trade to the Eastern Islands. Treaties closely knit the three kingdoms on the Eastern Coast – Anga, Banga and Kalinga – and Champa controlled the alternate route to the east. Champa was an important trading partner for us and our gateway to the distant eastern markets beyond Indian shores. When we signed a treaty with King Udayan of Kaushambhi, we, therefore, ensured annexing Champa strengthened Anga. King Dadhivahan became the king of the merged kingdom, with Champa as his capital. King Dadhivahan was no great warrior, and Magadha swallowed up Champa, as you know. This gives Magadha a significant advantage in trade. However, this success does not satisfy them. The remaining eastern kingdoms of Kalinga and Banga now fear the Magadha war machine, but the word is that the Magadhans will turn towards us first.' He took a seat.

Now, it was Jayaraj's turn to speak. He was responsible for the management of treaties. He said, 'Sirs, I wish to draw your attention to the organisation of the eight clans and the dangers that face us. A few years ago, Magadha had eight thousand villages. Today it spans a vast swathe of land, and we have lost count of its villages. Only a few islands of independence subsist in their immense domain. Of these, Vaishali is the one that offends their sensibilities the most. We need to understand that King Prasenjit inflicted a blow on them, but it was Bandhul Malla and his sons who achieved that prodigious feat. The old Prasenjit faded away like a faint star. Emperor Bimbisar considers destroying us as necessary, and he senses the time is ripe for an attack. Until now, the combined republican forces of the Vajji Clans, the Malla Unions and the Kosi-Kolon formed a solid alliance. We still feel it is a strong pact...' Jayaraj mulled over his next few words before continuing.

'As you know, Gentlemen, there are sixteen large divisions in this land. Those of us present here forged our alliance long years ago, and it has stood us in good stead. Now, to counter the raw power of Magadha, we need to add Chetik to our treaty organisation. They have reasons to ally with us, but we face a problem. Bandits infest the route to their capital, and getting officials across is difficult, but we must do so quickly and with the necessary precautions.

'Now King Udayan of Kaushambhi is an important figure, and we have every reason to believe he will remain our steadfast friend. The Kurus and Panchalas in the north also will support us, as they did in the past.

'King Avantivarman of Mathura and King Chandamahasena of Avanti will not side with us. But Avantivarman will not go to battle against his son-in-law, Udayan. Emperor Bimbisar has married his daughter to King Udayan, but we can count on Minister Yogandharayan's diplomacy to make sure these two powerful kings will not add to Magadha's war efforts. This is a crucial matter, however, and we cannot leave it at that. We must do one thing: we know King Udayan is Ambapali's slave. We must ensure she uses her influence to shape the behaviours of the two kings.'

There were whispers in the assembly. Jayaraj waited for them to subside. Then he continued. 'Now, Gentlemen, we also need to consider the far lands.

Let us discuss Gandhar in the west, first. As you may know, at one point, Gandhar sent an urgent appeal for help to Magadha. Emperor Daryush of Persia is the Bimbisar of the West. He has already annexed the western part of Gandhar. Magadha and Vaishali both sent their men to Takshila for education, and they naturally came back with fondness in their hearts for their old university. But when Gandhar most needed aid, wars had already bogged down the Magadhans. Singh advised Gandhar that Vaishali, with its republican ethos, was a more natural ally than Bimbisar's Magadha. He explained Bimbisar was not too different from Daryush. When Gandhar approached me, I took quick action with this assembly's concurrence. Our young men distinguished themselves in battles in the Indus Valley. We can now call in Gandhar's debt to us, despite the many strong ties between Gandhar and Magadha. This is important.'

He waited for questions, but no one raised any. He continued. 'That leaves a few essential figures. We supported Kalinga against the southern kingdom of Assak. We made the right choice there. Kalinga will support us, and while Assak remains our enemy, they lack the clout that Gandhar, for example, has. I believe we can neutralise them militarily. As for the Kingdom of Kamboj, we know we can buy their loyalty – more so than the Magadhans who may offer more money, but do not have the relationships that we have. From a geopolitical point of view, Magadha has formidable military abilities. But we think we need to take on Magadha only, and no other major kingdom in India. We did what we could in diplomatic and policy terms.' Jayaraj sat down to whispers of approval.

The man next to him, a Gandhar, Kapyak, invited by the assembly, rose. He spoke in a booming voice that echoed in the hall. 'Gentlemen, I am privileged to be here before you. I am here to testify of the great valour and the considerable contribution of the eight clans to Gandhar's cause. The chief minister of Gandhar sends his best wishes and his gratitude to Vaishali.

'I was part of the Vaishali army division, and Acharya Bahulashavya himself inspected it before the start of the campaign. Please do not consider this a vague expression of benevolence. Let me affirm we owe our survival to you. We see a likeness of republican and democratic values between yourselves and us. I would also like to explain Vaishali division's contribution to the war. The division's task was to defend the Indus riverbank along the route from Pushklawati to Takshila. King Shas mounted a fierce campaign with a joint army. His army outnumbered the Vaishali division, but they fought back each of three Persian attempts at crossing the river. When the Persian forces retreated, defeated, your men crossed the Indus in a lightning tactic and captured the Persian army chief. Our army chief himself has committed to repaying the debt that Gandhar owes you. I am here to strengthen your hands. Gandhar is with you!'

A round of applause greeted this statement. Kapyak waited for it to finish. Then he said, 'I say all this because I know the one who led your men from the front and took part in the daring capture of the Persian army chief is a modest man. You know him well. His name in Singh! As you know, he married Rohini, daughter of Acharya Bahulashavya. The acharya saw the young couple loved each other and was happy to formalise the union. The whole Republic celebrated their marriage. Even today, you will hear stories of the celebrations.

'Acharya Bahulashavya and the council of Gandhar further cemented the ties between our two republics by sending here a company led by this insignificant man to further cultural and economic relationships. I will conclude by saying that within a few days, say four days, a powerful force of our elite soldiers and best physicians shall arrive at Vaishali.'

The applause this time was even louder. Kapyak bowed and took his seat.

Sunand stood up once more. 'Gentlemen, you have heard Nagasen, Jayaraj and Kapyak speak. I trust they reassured you, but Singh's and our men's valour is not enough to ensure our survival. Nor is the support of our friends.' The hall fell silent.

'I am sure', Sunand continued, 'you have given thought to the situation in all its aspects. You are experienced men of the world, and the Republic looks to you for guidance and wisdom. I will now put forward the necessary proposals before you: first, land and treasury security; second, infantry, cavalry and navy organ-isation; third, finance management and arms production means; and fourth, diplomacy, propaganda and espionage.

'Gentlemen, on the first point, I propose that Arya Suryamall lead the de-fence of Vaishali. He is already our Chief Security Officer. He knows the lay of the land better than anyone in Vaishali. I need not say more about him. Those who accept his nomination may please remain silent. Those who object may speak up now.'

The hall was silent.

'I ask a second time. Anyone who objects may speak now.'

The silence deepened.

'And I ask a third and last time. Those who agree with Suryamall's election may remain silent. Should anyone here have an objection, voice it now.'

No one raised a voice.

'Assembly members, Suryamall will be our head of Defence. Now, on the second of my four points, I propose Arya Singh for the overall command of the infantry, cavalry and navy. I ask for the first time: does anyone object to this proposal?'

The hall was quiet. Sunand repeated the question, but no one spoke.

When Sunand said it a third time and the silence continued, but Singh rose.

'Please speak, Sir', Sunand said to Singh.

'Gentlemen, thank you for your attention. This assembly wishes to honour me, and I am grateful. But I have a suggestion. I suggest that Army Chief Suman leads the armed forces on the ground and that I and others serve under him.'

A few members spoke up now. 'Well said', one of them declared, and there were more words of assent.

Sunand nodded. 'Very well, we need to vote since an opinion contrary to my proposal has been voiced. Please follow the procedures. A member of the staff will come to you with coloured sticks. Select the red stick if you support my proposal and the black one if you support the amendment put forward by Arya Singh.'

Singh stood up again. Sunand looked surprised, but said, 'Singh wishes to speak again. Sir, you may do so.'

'Gentlemen, I wish to clarify my position', Singh said. 'I do not oppose the original proposal. I only want to submit that Arya Suman is an experienced commander and master strategist, and not only a grey-haired veteran. The young men of Vaishali and I am one of them, see it as an honour to serve under him. I will be more comfortable serving under him than commanding such an outstanding personality. That is the intent behind my speaking. I ask that you please consider your choice in this light.'

Mild applause and murmurs of approval greeted the young man's words. The staff were fanning out, offering the sticks to the assembly members, and keeping the rejected sticks. When the scurrying was done, and the rejected sticks were piled up before the centre, the black sticks were clearly far fewer.

'The assembly agrees with Singh', Sunand said. 'Commander Suman will supervise our forces, and he shall set up his organisation as he chooses.'

The council appointed Bhadriya head of war production and Jayaraj, head of diplomacy in a similar manner. Sunand requested to appoint Singh assistant, and Kapyak, head of the navy.

After these appointments, Sunand said, 'Gentlemen, we should now address a matter of grave concern. We will require money and food to survive a long-drawn war. We do not have enough, in my opinion. It is as simple as that. We need to solve this problem today.'

Suryamall stood up, and Sunand nodded to him. He said, 'What can we do without money? And what is the solution?'

Sunand looked at Bhadriya, who rose and said, 'At this hour, we have only one solution, as we all know. We must take loans from the merchants.'

'But why would the merchants give the State credit?' Swarnasen interjected without standing.

Bhadriya said, 'Because their safety depends on our survival. At least I hope they will think so. We do not ask for charity. We can quote Emperor Bimbisar's example to them. Magadha has built its armaments on strong ties with its merchant class.'

Commander Suman then stood and waited for permission to speak. He said, 'Gentlemen, may I have your ears? Vaishali today faces an unprecedented danger. It appears the enemy realised our army suffers from decadence, and our finances are not in order. There are visible signs of decay. The fortifications have not been repaired for a long time, the moats dried up and squatters farm on some of them. We need to change our ways of working and to move on a war footing.' He looked at Bhadriya.

Bhadriya said, 'Gentlemen, I propose we issue twelve-year bonds totalling one hundred million gold coins to the merchants at the prevailing interest rates. My department will discuss the details with representatives soon. I trust we shall find a solution.'

The chief of the Kosi-Kolon rose, and Sunand gestured to him to speak. 'Gentlemen, the eighteen republics of Kosi-Kolon shall provide funds of thirty million. Further, we shall send our half of our combined cavalry to fight for Vaishali. This army shall provide for itself.' He sat down to thunderous applause.

The head of the Mallas, Rohak, spoke up to offer Vaishali a thousand elephants, a thousand chariots, twenty thousand cavalries and fifty thousand infantrymen. He stated the Mallas would fully fund those forces. The offer won another round of applause.

On a signal from Sunand, Suman stood to announce the names of those nominated to the war council. He declared that from that instant onwards, the council would meet daily, or more often if needed, to conduct proceedings in secret, reporting only to the chief minister.

The assembly was declared closed.

CHAPTER 114

THE WAR ROOM

Along the back of the assembly hall was a complex of catacombs leading to an underground room meant to be Vaishali's war room. This room, called Mohangrih, led through secret passages to a busy abbey that drew thousands of devotees every day. A towering statue of the abbey founder was the centre of attraction for the visitors. From a dark recess of the abbey's main hall, a secret door led into Mohangrih. The residences of the leaders of the assembly also had secret passages connecting them to the war room. A senior leader controlled each of the entry points. Even their family members and most trusted knew nothing of these passages. The code of the Vajji Union was that only the men who had bathed in the Holy Lake could learn of the passages to Mohangrih. The punishment for non-sanctioned knowledge was death, irrespective of the offender's status. Since two executions had been carried out on this account, no one in Vaishali took the code of secrecy lightly.

Sunand's announcement of secret meetings was a signal to the war council they should start their work in earnest. Seven oil lamps lit Mohangrih. The nine men who held Vaishali's fate in their hands – Suman, Sunand, Singh, Nagasen, Jayaraj, Kapyak, Bhadriya, Swarnasen and Suryamall – sat in a circle.

Nagasen, the Foreign Secretary, started the consultation. 'Gentlemen, as you will guess, I had prepared for this meeting in advance. I only needed to wait for official confirmation of the war council through our democratic process. I will repeat what I said earlier: Emperor Bimbisar plans to attack Vaishali. We have ample proof of this.

'More importantly, the ousting and exile of the great Acharya Varshkar is an act of deceit. Varshkar, as expected from him, has played his part well. He has become the public face of a centre of learning and charity, where he poses as a savant who abandoned immense worldly power to lead a celibate ascetic's life. People throng there, and it gives him suitable cover to conduct espionage right under our noses. He has set up a vast network – its members pose as craftsmen, businessmen, merchants, circus entertainers and prostitutes. Magadha has taken advantage of our open-door policy to build this network. It is, of course, controlled by that man with a razor-sharp mind, Varshkar.'

The war council received this statement with silence.

Sunand said, 'You mentioned proofs. What are they?'

'There are many. Let us discuss one. Did the news of the incident at Brahman Somil's place reach you?'

'About the Chandal sage and his curse?'

'Indeed, Sir. We can only infer Varshkar provoked and enacted it. Who else could have done it? As you know, several of our citizens died in that episode, but Acharya Varshkar thinks big. What he achieved was to make the one-eyed Chandal a figure of fear and reverence. Our people go to him to confide in him and seek his blessings. Could there be a better source for intelligence?'

'Perhaps not. But I asked for proof. Can the Chandal not be who he claims he is?' Sunand said.

'He could, but we know who the Chandal is. I will ask Arya Jayaraj to speak on that.'

'He is none other than Prabhanjan, the famous – or infamous – Barber of Rajgrih.' Jayaraj said in a matter-of-fact tone.

'What is that?' Sunand asked, his eyebrows knit. 'Barber?'

'Yes, Barber', Jayaraj said. 'But he is a legend, he is no ordinary barber. The Barber Prabhanjan is one of the most accomplished intelligence agents in this land, and the woman with him is a talented prostitute named Magadhika.'

Sunand lowered his head, closed his eyes and sighed. When he looked up, he said, 'The deaths of the Brahmans – I suppose poison achieved that?'

'Yes, the physicians confirmed it', Jayaraj said.

'Perhaps merchant Nandan is part of all this?' Sunand said.

'That is correct', Jayaraj said. 'But that is not all. You must have heard of Bhadranandini?'

'No, I cannot say I have', Sunand said.

'People think she is a prostitute from Vidisha. Her charms have our men swooning – she seems to hold Vaishali's life in her hands.' Jayaraj said.

'I guess she is not what she claims to be?'

'That is right. She is – as you guessed – a Magadhan snake woman. Her name is Kundani, and she killed King Dadhivahan when the Magadhans crushed Champa. Let me clarify this: many of my agents confirmed she is a snake woman. A man kissing her will die immediately of poison.'

Sunand stood up and paced the room while the others leant forward. Suryamall stroked his chin thoughtfully.

'And you say you found all this out through trusted men?' Sunand asked Jayaraj.

'As for Kundani or Bhadranandini, I have done more than that. I met her. So far, she had only driven men crazy and sucked up an incalculable amount of money from Vaishali. But surely, she is waiting for a signal to do something bigger.'

Nagasen said, 'And now, the head of Finance, Bhadriya also has news for us. So does Suryamall. Let us hear Bhadriya.'

Bhadriya spoke in a deep voice that echoed in the room. 'Sirs, you probably know of Kritpunya, the wealthy Champa merchant who settled in the main market.'

'Yes, a member of the assembly introduced him to me', Sunand said. 'And at one point a servant of mine pointed out his son's entourage. He sounded like an engaging and sincere trader! Is he…'?

'Yes, he is Varshkar's man. He has been buying up promissory notes issued by our corporation wherever he can. He has travelled to every kingdom of the land and cast a wide net. I have no figures on how much he has collected. But the plan is for him to bring our trade to a halt on Varshkar's signal.'

Sunand sat down, and Nagasen said, 'Now I will ask Suryamall to speak.'

'There is the matter of the bandit Balbhadra. We still call him a bandit, but he has grown in stature, to be honest. He is, in fact, a seasoned Magadhan warrior, whose ranks have swollen to ten thousand men. Further, we estimate they have reinforcements of fifty thousand men in the forest areas around our borders. These men belong to a single Magadhan army division. Some even infiltrated into our land disguised as ordinary farmers. They are waiting for the call to arms.'

Chief Suman rose, his forehead creased, and his lips pursed. 'In short, we no longer know who our friends and our foes are!' he whispered.

'Sir, that is true', Nagasen said. 'As you have deduced, the emperor need not mount an armed campaign to annex Vaishali. The web they spun has ensnared us. They have already done enough to crush us.'

Singh rose and waited for Sunand's nod to speak. He said, 'Minister, Sir, we apprised you of the enemy's vast conspiracies through a few examples. Now, let us look inwards at our own might. Wine and lust consume all of Vaishali's men. Our life force is spent at the Palace of Seven Worlds. The merchants we used to consider as masters of the commerce universe are not likely to finance us – at least that is what I sensed from market rumours. The finance minister can throw more light on the condition of our treasury, but he told me it is pitiable.' His voice had become hoarse. He lowered his head for a few moments before steeling himself to continue.

'Our army, praised in the assembly, has let discipline go slack. Our officers wasted themselves in debauchery. Their leaders did not set good examples.' Here he looked at Swarnasen, who did not return his gaze.

Sunand closed his eyes and locked his fingers behind his head. 'Does the finance minister have something to add?' His eyes were still closed as he spoke. He seemed to be in a trance.

Bhadriya stood and said, 'Only this, Sir, that if we go to war today, we cannot expect resources from the treasury. Tax collection has slowed down, and Balbhadra's campaign of terror has worsened matters. Perhaps Prince Swarnasen, who heads the army's depots, can raise the needed resources?' He looked askance at Swarnasen.

Swarnasen got on his feet without haste. He said, 'The main point is that if we cannot contain Balbhadra, we are finished.'

Kapyak raised his hand to speak and stood erect when Sunand gestured towards him. 'Sir, I need to reveal an important piece of information. The Magadhans have established a large army presence across the Ganges in Pataligram. They have used brute force to throw out the villagers from a long stretch of riverbank. They lined it with wooden forts every two furlongs. Pataligram has already become a formidable military centre, and our navy's supremacy is no longer secure.'

Sunand nodded, rose and started pacing the room. Then he turned to the group and looked at Nagasen. 'Nagasen, what do you recommend? I am sure you – and the others – are not planning to let Vaishali burn?'

Swarnasen staggered to his feet. He shouted, 'I suggest we capture immediately that wily Brahman and all those spies!'

'We can do that. But it will be an explicit invitation to war. A war that we have not prepared for', Chief Suman said calmly.

Nagasen nodded. 'That is right', he said. 'We need a three-pronged plan. First, we must send a messenger to Rajgrih. This messenger cannot be ordinary, he will need to be high-bred, sophisticated and a great diplomat. And he should go with a family and a large delegation of supporters. He should draw attention to himself and his family and proclaim our interest in long-term relations with Magadha. He should make a case for the avoidance of conflict, now that Magadha has annexed Champa and fulfils its commercial needs. And he should provide cover for at least two high-calibre spies to do a thorough military reconnaissance of Magadha. So far, our spies tell us what moves they make. We lack deep insight into the chinks in the enemy's armour and their financing.'

Sunand had seated himself and was much less perturbed. He stroked his chin as he listened with attention.

Nagasen continued. 'Second, we must keep the current secrecy level. Not a word must leak out that we are taking concrete actions. We must appear dull and lethargic. The enemy must not detect any signs of the vitality we will infuse into our defence today. Most of all, the Magadhans must stay under the illusion we do not know of their preparations and their spy networks. They should keep thinking they have trounced us and we are rotting away with every day.' He looked at

Sunand, and then at each of the war council members. Sunand raised a finger as if acknowledging an exceptionally good point.

'Third, we regain our strengths, but do so with no swaggering or hand-waving. We only need to chasten our best officers once and to have their seniors set good examples. They are not bad men. Their swords and arrows drew blood in battles all over the land. There is a reason why we have never faced an attack such as the one that Magadha is planning now. It is our men. We should sort out the state of our finances. We let matters drift for long, but we can set them right without too much fanfare. We need not go all over the marketplace to ask merchants for loans. We can approach a select few and use the proper amount of coercion.'

Chief Suman said, 'This is a well thought out plan. I propose that young Nagasen lead the mission to Magadha.'

'Sir, I feel my absence in the next few days will be harmful to our cause. May I propose that friend Jayaraj be the one? We will surely miss him too, but let us discuss how to minimise the impact of his absence from this room.'

'I will go, Gentlemen', Jayaraj said. 'But I need a free hand to carry out this mission as I like. I believe we should send a visible face from one of the old families – perhaps a close friend of Swarnasen with similar interests.' He let a smile flicker on his face. 'He should reinforce the Magadhan impression of us Licchavis. We must convey the message the emperor should consider forgiving the great man who lives humbly in our midst.

'I will travel in disguise. Overall, our mission must suggest we are scared, unprepared and unwilling to prepare for battle. We must not make my absence public, it is important. You can easily claim my thankless and impossible task overwhelms me.' He looked at Kapyak. 'Arya Kapyak, I would like you to act for me in addition to your appointed role.' Kapyak joined his palms in a namaste.

'That is excellent', Chief Suman said, stroking his white beard. 'Our tomorrow will differ from today.' He turned to Singh. 'Singh, I request you to coordinate the army's rejuvenation. I will continue to be the public face, and I will make it a point to show no great energy.'

'It shall be done, Sir', Singh said. 'I only have one condition – my detailed plans will also remain secret.'

Sunand stood, and the others followed suit. 'We are agreed', he said. 'We need to resolve the matters of finances, logistics and supplies. Arya Bhadriya will need to work on that, and he will receive our full support. Arya Jayaraj, you shall return within one month. We shall hold the next meeting of the full council then. Until then, I shall work personally with Bhadriya, and each of us knows what he has to do.'

CHAPTER 115

THE OUTSIDER

The mission to Magadha was launched with much fanfare. The cynics saw it as a sign of a jaded republic trying to buy its powerful neighbour's favour. A message was sent to Acharya Varshkar that the mission would praise the acharya's exemplary conduct, and request the emperor to forgive him. Varshkar received the message with a stony face, without comment. He wrote notes at a furious speed that midnight. When he was finished, he called up Somil and ordered him to get the notes over to Nandan right away.

Nandan, woken from his sleep, took the sealed notes inside and read them. In no time, he had washed and scurried out of his house even as his neighbourhood slept. He rode to a suburb of Vaishali where a man called Upali stayed. This Upali was a potter of exceptional skill who had recently migrated from Sravasti. Nandan handed over the notes, sealed again, to Upali and returned home before sunrise.

At sunrise, three men left Vaishali from its three doors. They travelled on foot. One went to the north-east and handed a command over to Magadhan Chief Udayi in his tent. The second marched to a crafts village where the Magadhan policy planner Dhruvavarsha hid and gave him a scroll. The third reached Magadhan Chief Sumitra and delivered a similar scroll. The three messengers returned to Vaishali without tarrying.

Unknown to them, a skilled spy shadowed each of them. The spies did not bother to trace their steps back to Vaishali. Following a plan, they skirted around the crowded areas coming alive with the morning and met at a deserted abbey. A village youth was lolling under a large banyan tree at the gate. The spies reached within moments of one another. They saluted the youth, delivered their messages in whispers, and he replied to each of them before sending them off in different directions. Then he closed his eyes as if in deep concentration. After a while, he pulled out a big parchment and sheaves of paper from an unimpressive cloth bag beside him. He pored over them and muttered to himself.

He rose and stretched lazily. He reached into his bag again, found flint stones and struck up a fire with which he destroyed all the material he had so carefully studied. Now he again mumbled. And some words were audible. 'Yes, only my sword and I!' he said at one point.

He started off on the route to Rajgrih. The sun had risen, but the trail ran through a lonely forest. Most parts along the path showed no sign of inhabitation. Once in a while, a cluster of huts broke the monotonous wooded landscape. The man walked at a fast pace, kicking up dust. It was sunset when he reached a small village known as Bhindigram. His steps slowed a little, and his face showed signs of tiredness, now that a basic comfort level was within reach. He saw a small abbey and wondered if he should rest there. Nearby was a house with a large boundary wall. He walked to the house and waited at the open door, calling out softly.

'Householder, may I seek shelter here tonight? I am an outsider. I have travelled long and far, and my feet refuse to carry me. I need food as well. I am hungry, and I do not have my own food. I will pay you in gold.'

The master was a wizened old man. He said, 'If you have gold, you are welcome, friend. We get very few visitors here. Today, as it happens, there are two more like you.' The old man pointed to a thatched hut in a corner of the courtyard.

When the young man reached the hut, he saw two others squatting on the floor, chatting amiably. 'Friends, I am an outsider like you. I need shelter, and I am lucky I found it.'

'You are welcome, friend, sit with us. We are lucky to have more company,' one of the men inside said. As they expanded their circle to let the third visitor in, they continued to chat in general terms, but their eyes communicated they had serious matters to discuss.

'Where are you from?' the new arrival asked.

'To the craft village.'

'But where are you from?' the man asked again, with a laugh.

'Oh, from Champa.'

'Champa? But why on this path then?'

'We had work, friend.'

'Aha, work.' the village youth laughed again. 'That is well, just as well.'

One of the other two gave him a hostile look. 'Is something funny?' he asked.

'Oh no, nothing funny, friend. I just tend to laugh.' He chuckled again. 'Oh, by the way, is any of you good at telling stories?'

'Stories?' The men were clearly uneasy with the newcomer's manner.

'I would love to hear a good story,' the villager said. He laughed again.

'What is funny?' one of the two men said. He was furious now. 'Are you a stupid villager?'

'I am actually a villager, Sir', the young man replied, ignoring the insult. 'And you two, Sirs?'

'We are citizens. From the city', one said coldly.

The villager laughed even louder. One man reached for a stout stick beside him, but his friend clutched his hand. 'Do not…Let him laugh. How is that a crime? It does not harm us.'

The man nodded as if he saw the point. He glared at the villager.

The footsteps of their host arriving with a rough wooden tray full of food broke the tension. 'Gentlemen, soldiers are combing the area outside. I wonder if they are looking for you?'

The two city men looked at each other, and then at the villager.

The villager chucked again. 'I must confess I am waiting for them. They will get here, by and by. We are looking for a few Magadhan spies. Vaishali has just passed a death sentence on all of them. Let me see where they are.' He rose, picked a fruit from the tray and strolled out.

The two other visitors had turned pale. 'We should see what is happening.' They stood up and rushed outside, leaving the master of the house looking on, with the tray in his hands.

CHAPTER 116

THE SHADOW MAN

Yet another terror stalked Vaishali. People were talking about a strange, long black shadow with the shape of a man strolling in the outer areas of the city in the early evening. The consensus was that the shadow had no body attached. But it was rumoured that the shadow had been heard speaking. The shadow seemed to be able to fly, to leap the river and mountains. The whispers multiplied. It turned out that people had heard him speaking in a hoarse, unearthly voice.

Groups of shadow watchers formed among all ages and genders. They had a herd mentality. People reported that on full moon nights, the shadow came over the mountains and across the forests towards Vaishali, circled the city walls, and then vanished into thin air. Perhaps it soared towards the stars. The shadow became a subject of heated debate between believers and non-believers and, irrespective of their convictions, an object of fear for most citizens. On several occasions, women collapsed in terror after they thought they had seen the shadow.

All agreed that for all the fear the shadow evoked, it had never harmed anyone. People hallucinated, went into spasms or fainted – but the shadow himself never physically touched a hair on anyone. People also noted he never hovered in the inner city.

The fear of war also loomed over the city. However, much the leaders of the assembly tried to control things, they could not keep secret the preparations for war. The fearful atmosphere created fertile circumstances for the legend of the shadow man to take root and grow stronger in the minds of the citizens.

Commentators and experts detected a pattern in that the shadow man was most often and regularly seen when Kritpunya's son went out on his daily evening ride. The sightings occurred at the far end of the ride when they were far from the city centre. The boy and his servants had actually been the first to report seeing the shadow man.

One day, the shadow man broke with tradition and touched the boy as he was riding. The witnesses stated that it was immediately obvious the shadow came over the boy and hovered above him. Then the boy let out a strangled cry before fainting. Later, the boy said that he had felt an icy grip on his throat. It took a long treatment under the best physicians to heal him. He refused to step out for his ride after the incident. The abrupt halt to the spectacle did nothing to improve the citizens' morale.

CHAPTER 117

THE GRAND WEDDING

Merchant Kritpunya was planning his son Pundrik's wedding, a ceremony designed to be extraordinary. Pundrik's bride-to-be was a beautiful, tender girl named Mrinaal. Her father, Dhananjay, was among the richest merchants of Vaishali – and of India. His forebears had lived in the city for many years. People deemed Dhananjay's wealth to be immeasurable but often speculated that if it came to counting, he would have more than a billion gold coins. The wedding extravaganza lived up to the expectations. People watched erecting structures for the celebrations, sprucing up the houses, beautifying entire streets, and guests streaming in with gifts from far and wide. The spectre of the shadow man lost its grip on the city. High-spending visitors meant increased demand for all kinds of entertainment, and for a few days, the pall of gloom over the city gave way to cheer and revelry.

The wedding ceremony took place. The bride and the groom had completed the circumambulations around the sacred fire and taken their sacred vows. The groom's side returned home in a grand procession with the bedecked, shy bride. Kritpunya had constructed a wing in his mansion for the newly married couple. He had spared no expense to make it the most lavish and comfortable palace.

The ceremony of the bride's entry into her new home was in progress. Vaishali's elite had converged at the spot. Pundrik's merry friends were busy feasting, regaling the bride with their stories and helping to manage the mountains of gifts brought to the grand occasion. Outside, in a large illuminated tent, the feasting continued. Food and drink flowed freely. Observing the traditions, Brahmans received silk clothes, shawls, cows, and gold-adorned slaves. Kritpunya's reputation had only grown since his arrival in Vaishali, and he did justice to it with generosity and good taste. Pundrik gracefully endured the sometimes bawdy jokes of his friends. Music and incense wafted through the air, making it heady. An army of servants kept the supplies flowing. Spirits were high.

At the end of the night's first watch, the music was still playing, but the crowd had disappeared, and the commotion subsided. Those who spoke had a tired tone. Only family, a few close friends and servants were still present. The grand bedroom in the new building had been decorated with taste, and sheer silk linen and with flowers adorned the bridal bed.

Pundrik entered the room, stiff with exhaustion but with his heart pumping wildly. He was dressed like the prince that he was. He paused before a large mirror to check everything was in order. He calmed his feverish heart by breathing deeply, as an experienced friend had taught him. The bridesmaids pushed Mrinaal into the room, whispering naughty things into her ears, and then shut the door. The couple could hear them jostling outside, craning to listen to what happened inside the room. Mrinaal stood near the closed door, shy and uncertain. Pundrik looked at her, nonplussed now that the moment he had expected had finally arrived. He found himself even more aroused by Mrinaal's shyness but did not bring himself to act.

The music stopped suddenly, creating a shock wave. A silence descended on the entire complex, and Pundrik and Mrinaal stood rooted in shock. A scream shattered the silence. What followed was pieced together from confused and conflicting accounts. An invisible man snatched the musicians' instruments. Soon, a guest saw the shadow man, screamed and lost consciousness. While others tried to revive her, more people saw the shadow man float along the roof towards the bridal suite. By then, Pundrik had grabbed a dagger and opened his room door. The giggling crowd outside had fled. Mrinaal saw Pundrik step back, looking scared. Next, he fainted. A dark-looking mass entering the room was the last thing she remembered.

CHAPTER 118

THE DILEMMA

Mrinaal woke up with a heavy head. She lay there, panicked, for many moments as she tried to accept her strange surroundings. Her mind started working, and she recalled the chain of events that had led to her waking up in this strange room. She looked around and was relieved to find she and Pundrik were in bed. Pundrik slept with a smile on his face. There was no trace of the shadow man. Everything in the room was in order. It did not signal he had witnessed anything untoward. She looked again at Pundrik's peaceful face. The shadow had left no mark on him. She tidied her clothes and walked to the window, which she opened a little.

Outside, the sky had paled. She turned back to admire her sleeping husband. He looked even better in dawn's light. A smile played on her lips. It was as if the shadow man's inauspicious visit man had not blighted them. She walked around the room to familiarise herself with it, touching the objects, peering at some of the smaller, expensive and exotic artefacts.

A polite knock sounded on the door.

She opened it softly. The maid standing outside saw the smile on Mrinaal's face and contented look on Pundrik's, and her eyes twinkled as she laughed. She clapped her hand over her mouth, not to appear insolent, and gestured to Mrinaal to step out. When Mrinaal did so, she found herself surrounded by many of her ladies-in-waiting. They looked at her keenly and seeing the events of the night had cast no shadow on her relieved them. They were about to deluge her with questions when they halted. Mrinaal turned to follow their gazes.

Kritpunya was striding down the corridor, looking worried. He showed signs of relief when he saw Mrinaal standing hale and hearty. He greeted her but did not stop. He went straight into the room, and his chest heaved as he took a deep sigh at the sight of Pundrik snoring peacefully.

The mood lightened as Mrinaal and the women also entered the room. First hesitant, the questions then sprang up as if someone had opened the floodgates. The maids did not usually speak so much in front of the household head. But the night's events were not usual.

What was the shadow man's origin? They had heard of him neither in myths nor in grandmother's tales. He had never featured in the threats mothers used to put their children to sleep. Could it have been a mass dream? If not, where did the shadow man disappear? The questions kept coming, but no one had answers. More people came into the room, a Brahman among them.

Pundrik stirred and rose to rest his back on the bed rest. His eyes were still drowsy. They sought Mrinaal's eyes by instinct, and the couple's eyes lit up when they met. Then, Pundrik registered many visitors surrounded him, including his father.

Kritpunya rushed to him and said, 'Son! I am so…Did you see anything last night?'

Pundrik gave his father a wan smile. He had a curious expression. The Brahman interjected, 'Master, that shadow man was a bad dream, a figment of our collective imagination. It has been known to occur. I shall recite mantras and conduct a ritual to pacify the spirits that caused it to happen. Please do not trouble the bride and the groom.'

Kritpunya had seen many vicissitudes in his life. He decided to accept this challenging time with patience. He performed a small ritual in which he washed the limbs of his son and daughter-in-law, and left the room.

Pundrik hardly had time to spend with his new bride. He was soon parted from her and taken to a separate chamber where he received a back and limb massage by a trained masseur. He bathed and dressed, perfumed himself and put on his ornaments. When he stepped into the room where his close friends were waiting, they greeted him with loud cheers and laughter. Some asked him pointed questions about his night, but those who knew of the shadow man put a stop to that line of teasing. Pundrik parried off their queries with an enigmatic smile, one that did not light up his eyes.

Some persisted. One said, 'Well, friend, perhaps you had had too much wine? That may be why you do not seem to have exciting enough stories for us?'

Another said, 'Oh no, let him be. Give him more time – he has just woken up from an exhausted sleep!'

Now Pundrik spoke for the first time. 'The horses', he said.

It was as if he had doused his friends with cold water. Pundrik's words seemed to come from a distant, alien species and not from their newlywed friend's mouth. The timbre of the voice was completely unlike Pundrik's. His friends gaped at him.

He repeated the same words that made no sense to his shocked friends. Then he stood and walked listlessly to a door. He looked unaware he owed conversation to his friends. He passed the door and left the room. His friends stood rooted and stupefied. Then, they saw his footsteps falter and become unsteady, like those of a drunkard. Two of them raced to his side. One grabbed his arm to steady him.

Pundrik had stopped his daily outings after his terrifying encounter with the shadow man. Now his strange, unearthly tone and his insistence on walking towards his beloved horses perplexed them. The stiffness of his bearing also stunned them. His amiability and humility had vanished. He walked like one possessed by a spirit.

His servants could not refuse him. They ran to fetch his favourite horse. A servant fled to apprise Kritpunya of the development. The merchant dashed out to the courtyard, his arms flailing. He asked Pundrik to stay at home. Pundrik gave his father a blank smile and looked past him.

Kritpunya shrank back at his strange behaviour. His panicked thoughts reflected on his fallen face. What had gone wrong with his dashing son? He seemed under a spell. The servants made out the words 'shadow man' as Kritpunya, uncharacteristically, muttered to himself.

Meanwhile, the bride was recounting the story of the shadow man's dramatic entrance to her maid. The servant was horrified. 'Then it was not a dream or an illusion! The shadow man was here! But where did he go?'

Mrinaal confessed he had fainted and collapsed in a heap when the spectre had attacked them. She only woke up in the morning and did not know what had happened during the time she lay unconscious. It gradually emerged everyone had lived the same experience. The night was a blank in their memories.

Kritpunya and his wife conferred in hushed whispers on the state of affairs. At the end of their discussion, Kritpunya said, 'Enough is enough. I will send word to Arya Varshkar. Let me call merchant Nandan.'

CHAPTER 119

PUNDRIK'S RIDE

Pundrik rode the horse like he had never done before. His servants tried to keep up with him, but it was no use. It was as if horse and rider had fused into a supernatural entity. The servants had never seen anything like it before. Except for the clouds of dust that it kicked up, it was as if the horse was floating rather than galloping. After a while, they reined in their horses. The clouds trailing Pundrik's horse had melted into the horizon. The servants came to a fork in the forest path and had to stop there.

It was a long time before Pundrik returned, his face betraying no sign of emotion. When he got close to his servants, he smiled as if nothing had happened. The servants immediately formed a protective ring around him and led him back to the palace. As Pundrik dismounted and walked into the house in his strange new gait, the servants ran to Kritpunya to tell him what had happened. Kritpunya's forehead was now lined with worry. His servants had never seen him in this mood. He sent for Pundrik and tried to converse with him, but it was no use. Pundrik continued to exhibit his unnatural self.

As Kritpunya sat despondent and tense in his room, his wife joined him. She said that it was likely some kind of fever that had descended upon their son as a side effect of physical pleasure. She hoped that it would be a passing phase and that sleep, rest, food and the consummation of his desires would cure him over time. People would smile when they remembered this strange phase of his behaviour.

Pundrik withdrew into a shell in the next few days. He dissociated himself from his friends and stopped speaking to his parents. To his bride, he was polite but distant. His friends, puzzled by his cold treatment, stopped coming to visit him. They speculated on his state of mind, and some of them concluded that his mother was right; there could not be a medicinal cure for Pundrik.

The bridal suite was soon barred to all except the newlywed couple. When young Mrinaal was asked about matters, she said that he only slept, ate and drank wine. He did not speak much, if at all. His appetite was shrinking.

Varshkar had received news of these developments without any reaction. Nandan's servant had relayed a message from Kritpunya to him. Later in the day, however, he brought up the matter of the shadow man with Somil.

'Somil, this shadow that looms over the city's fringes – the one that you had told me about – are there still reports of sightings?'

Somil thought for a while. 'No, Arya, I have not heard anything in quite a few days', he said. 'I cannot say exactly how many days, but I do know it has been quite some time.'

'I see. Can you find out more about it please? Can you also ask Nandan to instruct Kritpunya that he must keep a tight watch on his son?'

CHAPTER 120

GAURPAD, THE CHEMIST

The world-famous chemist Gaurpad was in his element. He was in his laboratory, lecturing his students – young men from all over the land and from abroad. Even as he spoke, some groups of students were conducting tests assigned to them in corners of the laboratory. The colours and features of the students in the lecture groups showed signs that the world from Greece to China, and all the lands and islands in between, was represented here.

'So, scholars, is there an answer to the question from your friend from Kapisha? It is an interesting one for us. What are living beings and non-living objects made of?' Gaurpad said. He looked around him at the semicircular ranks of his keen-eyed students. Their eyes were bright, but no hands went up.

'They are made of the basic elements that combine in various forms. Matter results from the mixing of the elements in three different forms. Some forms of matter are made up of one kind of parmanu, atom, the particle that is the smallest building block of the world. The forms of matter made of only one kind of atom are called the basic elements. Other forms of matter combine atoms to form the anu, molecule, in a chemical reaction. We call these compounds. The third kind, mixtures, combines elements, and compounds in physical unions. This is what makes the world.'

A pale-faced Chinese-looking student with a ponytail said, 'Sir, what is the difference between the anu and the parmanu you mentioned earlier?'

'Think of it this way: the atom does not have an independent existence as such', Gaurpad said. On the other hand, for any compound, the smallest particle that retains all its properties is the molecule. In nature, the atom must exist in a stable form as part of a molecule. It is molecules that practically represent nature, and not atoms. Atoms and molecules have weights, and different types of atoms have different binding efficiency when it comes to combining to form molecules. In some cases, the binding is such that is stable.'

'Sir?' A dark-complexioned student from the island of Sri Lanka raised his hand. 'If all matter is made up of these substances, and if we master the science of their combinations, then can we continually put them to our use as we wish?' There was a tone of wonder in his voice.

'Young man, some of the substances are accessible to us, and others are not', Gaurpad said.

Another student asked, 'Master, are atoms eternally indivisible?'

'No, no, that is not the case. Some atoms break of their own accord and combine with others to convert into different types of atoms. Chemical reactions can stimulate such changes. Today, we believe that we can convert "nag" atoms into a form of mercury, from which gold can be obtained. A lot of research is being done on this, and a breakthrough is not far away. The trick is to put the smaller atoms into larger atoms, giving a stable mutated atom.'

The class listened to this in silence for a few moments. Then a hand shot up from the back. 'But Sir, how is all this done?' The question came from Kapish, a student from Gandhar.

'It requires energy from light rays, and also electric energy such as the kind you see in a bolt of lightning. Atoms consume these forms of energy when they disintegrate and release them when they combine to new stable forms.'

It was clear certain students had not grasped this. 'Not how are such processes achieved, Sir?' another student asked.

Gaurpad nodded as if to show that he understood the difficulty of the topic. Gesturing with his fingers to illustrate the concepts he described, he spoke slowly, searching for the right words. 'Students, think of it this way. The molecule of every compound is like a small – no, a minuscule solar system. You were taught earlier that the earth and the other planets perform their peregrinations around the sun, each in their own paths. The sun itself is not still, and it traverses the universe. Within a molecule, the particles that carry an electric charge revolves around a core particle. What is in the space between the central core and the revolving particles?'

The students were silent.

'Nothing! Vacuum!' Gaurpad eyes shone, and his voice became high-pitched. 'Thus, what we perceive as solid is largely composed of empty space! Does the Bhagwat Gita not say *anorianiyan mahto mahiyan*, smaller than the smallest and greater than the greatest? This unity in the cosmos reflects on the eternal truth that God is greater than the greatest and smaller than the smallest.'

A Magadhan student sitting in the front row raised his hand and spoke. 'Master, should we consider the nothingness to be the sky? Vacuum implies nothingness, but the sky is not nothing. It is – we know that.'

'Perhaps we have veered into philosophy from chemistry. But the sky is not nothing. A fluid pervades all our atmosphere. It ties together the atoms, this earth, the planets and the universe. This life force, shakti, provides energy to the living and the non-living world.'

'What is the balance between this life force and the material world?' a Tibetan scholar asked.

'Son, matter itself has two forms. The material form and energy form. Material has weight and volume, energy has the power to achieve work. Energy depends on the material. Now, the material can be in three states: solid, liquid and vapour. Heat energy can change these states. What is special about these states? You may recall we discussed that solids have hardness, liquids achieve level-ness, and vapour tends to occupy the available space. The material world exhibits changes in these states, but the totality of material and energy remains the same.'

The Tibetan frowned with concentration. A student from Tamrapali spoke. 'What are the forms of energy, Master?'

'Force or mechanical energy, heat, light and electricity', Gaurpad said.

'But when we can obtain mercury from the nag atom, and gold from the mercury, why don't we just get gold from mercury?' a boy in the middle asked in an excited tone.

Gaurpad smiled. 'I see that is always an interesting topic.' He launched into a complicated discussion of the current research and its limitations, and on why attempts to generate gold from mercury were sure to fail after centuries of efforts from the best human minds. Gaurpad always made it a point to let his tutorials meander where the interests of the young men took them. For his formal lectures, he followed a more rigid approach to content.

As the discussions ranged across disciplinary boundaries, one student asked, 'Master, are ageing and death not the destiny of all human life?'

Gaurpad locked his fingers and looked at his palms. 'Well, it depends. It depends on whom you ask, even in the community of scholars of chemistry. In my view, old age and death are not necessarily the end of all of us humans. You know well by now that our bodies are made of materials including minerals and salts. These are spent in maintaining the body. When the rate of depletion exceeds that of building up these essentials, the result is what we see as ageing. That is why different individuals with the same health, and born at the same time, age differently. If we control our constitutions, we can delay ageing. Can we postpone it forever? In principle, there should be ways.'

Gaurpad raised a finger to make a point but froze as a deep voice echoed in the hall.

'I am here, I am here, Gaurpad!' the voice said. A shadow blocked the doorway, and then a figure entered.

It was that of an imposing man dressed in all his finery. His silken clothes glimmered in the soft light, and he smiled at Gaurpad.

CHAPTER 121

THE UNEXPECTED

Gaurpad was stunned. The voice that the visitor spoke in seemed to have come down from centuries ago. The great chemist and scholar Gaurpad rose slowly, as if he was in a trance. He went to the visitor and fell at his feet. The class gasped. Some students in the back rows rose to their feet, watching the spectacle with eyes wide and mouths agape.

The young scion slipped his foot out of his red shoe and touched the prostrate chemists' forehead with his toenail. 'Rise!' he said.

Gaurpad staggered to his feet and stood bent before Pundrik, hands joined in a namaste. The students were now whispering and nudging each other. This was not a sight that they would have considered to belong to the realm of the possible.

The man drew himself up to his full height and waved at the students in an imperious manner. He did not say a word, but it was clear that he was dismissing them. They looked at each other in wonder, and some of them turned to look at Gaurpad for direction. None was forthcoming. Slowly at first, and then in a stampede, the students left the hall. Their queries and exclamations merged into an inchoate mass of noise along with their hurried footsteps.

The man looked around, seated himself on a high seat and gestured to Gaurpad to take a seat as well. They spoke in pure Sanskrit.

Gaurpad said, 'God of gods, you are here?'

'Did you not see it?'

'I did indeed, lord!'

'Then why did you not come?'

'I was full of doubts, lord.'

'Perhaps you thought I was no more?'

'No, lord. I – I was wondering if it was you.'

'You mean – because Vaishali is inaccessible for me?'

'The universe is yours. But what made you bless Vaishali?'

'That Kritpunya…He robbed me of a fortune in Kalika Island. He had no right to. I must set him right.'

'And that is why you have deigned to come this way? I see, Lord.'

'That is not all, Gaurpad.'

'Not all?'

'I am curious. About Ambapali. I have heard she is unforgettable. Is she?'

'That she is. But she is not a goddess fit for you.'

'Is she fit to be known?'

'That she is!'

'Then I will know her.'

'There is another one, lord!'

'Another one?'

'Fit to be a Goddess?'

'Indeed, lord. But…she is a snake woman.'

'Hmm. I shall destroy her pride. Who is she?'

'She lives in Vaishali under the name of Bhadranandini, the prostitute.'

'I see. I shall enjoy her as well.'

'She will die, lord!'

'Yes. Let her. When will the war happen?'

'Soon.'

'Good. I will feast on blood. I have not drunk much since the war of the Kurus. How many soldiers do you think?'

'I think three akshauhini formations will perish at the least. So just under half a million.'

'Good. Good. I will wait for the feast. I have waited long.' The strange man got up. A chilling smile played on his lips, and his eyes had a strange shine. 'You will keep this secret?' His tone was contemptuous.

'Of course, of course, lord!'

The visitor, a man possessed by a spirit, sauntered away. Gaurpad stood rooted, hands joined in a namaste.

CHAPTER 122

FATAL ATTRACTION

The night was quiet. A loud boom shattered the drum at Bhadranandini's mansion. The guards gathered around the one who had called. It was the scion Pundrik. He had ridden there on his white steed, which looked divine in the soft light.

He threw two bags at the head of the guards. 'The larger for your mistress. The smaller for you.'

The guards looked at one another, and their leader took a step back. They hesitated to speak.

'What is the matter?' Pundrik's voice was stern.

'Only this, Sir, that Lady Bhadranandini no longer entertains guests.'

'And why is that?'

'Sir, as you know, the war…She must obey the standing order from the assembly.'

'Hmm. I do not care for those orders. I order you to take me to her.'

'But Sir –'

'Have I not paid you more than the fees?'

The guard's forehead was damp with sweat. 'Sir, you have.' He looked at his men, but none showed any inclination to speak. 'Sir, I wish to return your gold, I cannot disobey a wartime order.'

Pundrik's hand moved in a fluid sequence. Next, it held a long sword that glimmered in the pale moonlight. The guard took a step back.

'Sir, we must follow orders. Our mistress…'

'I am her master!'

The head guard felt a hand on his shoulder. It was one of his men. 'Come this way', the man said and took the sword-wielding Pundrik into the mansion. The maids melted into the aisles when they saw the man with the naked sword.

The man strode into Bhadranandini's chamber. Only then did he sheathe his sword and stand smiling before the famous woman.

Kundani affected anger. She said, 'Sir, do you not care for the orders?'

'No, beautiful lady! I care only for my pleasure!' Pundrik said.

'But I cannot welcome you', Kundani said.

'Ah, we can dispense with the formalities. Sit.'

'I cannot sit with you.'

'Then dance.' Pundrik laughed.

'You are a gentleman, but you do not behave honourably, Sir.'

'That is exactly what I could say to you, Lady! You do not behave honourably!'

'On what grounds?'

'I have paid your fee. I have the right to enjoy you.'

'Do you think the sword entitles you to that?'

Pundrik threw the sword to one side. It fell with a clang. He raised his arm in a disarming gesture and grinned at Kundani. 'I thought you were not the type to fear a sword!' he said.

Kundani's confidence faltered. 'If you decide to use force, you know you can do it.'

'Force? Are you charging me with intent of rape?' He smiled. 'I only ask for my dues.'

'And will you drink?'

'Oh, I want to do it all tonight. It is a special night. For a sensuous woman like you, it is no night to be alone. I am already a fortunate man tonight and knowing you will only make me happier.'

Kundani looked hard at this abrasive, brash man. She hid her feelings and gave him a dimpled smile. 'You are a strange man, Sir!' she said.

'Is that so?' he said.

'It is, indeed.' She smiled with practised duplicity. She signalled to a maid to get wine. She bowed slightly towards her guest and gestured for him to sit.

Pundrik made himself comfortable and pulled Kundani gently by her hand until she sat next to him.

'You could conquer the world with your beauty!' he said.

Kundani laughed. She handed Pundrik a bowl of wine.

'Bless it with your lips, Lady!' he said.

'No, Sir. That is not my custom.' Kundani's smile stayed fixed, but her facial muscles showed the slightest signs of strain.

'Oh, but who cares for customs, dear? It is time for pleasure. Do as I say!'

'Is that an order?'

'No, a request.'

Pundrik burst out laughing at his own wit. Kundani eyed him wearily. Did the fool want to die? She wondered at the strangeness of his character.

He raised the bowl to her lips. She blushed and sipped the wine, delicately at first and then gulping all of it.

He stared at her. 'You did not leave a drop for me!'

'There is more', she said. She poured out a fresh bowl and handed it to him.

'But why a different bowl? I wanted to drink from the same one!'

'That is not possible.'

'Not possible!'

Kundani beamed at him. 'I am afraid so, Sir.' She pushed her bowl away.

Pundrik said, 'I see. You do not wish to be kind to me. You do not want to please me.'

'But I am bound to please you, Sir. You will find much pleasure here.'

'What I want now is to drink from the same bowl as you. Allow me to taste the nectar of your lips!'

'You do not understand, Sir.'

'Do you think I am a fool?'

'What if I say I do?'

'Well, I would forgive you for that if you do as I say. Now.'

'And if I don't?'

'I will not forgive you.'

'And what will you do, Sir?'

'Kiss your lips.'

Kundani's smile vanished. 'That is enough, sir. Please – you must not cross the limits I have set for this establishment.'

'Just give me that bowl, dear.'

Kundani lifted the bowl.

'Oh, and drink from it first', he said.

Kundani steeled herself, drank from it and handed him the bowl. Her heart was throbbing at the thought of what would follow.

Pundrik gulped the wine down greedily, unable to conceal his triumph. He rotated his head, beamed and stretched his arms. 'This is life', he said. 'More!' He handed the bowl back.

Kundani's face was white. She took the bowl and sat still, shocked. Who on earth was this, who could drink from her bowl and stay alive? Her hands trembled as she filled the bowl and handed it to him. Her tormentor pretended not to notice the effect he had on her. He drank up in a moment and returned the bowl, signalling with a move of his head that he wanted more. As Kundani took the bowl, he leant forward and stroked her neck.

Kundani stood on her feet, feeling a fear that she had never thought she would experience.

'Are you angry, dear?' He smiled innocently. His speech was not slurred.

'Who are you?' Her voice was faint.

'Your lover! Who thirsts for you! Do not stand so far away, Lady. Come and give me more wine. Here, let me...' He rose steadily, poured the wine himself and gave her the bowl, holding it in two hands. 'Make it richer again, dear!'

She could not look him in the face. She took the bowl and drank half the wine in it, felt drained and weak and collapsed onto him. He steadied her and took the bowl. In an instant, he sat, and she was in his lap.

She felt a surge of craving, a feeling so alien it shocked her. She looked at the man through blurred eyes. Who was this conqueror of death? What gave him the capacity to make her powers defunct? She reached for more wine and drank half of the bowl, spilling some. Was he laughing at her? Never mind. She pushed the bowl into his hands, he gulped the rest of the wine down and took a long, deep, breath.

An animal instinct guided her to move her swollen, quivering lips towards his. For the first time in her life, she felt a tremor of pleasure so deep she could never have imagined it. That was the last thing she felt. The next instant, her head lolled, and she went limp.

'Too soon!' he said as he lowered her to the floor gently.

He picked up his sword and strode out towards the gate. No one stepped forward to challenge him. When he stepped out, he reached in the folds of his clothes and tossed a bag of coins to the guards. He nodded without a word.

Soon, he was on his milk-white horse, trotting away as if nothing had happened. A woman's hoarse scream rent the air, but it did not seem to affect him.

CHAPTER 123

THE UNINVITED GUEST

It was Ambapali's birthday. The day had become a community festival for Vaishali, and the assembly was closed. The Palace of Seven Worlds glittered with lights, scents and colours. A thousand floating lamps on the Blue Lotus Lake made it look like the stars had descended onto the earth. Ambapali had ordered to throw the outer gates of the Palace of Seven Worlds open for all. The Palace was full of wide-eyed, shy commoners.

No one knew this was the last time the Palace of Seven Worlds would dazzle so.

In the seventh and innermost compound, Ambapali and her maids and slaves entertained the cream of the city. The dance and music performances reached their usual dizzying levels, heightened by free-flowing wine and good humour. Clerks and caretakers worked at a furious pace to keep track of the gifts that never seemed to stop and came, as usual, from wealthy men from every known corner of the world. They included elephants, jewels, arms and fabrics. A long corridor was used to showcase the gifts, and their sight reminded onlookers they were at the centre of the material world. The radiant Ambapali had by then gained semi-divine status. She gave her attention to her guests, taking special pains to soothe the men visibly embarrassed by their competitors' largesse.

The evening air was heavy with the enticing flavours of roasted meat and heady wines. Perfumed lamps cast soft lights on the bodies of young and beautiful women of all colours and races. They sang and danced, kept wine bowls brimming, served the kitchen's delectable produce and engaged visitors in conversation, dice games and whatever else the men fancied.

Ambapali's dress was a milky white and covered her well while highlighting her form. She moved between the groups with effortless grace. It was close to midnight. The select few the cream of the city – remained in the compound, mostly in horizontal positions. Some of them had succumbed to sleep.

Swarnasen was drunk. He said, 'Lady Ambapali, this is bliss! Supreme bliss! I only have one unmet wish.'

'Why do you not fulfil it?' Ambapali asked.

'Ah, that is the pity. I cannot.' Swarnasen raised his bowl to his lips, realised it was empty and handed it in a jerky motion to Madlekha, who filled it and handed it back with a smile.

'Now that is most intriguing', Ambapali said.

Swarnasen's eyes were sleepy. 'Oh, I wanted it so much', he said.

'Dear Prince, what might remain an object of your desire?' Ambapali's eyes twinkled, and Madlekha suppressed a smile. 'Suryamall, Priyavarman – friends – come here! Our prince has an unfulfilled wish. Should you not help him?'

A few of Swarnasen's friends staggered to them. His bowl was empty again, and he stared at it, lurching on his seat.

Somdutta said, 'What is it, Prince? Will a sip of this wine help you open up to us?' He offered a gold cup to Swarnasen.

'No, oh no. Oh my heart, it burns!' Swarnasen said.

'Give the prince more wine. It will cure his heartburn', Ambapali said, laughing, to Madlekha, who was her usual efficient self.

Priyavarman said, 'Let us all drink to the prince and his unfulfilled quest!'

The men drained their bowls, which were replenished instantaneously as if by magic.

Priyavarman yawned and said, 'Friend, now tell us, what you crave?'

'If Balbhadra had been invited here, I would have wet my sword in this wine and run it through his heart. Ah, we would have known peace!'

'So, that is your desire!' Priyavarman said. 'We would not have guessed. Well, Lady Ambapali, you really should invite Balbhadra – that is the only way the prince would stand a chance of fulfilling his wish!'

Ambapali's laughter was musical. 'But I only have the power to invite citizens', she said.

Suryamall chimed in, 'Friend, it is not such a great thing. Why do you not realise your ambition before sunrise today?'

Ambapali put on a mock-serious face. 'Friends, has any of you ever seen Balbhadra?'

They shook their heads.

'Oh! Then he could be here, enjoying himself, right under our noses!' Ambapali said, with exaggerated concern.

'What a disgusting thing that would be', Suryamall said.

'Why disgusting, dear?' Ambapali asked, putting on an expression of great innocence this time.

'Well…you know – if a bandit is right here among us, citizens', Suryamall shrugged.

Ambapali frowned, as is she was in deep thought. 'But I sometimes wonder whether perhaps, the birds and animals think us more savage than those living in the forest? We do have our faults, do we not?'

Suryamall's eyes opened wide at this challenging thought. He said, 'But…but what if you saw him, face-to-face? Would you not feel repelled?'

'Oh, I would offer him a bowl of the best wine with my own hands and consider myself honoured!' Ambapali said.

Suryamall's jaw dropped. 'Honoured!' he said.

'Why not, friend? He is, after all, a brave man.'

'Hmm, I can only certify that after he has engaged me in an open sword fight', Suryamall said.

'Since he has entered the land of the Vajji Union, that day will surely come. But who is this man, anyway?' Ambapali asked.

'Well, the chief minister has offered an award of ten thousand gold coins to the one who will answer that question', Suryamall said.

'But those ten thousand gold coins might become the price for the informant's head!' Ambapali said.

The men looked at Ambapali quizzically.

Then a clear and distinct voice spoke from a room next to the courtyard. 'If Lady Ambapali wishes to have the honour of serving me a cup of wine, this time is as good as any to do it.'

The words, pronounced distinctly but without shouting, struck them like a bolt of lightning. A man with an imposing, muscular body entered the room. He was tall and cloaked in black from head to toe. A hood hid his face. His naked sword glinted in the Palace's flickering lights. He steadily trod towards them, holding his sword high in his right arm.

The others had not recovered from their shock. Ambapali's mind was reeling. She thought she recognised the voice, but could not quite place it. Her heart thudded with fear.

Suryamall unsheathed his sword and leapt towards the intruder. 'If you are that bandit, you have a different fate in store than a bowl of wine. Prepare to die!'

'There is no rush, friend Suryamall! Let us follow decorum. I am the one whom you call a bandit. Allow me to fulfil Lady Ambapali's desire. After I have had the pleasure of a drink, I am open to proving my bravery as you wish. Does that sound reasonable?'

Balbhadra's spoke in a measured tone. Ambapali realised where she had heard this man before. She closed her moist eyes and took a deep breath. She stepped forward to hold Suryamall's hand. 'Wait, Sir', she told him. 'Our guest is right. Let me give him a bowl of wine.'

Ambapali stopped Madlekha with an invisible gesture and poured the wine herself. She gave it to Balbhadra with both hands, without bowing or showing emotion.

'I am honoured, Lady', Balbhadra said as he raised the bowl to his lips.

'It is I who is honoured, Sir.' Ambapali said. Her face was downcast.

'That is enough!' Suryamall shouted. 'Now stand back, Lady Ambapali!'

Ambapali stood her ground. 'There will not be bloodshed in the Palace of Seven Worlds. Please recall my constitutional rights', she said.

Balbhadra spoke again in a calm voice, as if he was addressing a formal meeting from a position of authority. 'Lady Ambapali, perhaps everyone here should have a chance to see their desires fulfilled. Now this distinguished gentleman, Prince Swarnasen, has expressed a long-felt yearning, one that seems to have troubled him.' He looked at Swarnasen, who had staggered to his feet and did not look steady. 'Friend Swarnasen, your sword, I see, is beside you. Take hold of it and try to fulfil your heart's true desire. Bandit Balbhadra stands before you.'

The measured, icy words struck them all dumb. Elation left Ambapali voiceless. Was she imagining it, or had the man who now went by the name of Balbhadra winked at her?

Balbhadra took a step forward. 'Advance, Prince!' he said. 'I have my own challenges – I have much work to do, Sir. Today is the birthday of the benefactress of the republic. It is a good day to fulfil the wishes of every citizen.'

It was clear Swarnasen was too drunk to fight. He reached for his sword and unsheathed it, but could not bring himself to take even a stance. His companions drew their swords.

Balbhadra raised his left hand. 'Gentlemen, Gentlemen! Let us do this the honourable way. First, the prince.'

While Balbhadra addressed the others, Swarnasen jumped unsteadily to pick up a spear lying next to him and threw it with all his might at Balbhadra, who sidestepped it easily.

Balbhadra looked at Swarnasen from head to foot. 'Now, tell me, Prince – should I not detach your head right here?'

'No!' Ambapali spoke in a plaintive cry. Her hand flew to her mouth.

Balbhadra nodded. 'I shall respect your wish, Lady Ambapali. But for what he has just done, the prince must go down on his knees and ask my forgiveness.' His manner continued to be cool-headed and detached.

Swarnasen cried out in a fury and launched himself at Balbhadra. The bandit parried and dodged him without effort. Swarnasen fell on his face. Balbhadra stamped on his sword hand to incapacitate it and then nodded. 'Well, that will do.'

Ambapali and Balbhadra were together now. Ambapali's heart raced, but she showed no emotion. The other men had formed a ring around them, but the bandits realised they were drunk, and they feared for Ambapali's safety.

'Stand where you are, each of you!' Balbhadra's voice thundered this time. The men shrank back. 'I have not come here to kill you, drunk womanisers!' He resumed his earlier tone. 'Look around yourselves. Look at the rooftop and each door here. My men are all around you, and I am next to the benefactress of the republic. Listen to me, fools, and do as I say.'

The Licchavis lowered their swords, following Suryamall's example.

Balbhadra spoke louder. 'Step forward one by one and lay down all your jewels and ornaments before me.' His voice carried through although he lowered it. 'If one of you holds back a single valuable piece, my men will cut off the limb bearing it. Prince Swarnasen, you will lead the procession.'

The men of Vaishali did as he said. Most of them moved unsteadily. Ambapali and Madlekha gave up their ornaments as well.

'That is well. Very well', Balbhadra said.

The chief usher came trembling into the compound, and said, 'Lady Ambapali! Thousands of men dressed in black surround The Palace of Seven Worlds…I do not know…'

Ambapali took a deep breath. Without looking at Balbhadra, she said, 'Tell our staff not to resist. Open all locks and doors as these invaders command.'

The chief usher stood rooted for a long time. He tried absorbing what he had heard and taking in the abject spectacle of the cream of Vaishali caught drunk and unprepared, cowering before this invasion of bandits. His shoulders drooped as he walked away.

Ambapali now addressed Balbhadra. 'My Uninvited Visitors, the next courtyard displays the gifts of this special day. Further, if you ask my staff to open specific rooms, they are bound to help you. I have nothing more to say.' Only Balbhadra could see she showed no trace of unhappiness. It was almost as if she had received the best possible gift on that auspicious day and was trying her best to mask her joy.

Balbhadra said, 'Lady Ambapali and the so-called gentlemen will now move to that corner of the compound. Quick.' The objects of his command followed it without a murmur. They were quickly ringed by Balbhadra's men.

Soon, a contingent of men dressed in black filled up the space they had abandoned, each carrying a pack neatly strapped to their back and a drawn sword. Their movements were precise, unhurried, and conveyed a sense of discipline.

Balbhadra looked at them and said, 'Men, what have you taken today? Let us give the elite of Vaishali a brief inventory.'

'We have confiscated all the grain and useful food stocked here', one of the shorter men replied.

'And why have we not taken anything else?' Balbhadra asked.

There was silence in the compound. The hum of insects seemed to turn louder. 'We are bandits, I am given to understand', Balbhadra said. 'The officials of the city sent armies against farmers, robbed their food in the name of war readiness and left their children hungry. My men and I have set this injustice right.' Balbhadra raised his sword and laughed. 'Victory to Lady Ambapali, whose granary will feed hungry mouths in hundreds of villages.'

The men of Vaishali stood silent and shamed. Ambapali closed her eyes and controlled her exultation.

'Lady Ambapali, this republic is not different from an empire when it comes to its treatment of the common man and woman. Its values have eroded. That the assembly executes its decision-making through a system of open discussion is not enough to provide superior governance. Does the assembly have the pulse of the people?

'Do you not have poverty and slavery on the one hand, and drunk, womanising courtiers on the other? Look at these men: their diamonds are like pebbles to them. And here they are, feasting and making merry after sending their army to scoop up every grain of food from those who live from hand to mouth.'

Balbhadra raised his sword, and its point glittered in the soft light. 'Men, we will retreat as we came. My gentlemen friends, take note we will continue to enjoy the company of some of your notables. Do not move till you know the last of us has left. If you do, I will not stop my men from finishing you off, and sacking the Palace of Seven Worlds. History will immortalise you as drunks who dishonoured your great republic.'

He lowered his sword, and an orderly retreat began. Soon, the last of the thundering hoofs had retreated into the darkness outside the Palace of Seven Worlds.

CHAPTER 124

THE LONE SPY

ayaraj had scouted the region during an earlier mission. He knew from his sources that up ahead was a village of the Malla and Kolo tribes and that he would find some sympathisers there if he was discreet about it. He approached the village through the dense forest that lay before it. He was on foot. He had a reputation for cool-headed bravery and had done much to earn it. He kept his hand close to his sword's hilt, and his ears pricked for any animal or human sign. He knew he had little time to complete his mission, critical to the survival of his homeland, and he must cover as much ground as he could. Soon, the path widened, and he sensed that he was close to the crossing of the three paths that he wanted to reach.

His feet were sore, and his back ached. He decided to stop for dawn to break out. He saw a small platform built along the path and occupied a corner of it. He tucked himself inside a sheet and fell into a light, alert sleep. He awoke by instinct, as the sounds of the birds and insects changed. The sky was a paler shade of indigo, and the stars were about to fade. He walked towards the village, towards food, shelter and his first intelligence gathering.

At the crossing, a caravan of traders joined him. It happened so that he could not have avoided it. It would have been strange for him to ignore the friendly greetings of the travellers. They were six men, with four horses and a cart. They carried the much-sought-after Maireya wine in large wooden barrels. Jayaraj accepted their offer to climb the cart and enjoy a faster ride. He steered the conversation to generalities and cordial small talk.

Soon, four more horsemen joined the caravan. His companions told him they were part of the convoy but had been left behind, and Jayaraj knew he was in trouble. One merchant asked what Jayaraj did for a living. They had avoided the question till then. Jayaraj said he was a cloth merchant. The men in the cart looked at his sword and sniggered. Jayaraj kept an impassive expression.

They reached the village by sunrise. It was a large village, marked by several signs of prosperity. Large wooden buildings lined its main street, and some inhabitants had refined grooming. A large inn stood near the outer part of the village, next to a thriving food market. The men of the caravan invited Jayaraj to join them at the only inn in that area. After he visited the river to wash up and complete his chores, Jayaraj agreed to his newfound companions' invitation to join them for lunch.

Something about the way the merchants conducted themselves signalled danger to Jayaraj. He joined them for lunch as they sat on an earthen floor in the courtyard, but unsheathed his sword and laid it beside him.

One merchant, a tall and dark man with an impressive turban, smiled at him. His sparkling white teeth showed, but his eyes remained cold. 'What, Sir, do you eat rice with a sword?'

'No, friend', Jayaraj laughed. 'Well, it is just a habit carried forward from the jungle, where I made sure I did not let down my guard while eating. Even here, perhaps I might meet a hungry wild dog. Who knows?' He laughed again.

The merchants smiled, some displaying a convincing act. But Jayaraj knew when he was among enemies. A swarthy man with an eyepatch took his place in a far corner as lunch was being served. Though they did not exchange looks or words, Jayaraj guessed that his entry was no coincidence.

'Young Sirs, I am a Chandal by birth, and an ascetic by nature. I do not cook my food, and I only live on leftovers. Will you not give me some of the food you leave?'

Jayaraj marvelled at the inexhaustible resourcefulness of the monstrous Acharya Varshkar as he understood the situation that he was in. The humble monk in front of him was the famed Prabhanjan, the barber and master spy. The wily Brahman, Varshkar, seemed to have a thousand arms and eyes. How else could Prabhanjan be on his track so soon?

There was hope, though. The Magadhan intelligence must know that he, Jayaraj, was an undesirable alien. Still, they had most likely not yet guessed they were up against Jayaraj himself. Else Prabhanjan would have bothered to use a different guise.

The merchants rose as one to greet this latest entrant into the scene with respect. They said they would gladly share their food with him, and he needed not to wait for their leftovers. Jayaraj joined them in paying his respects to the 'sage'. They gathered around him, giving him a mat placed higher than the others. As they ate, Prabhanjan launched into philosophical and religious discourse. Jayaraj acted as if he was hearing Prabhanjan out, impressed by the latter's verbal abilities, but thought feverishly about his predicament and how to get out of it. Soon, he had the outline of a plan ready.

'Friend, I would like to buy a horse. Where can I get one?' he whispered to the man sitting next to him. The man relayed the question to his neighbour, and they squinted up at Jayaraj as if wondering what he was plotting.

'How can we be of help, Sir? We are newcomers ourselves', the man next to Jayaraj said.

'Will one of you not accompany me? I would be far more comfortable with a friend by my side', Jayaraj said.

The men conferred among themselves. Shortly, one of them rose and gestured with a shake of his head that Jayaraj should follow him. He seemed to be the strongest of the group.

They walked out to the main street. Jayaraj's escort was a taciturn, bull-like man. Jayaraj motioned to a large house at a crossing. 'Friend, this sign says it is the headman's house. Why not seek his help?'

The man shrugged as if to say that he had no strong opinion on the matter. The prefect was a rotund, bald man who seemed satisfied with his station in life. He stroked his belly as he listed to Jayaraj. In an instant, he had found the solution. There were no horses available, he opined, but he did have a very strong pony, and he would highly recommend it.

Jayaraj kept himself from smiling at the audacity of the headman. He did not bargain down the price of five gold coins that the headman demanded. He said he would get coins from the inn and requested that he be allowed to ride the mule to test it, as well as to save time. He said that his companion would stay behind while he made the trip to the inn and back.

Of course, as soon as he was out of earshot, he goaded the pony to trot along the highway to Rajgrih. He had his sword and a little gold with him, and that was all that he needed to carry. As one look at the pony had told him, the headman had grossly exaggerated its qualities. It was, however, more than adequate for Jayaraj's escape. He would have an hour's lead by the time Prabhanjan's men started off on a chase, and they would surely expect him to flee away from Rajgrih, rather than towards it. By night, he had reached the next village on the highway. He was satisfied with what he had achieved.

He chose to stay at a run-down inn. One look at the inn and its keeper had told him that this was not a popular place, and he could count on his money to keep the man silent. He also had a good view of the road from the room that he chose for himself. He paid the innkeeper double the amount due for his stay and for a light dinner. As he lay back after eating, scanning the road for the caravan, he was startled by a familiar and creepy voice.

'I am a Chandal ascetic, good sirs. Will you not feed me your leftovers?'

Jayaraj realised that he had let down his guard. He had dozed off, and that infernal spy Prabhanjan had again pounced on him like a ghost. He dragged himself to his feet and stepped out after checking from a few vantage points that there were no other men visible outside. It was only the scoundrel Prabhanjan.

The innkeeper had not reacted to Prabhanjan's demand. He just stood there, unsure of what to do. Something in Prabhanjan's demeanour told him that shooing away this beggar would not be easy.

Jayaraj stepped forward. He said, 'Sir, I have eaten, and there is no one else here. Allow me to give you a gold coin.'

'I do not touch gold!' Prabhanjan spluttered.

Jayaraj pretended to be crestfallen. 'Well, Sir, in that case, you must ask a family man in the village. We have nothing to give you.'

'Or perhaps I may as well sleep hungry? Very well, it shall be as you say. I will sleep here', Prabhanjan said, eyeing the innkeeper as if to challenge him. The innkeeper shook his head dolefully.

Jayaraj shut his door and drew the chain across it. He peeked through the window at the silhouettes of the innkeeper and the spymaster. Prabhanjan was now engaged in an earnest discussion with the innkeeper. Something clicked in Jayaraj's mind. He realised that the innkeeper must work with Prabhanjan. That was the reason Prabhanjan had found his way here so soon, and also why he had felt comfortable in making himself visible without more men to back him up. It was likely the innkeeper was not as unathletic as he looked.

Jayaraj pondered his options and realised there was only one way to end this cat-and-mouse game. He tied his money bag tightly to his waist, put together his other meagre belongings and drew his sword. He put out the dimly flickering earthen lamp in his room. When he looked outside again, he saw that the two men now had swords by their sides. They were nodding and gesturing as they spoke to each other.

Jayaraj deepened his breath and produced snoring sounds. He saw the two listen carefully for a long time and then walk tiptoe to his door. He stepped behind as the two men burst inside, smashing the door with the practised moves of soldiers. Prabhanjan was at his bed, with his sword arm raised. Jayaraj quickly went for the innkeeper's jugular and reduced the man to a lifeless heap.

Prabhanjan whirled around, on his guard at once.

'Sir, it is dark here.' Jayaraj said. 'Your friend has attained nirvana in this dark. Let us step out to the faint moonlight outside. I will gladly send you on your way to nirvana as well. You will like it better in the light.'

Prabhanjan grunted. 'Death. It comes and goes. I have met it a few times by now, Sir. It is a part of my job – and yours.'

'Words of wisdom, indeed! From none other than the Chandal saint!' Jayaraj chuckled to provoke his opponent.

'No, Sir. This is Prabhanjan speaking. Now that I have picked up a sword, I am a soldier. And I speak the truth.'

There was no more talk. Jayaraj quickly withdrew into the courtyard behind him so that he was not disadvantaged by being silhouetted. Within the first few movements, each of the two opponents realised that the other was no pushover. Death was, in fact, just a hair's breadth away for either of them. Both of them avoided any brash shows of muscular strength. They circled, thrust, dodged, and parried. Jayaraj felt the sweat soak through his clothes and saw Prabhanjan sweating profusely as well. He prepared for a long-drawn battle. Just then, Prabhanjan attacked, but his foot slipped on a wet patch. He lost his balance, and it took a few moments for him to regain his balance. Those few moments were all Jayaraj needed. He swung his sword with just enough force to maim Prabhanjan's shoulder. Then he brought it in a wider and stronger arc to detach his tormentor's head from the rest of his body. Prabhanjan's hand continued to wield the sword even as his head hit the ground. Jayaraj almost fainted at the sight of the headless swordsman and the fountain of blood. As Prabhanjan's trunk hit the ground, Jayaraj collapsed in relief. He had to stop himself from shivering. He rose to his full height and drew up his shoulders. He took deep, long breaths with closed eyes. Then he moved quickly to get his pony. In a short while, he was riding towards Rajgrih.

Vaishali had drawn blood on Magadhan soil.

CHAPTER 125

IN MADHUBAN

albhadra rode out in front with his sword drawn. He rode fast but showed no sign he was desperate. Ambapali followed him, and right behind her were Swarnasen and Suryamall. Swords at the ready, five of Balbhadra's men, each of them heavily armed, hemmed them in. They crossed the deserted Royal Avenue without incident. The bandits had counted on surprise and had judged their enemy well.

Ambapali wanted to speak to the leader of the bandits. Her heart ached with longing to be by his side. But he showed no signs of wanting to talk. He pressed on at a steady pace. Ambapali was glad the darkness hid the flush of her face. She thought of the lion's attack and fantasised she was alone in the same hut with the love of her life. She remembered the feel of the ground below her feet as she danced with no sense of control.

She could not stop herself from speeding to catch up with Balbhadra. 'Sir, how much longer do we have to ride?'

'No longer', the bandit said in his laconic manner. 'We are there.' He called out, and the horses slowed to a canter before stopping. A dark shape moved to their right. It was a man who could have passed as a ghost.

'Is all well?' Balbhadra asked.

'Yes, Sir', the man replied in a soft whisper. 'It happened as you had predicted.'

'Good. Go to work.'

The black shape melted away. Balbhadra led the riders up a gently sloping path to a plateau where he dismounted and signalled the others should follow suit. He helped Ambapali down. Suryamall and Swarnasen looked shaken at what they saw. On the rolling hills to their south, they saw an endless pattern of fires with groups of bandits around them. Most sat, but some roamed between fires on foot, and others were on horseback. They looked cheerful and at home.

Suryamall whispered to Swarnasen, 'We are in the bandit's camp. And it is massive. The intelligence we had was right.'

Now something changed in their field of vision. A line of well-groomed cavalrymen entered the scene from their left. Their gleaming weapons and armour shone in the soft light of the moon and the fires.

'It is our men!' Swarnasen said, in an exultant hiss. 'They followed us!'

Suryamall was silent. He tried to decode the meaning of the events unfolding before him – the Magadhans massing for an attack, the bandits carrying on as if nothing was happening. He looked next to him at Balbhadra, who stood head cocked to one side, arms folded across his chest as if he was watching a spectacle of mild interest.

The Licchavi horsemen broke into a gallop, and the thudding of horse hoofs shook the ground. Suryamall and Swarnasen turned to look at Balbhadra again. He stood unmoved. 'Has he lost his senses?' Suryamall hissed. 'If only I had my sword with me!'

Now the Licchavis broke into a thundering charge. Suryamall's feverish eyes drank in sight, but soon he was frowning in consternation. The Licchavi cavalrymen seemed to charge into vacant space. Their lances and swords met nothing but wind. The scores milling around bandits had vanished as if wound up like toys waiting to be sprung away.

Swarnasen prodded Suryamall and asked, wide-eyed, 'What happened here? What sorcery is this?'

Suryamall lowered his gaze. He swallowed to hold back his emotion. When he spoke, it was in a hoarse voice. 'This is destruction. And I have to stand by…These are no ordinary bandits. They are trained soldiers.' He pointed to a corner of their field of vision. There, from a broad ridge, an endless line of black-clad horsemen snaked out to cut off the rear of the Licchavi brigade. Soon, they had enveloped the Licchavis on three sides, and then encircled them. As the Licchavi struggled to form a defensive circle, the bandits cut them off into small groups.

Swarnasen saw Suryamall had closed his eyes tight. He could not bear to see what would follow.

The Licchavis had started falling. Some were pushed into the fires, and their screams echoed over the din of battle.

Swarnasen turned to Balbhadra. 'Sir, please stop this massacre. This is not a battle any more but slaughter.'

'Do you surrender?' Balbhadra asked.

'Yes. Spare our men', Swarnasen said.

'Very well, let us end the fighting. Friend Suryamall, bring your officer to me.'

Balbhadra took out a conch and blew it. Men shouted out commands, and the bandits drew back from the slaughter. Suryamall rode down into the field.

Balbhadra's men parted to make way for him. Suryamall greeted his officer with a lowered head and a half-hearted acknowledgement of the officer's salute. The two of them rode back towards Balbhadra.

Balbhadra nodded to them and signalled for the group to follow him. He turned and rode along a slender path that grew thinner as it wound between rocks. Soon, they entered a tunnel and Balbhadra had to dismount and lead his horse by the reins. The others followed suit. They walked along a narrow but airy and well-lit cave path.

Without warning, the path opened into a lush green meadow. They faced the east, and a soft light bathed the landscape before them. Yet, the four prisoners from Vaishali were not admiring the natural beauty before them. The sight of five thousand horsemen dressed in black and arranged neatly in formation stunned them.

It seemed Balbhadra had brought them to that spot to show them his might. After he had let them take in the sight of his formidable army, he showed them back into another side of the cave. There, they found incongruously lavish couches made out for them. There were silk sheets and bolsters. Next to the couches were tables laden with fruits, sweets and drink.

'Lady Ambapali, friends, you are my guests today. Be at ease, and I hope you will partake of our humble offerings of food and drink. You must forget the nightmares of the night.' His eyes smiled at them.

He turned to one of his men. 'Lady Ambapali must be upset. We have troubled her no end. Find a place where she can rest.'

The man who had been ordered so bowed before Ambapali and led her away.

CHAPTER 126

THE IMMERSION

The man who had been tasked with taking care of Ambapali introduced himself as Samba. He handed Ambapali over to a statuesque, dark woman named Vama. Ambapali was impressed by Vama's demeanour and her refinement. She noticed that the cave had been furnished like a room in a palace, except that the floor was made of mud, and the walls were of irregular stone. Her mind was reeling from the events of the night, but she thought she might find solace here.

'Who are you, Sister?' she asked the black beauty.

'I am a masseuse, Lady', Vama replied.

'You are a lucky woman. You serve a great man', Ambapali said.

'I am glad you think so, Lady Ambapali. And you know this – I have heard your name many times, and my eyes are blessed to see you in person. Come, Lady, we have little means here, but I will do what I can to please you. Let me massage your limbs.'

'Very well, Sister', Ambapali said.

Guided by the Masseuse, Ambapali sank onto a massage table. Only then did she realise how weary her joints were. The perfumed oil, Vama's fingers, her astonishingly strong wrists, and her soothing small talk made Ambapali feel both relaxed and energised. When she was finished, Vama asked Ambapali to sit up, still leaving the oil on, and wait for a while. She went out and returned with a basket of food and wine.

Ambapali said, 'You have magic in your hands and fingers, Sister. You have been wonderful. May I ask when your master, the king of the bandits, will be here again?'

'That is hard to say, Lady', Vama said. 'He comes and goes as he likes, and he has much to do. Why do you not enjoy this moment of rest and help yourself to this special meal?'

'No, Sister, I am not hungry. Call him', Ambapali said.

'Call him?' Vama laughed. 'He does not come when called. He may come on his own, though.'

'What does that mean?'

'It means he is not ruled by anyone else's wishes.' Vama's smile was sly.

'I see. I used to think the same for myself at one point. Will you tell him, though, that I must see him? If you get the chance?'

'I will get the chance.' Vama laughed.

'You are still the ruler of your own destiny, Lady!' a man's voice spoke from behind Ambapali. He turned around to see Somprabh standing before her. It took her a while to register his presence. The man she had ached to see was before her. She felt her heartbeat quicken.

She had seen Somprabh in different forms and guises. He had been the one who captivated her in his bare hut; he had also been the one dressed as Balbhadra, the bandit. Now she saw him as she never had before, clothed in fine civilian attire. A thousand thoughts came to her, but she had lost all her talkativeness.

Somprabh gazed at her with longing. He broke the silence first. 'Are you looking at me in anger, Lady?' he asked with a smile.

'Even if I showed anger at you, Sir, what difference could I make to someone as powerful as you?' Ambapali replied.

'Ah, but the powerless can be powerful in their own way', Somprabh said.

'And how many such people are there, dear?' Ambapali asked.

'To be honest, I know one. I can name that person if you say so.'

'Please feel free to name that person.'

'Listen, I know a person fearless in the presence of robbers. She invites them to take away all they can and expresses surprise as they only carry away food when they can take many jewels and much gold.'

'I see', Ambapali said, her face radiant with her smile. 'Will you not join me – do you not need food and drink?'

They sat down together, and the Masseuse vanished.

'Dear, who are you?' Ambapali asked. 'You are a man more than any I have set eyes on, I whose fate is to have many men swagger and grovel before me. I have seen no one as strong and kind as you. Let me say this: I believe you to have all the good qualities a human may have. So, who are you?'

Somprabh took a deep breath. 'I have brought you here to tell you that', he said.

'Then say it, dear. I recognised you the first time you spoke during your raid.'

'And I read in your eyes I could not hide my identity from you.'

'Hmm…and I am familiar with your ability to read eyes. Enough now! Tell me, please.'

'I am a Magadhan. My name is Somprabh.'

Ambapali recoiled.

Somprabh said, 'What is it? Do you hate us?'

'No, dear, no.'

'Then why…'

'I cannot say it.'

'Even now? After all that we just said?'

'Yes, even now. Even at the cost of my life. You must forgive me if you can, Somprabh.' Her doe-like eyes became moist.

'Dear Ambapali, can I not be of help to you in this matter?'

'No, dear. Ambapali is helpless. She has no recourse in this matter.'

Somprabh's puzzlement was written large on his face. His eyebrows were knit, his forehead furrowed. His smile was weak. He lowered his head and took a deep breath.

'Dearest Som, is there something I can do to make you happy?' Ambapali asked. 'Anything at all? You can even ask for my life, you know.'

Somprabh looked up at her and straightened himself from his slumped position. 'I need nothing beyond what I already have from you. Your affection is your greatest gift. Please forgive my trespasses. What else do I need?'

'But that is exactly what I wanted from you, dear!'

'Even better. We sail life's journey in the same boat.'

'The journey is perhaps full of tears and sorrow…'

'But that is fate. We cannot run away from life. We face it, you and I.'

'Yes, we face it. Som, may I ask you one thing?'

Somprabh gripped her hands gently in his warm and strong hands. 'This insignificant Somprabh is your servant, Ambapali.'

'Will you be there for me whenever I fall?' Her lips quivered, and her voice broke. 'You know my inner self. Behind my splendour, my aura, this sheen of confidence, I am a frail, weak woman. I need you to be my man. I want to be your slave. I want you to be my protector.'

She rose and opened her arms to him. Her eyes were closed. The last thing she remembered was the insistent pressure of his warm lips and thudding chest on hers.

CHAPTER 127

THE LONELY TRAVELLER

It was a crisp, fine winter morning. The inner city of Rajgrih was teeming with people. Many men were armed, and the crowd had unusual energy. The talk was of war, and groups of soldiers walked the market streets purposely, scouting for the best deals for those items they needed and the army would not provide.

Much of the talk was about the spectacular falling out between those two pillars of the state apparatus, the emperor and the chief minister. Many ordinary men seemed to have deep insight into the nature and causes of the rift. It was a poorly hidden fact the spy network had entered its most active mode and kept a watchful eye on the city. It was common knowledge that anyone could be a spy – beggar or woman, child or elder. Any place could become an impromptu centre for discussion of war-related issues. Past great battles, the merits of the navy, new tactics and secret weapons were among the favourite topics.

A horseman coated with dust brought his horse to a stop in front of an inn. The rider was broad-shouldered, muscular and tall. The horse was a magnificent chestnut specimen from the Indus Valley. The man who rode it was rustic in his appearance, but had a distinctive gravity and a presence, not least because of his apparent physical strength. He was slightly disoriented in the throbbing centre of the metropolis, but he remained confident, and his eyes showed fearlessness. He was impervious to the stares of the locals around him. Both man and horse were sweaty. The rider wiped his brow with the back of his hand.

He dismounted in a fluid move and led his horse to a clearing near the main gate and tied the reins to a wooden bar that seemed there for that purpose. He had the gait of a man with a stiff back and not used to walk. He walked straight to the innkeeper sitting behind a counter and sipping on a cup containing a hot drink.

Before he could say anything, the innkeeper had surveyed him from head to toe and shaken his head. 'Friend, I have no room', he said. 'We have an ambassador from Vaishali, and the gentleman has brought an extremely large retinue with him. They all stay here and occupy all the rooms.'

The visitor nodded. 'Well, then, consider me your own guest', he said. 'I greatly need rest. Here, ten coins.' He took out gold coins from a pouch and laid them before the innkeeper.

The innkeeper's eyes dilated, and his face transformed itself into a mask of amiability. 'Ah, ten…very well, very well. Yes. Now, it remains I have no room, but I can think of a way to help such a fine gentleman as yourself.'

'How so, friend?'

'I have a friend, a close friend who is an usher to the emperor himself. His house is close by, very close. And the house is pleasant. Very well-kept. Nice, indeed. And big. Very big. I will ask him to give you shelter.'

'That is a good plan, for sure.'

The innkeeper scurried to get his friend. The usher was a skeletal but very tall man with a grave air.

'So you are my host, Kind Sir?' the rider asked.

'Yes, I am.'

'And you have agreed on the share of money with your friend here?'

'Yes', the thin man said. His wizened face broke into a broad grin. 'Yes, all is fine. Please follow me.'

Jayaraj saw the size of the house had been exaggerated. Perhaps it was big by the standards of the inner city. In any case, it would do. It had all that he needed. When he yielded to sleep, it was a deep and dreamless sleep that descended on him.

CHAPTER 128

THE USHER'S INVESTMENT

When Jayaraj awoke, it was with a sense of complete disorientation. He reached for the hilt of his sword and drew some comfort when his hand gripped it. He sat up on his soft bed, and the memories of his mission came back to him. He recalled the walk to the usher's place, and the great relief his back and all his joints had felt as he sank into sleep.

He realised that he had been woken up by the sound of someone knocking on the door. Jayaraj cleared his throat and asked his visitor to come in. It was the usher who he now knew went by the name of Meghamali.

Meghamali said, 'Sir, you are obviously a good and kind man, and I am your servant. But this once, I need to ask you for a favour instead of serving you.'

Jayaraj suppressed a smile. 'How may I help you, friend?' he asked.

Meghamali lowered his head and took a few breaths before raising his eyes again and looking straight at Jayaraj. 'Well, Sir, my wife is very beautiful. And she bears a very good character. I married her two years ago. I spent all the gold I had collected till then in the wedding. From my in-laws I got nothing. Now, you see, I am in deep trouble.'

Jayaraj let his smile show. 'I see, indeed. But how can I help you get wealth from your in-laws, or from anywhere else?' he chuckled.

'Sir, the trouble is a bit different', Meghamali said. 'I…' He coughed, gulped, and composed himself. It took him some time. 'She has not returned home since last night.'

'Not since last night? Where did she go?'

'It is my misfortune, Sir, that I…She went to Sukhdas the merchant.'

'Sukhdas. I see. And who is that?'

'He is a nasty foreigner, Sir. He has come to Rajgrih with horses from Arabia and silk from China. I sent her to negotiate the terms to buy horses. I thought I could profit from having some horses in these times when war is on everyone's mind.'

'But why send your wife, friend? Why did you not go yourself?'

'My wife is beautiful, as I said, Sir and also very clever. And that Sukhdas is known to lose his harshness when he sees a pretty woman. He becomes weak in the knees and in his mind, and settles for an easier bargain.'

Jayaraj could not help tenderness develop in his heart for this simple-minded man. He kept his feeling to himself. 'So, friend, you do not hesitate to take advantage of your wife's good looks in this manner?'

'But Sir, I actually paid her greedy father at my wedding. I got no dowry!'

'I see. Let us forget the history for a moment and tell me about your wife.'

'Yes, yes, that is where I was, Sir. So as I was saying, she went to negotiate the terms to buy horses.'

'Yes, and I heard that. What happened next?'

Meghamali intertwined his fingers and looked at them. 'Well, that evil Sukhdas…He was smitten by my wife. He said that…if she spent the night serving him, he would give her a hundred horses and two hundred sets of silk. And if not, he would not sell them at any price.'

Jayaraj had seen many interesting aspects to life. He kept a neutral mask on. 'So, your wife of good character – what did she do?'

'She came to me, Sir, like the good woman that she is. She told Sukhdas that she needed my permission.'

'Hmm. I see. And then?'

'Then, I thought hard. And I said this: a hundred horses and two hundred sets of silk for a night of servitude…Let us be reasonable. It sounds all right to me. So I said yes.'

'And your good woman obeyed you?'

'Yes indeed, Sir. The thing is, she has sent the hundred horses, but she refuses to come back or to acknowledge my messages.'

'And has she sent a message to you?'

Meghamali's face fell. 'She has, Sir. Not that I understand it. She sent word that a husband who gives a hundred horses for one night of pleasure is better than a greedy husband.'

'And what do you say to that, friend?'

'I do not know what to say. I think it is a joke. She is fond of joking, my wife. She used to crack such jokes earlier as well.'

'I see, I see. And if you guess right, what would you want to do next?'

'I want my wife back, Sir. I cannot live without her. I will not eat, and I will starve to death.'

Jayaraj nodded, pursed his lips and sighed. 'That is true', he said. 'If you do not eat, you will starve to death. True indeed.'

'I am a respectable man, Sir.'

'Yes, yes. Well, respectable friend, spend this night alone. But sleep well and dream sweet dreams. I will work on this problem and solve it for you.'

The usher greeted these words with a fervent namaste. He bowed and left. As he walked away, Jayaraj heard him mumbling to himself.

CHAPTER 129

THE USHER'S WIFE

The next day, Jayaraj woke up fully rested. He felt a fresh energy coursing in his veins. He took out his flashiest clothes and asked Meghamali the way to Sukhdas's house. Meghamali had arranged for a young boy with a cherubic face to become Jayaraj's pageboy. The pageboy's name was Dhvall. Dhvall was a lean and energetic boy who seemed to hang on to every word that Jayaraj uttered.

Sukhdas saw an imposing man with a servant and accorded Jayaraj the respect due to a high potential spender. 'Sir, how can I be of service to you?' he asked.

Jayaraj smiled at him and said, 'I am looking for something special. I have heard that you are a great businessman.'

'Well, I try to do my best, Sir', Sukhdas said. I have endless supplies of horses and silk on this trip. I know that the horses are especially good investments in this time of war. Silk, as you know, is a good long-term investment. I have my own stock, and I also have a large network of supporters. As I said, you may assume that there is no limit to the stocks that I can muster.'

'That is what I have heard. So it is true. Very well', Jayaraj said. 'Tell me, have you sold much already?'

'I have done all right. I sell wholesale, and in some cases, I will also sell by the dozen. I do not sell in ones and twos.'

'That sounds sensible', Jayaraj said. 'How much would you charge for a hundred horses and two hundred sets of silk?' he asked casually.

Sukhdas's eyes widened. He peered at Jayaraj. He seemed to be performing some calculations in his mind.

'Well, friend? You did conclude a deal on these lines yesterday, did you not? It was a small deal by your standard, but perhaps you have not forgotten it?'

Sukhdas scratched his chin as he frowned. 'Are you a government official?' he asked.

'Hmm…I have not come here on official work. I am here in my personal capacity', Jayaraj said.

Sukhdas smiled. 'Tell me what you want, Sir. I will do what I can.'

'That is good. Business is the art of buying for less and selling for more. At least that is how I understand it.'

'Well said, Sir. Profit keeps us in business.'

'Indeed, indeed. Give and take, and make money.' Jayaraj laughed.

'Sir, we exist to serve wise princes such as yourself', Sukhdas said.

'So – coming back to my question – how much?'

'How much for what?'

'For the woman you bought yesterday.'

Sukhdas gulped. 'Which woman, Sir?'

'The usher's wife! Do you take me for a fool? Damn you!' Jayaraj glared at Sukhdas and bellowed at him.

Sukhdas reacted as if he had been slapped. He reeled and trembled. 'Bless you, Prince. I – I am completely innocent!'

'Do you think the emperor will forgive you even if you are? What an extraordinary thing to do! You can be sent to the gallows. It is a time of martial law!'

'But – but she came of her own will. I assure you that! She came with her husband's permission!' Sukhdas wiped his forehead with a silk cloth. His hands shook.

'Did she now?' Jayaraj said. He raised a foot and planted it on a small stool. 'Tell me, a hundred horses and two hundred silk sets were the price for one night, were they not?'

'That they were. And it was an honourable deal. And I am a respectable man, Sir. But the thing is, she does not want to go back to that greedy old man. Sir, that scoundrel makes her do lowly things. She has to deal with merchants on his behalf. He treats her beauty as an investment that he must make money from!'

'I see. I wish to see this investment of his.'

'I am a respectable man, Sir. I cannot command her here. But I can ask her if she is willing to come.'

'That is well said. Ask her.'

The merchant scurried inside. When he came out, he looked calmer. 'Sir, she will see you', he said. 'Come in, please.'

Jayaraj signalled the gawking pageboy, Dhvall, to wait. He let Sukhdev lead him past the reception room, through a curtained corridor and into a brightly furnished room. The woman stood in the centre of the room. He had expected a beauty, and he was not disappointed. She had large eyes, and luscious, red lips. Her limbs were slender, and her body shapely. Her eyes had a certain light that showed that she was completely fearless. Jayaraj could understand why a man with vast resources at his disposal may have given a small fortune for her company.

She spoke before Jayaraj could address her. She said, 'How may I help you, dear sir?' Her tone was firm. There was no question of genuflecting.

'Beautiful lady, I am your husband's friend', Jayaraj said. 'I have come to take you to him. It does not behove a woman of your class and character to stay here as you have chosen to do. Your place is by your husband.'

'My place may be there, Sir, but I am happy here. I do not know what he had told you, but I did not come here to fulfil my own desires, and the idea of coming here was not mine. You seem to be a righteous man. Tell me this: why should I go back to the greedy old man who sold me to another? Is he not the most unholy and shameless man? Will he not use me again if I go back to him? And here I am, comfortable, serving a man who gave away a lot for just one night with me. Am I not better here?'

Jayaraj nodded and did not say a word more. He joined his hands in a namaste to the young woman. To Sukhdas, he said, 'Friend, you have made a huge gain. Remember, a characterless man can hold on to neither money nor woman.'

He turned and strode towards the main door.

CHAPTER 130

THE MESSENGER OF THE REPUBLIC

mperor Bimbisar left no stone unturned in giving Kapyak, representative of the Vajji Union, a grand welcome. From the point at which he crossed the border into Magadha, Kapyak was made to feel like an especially distinguished visitor. His entry into each town on the way was marked with functions to felicitate him. In the capital, the most exclusive ambassadorial guest house was set aside for him. The Magadhan head of Policy, Abhaykumar, was appointed to personally take care of him.

Jayaraj made sure to stay away from Kapyak's highly publicised travel route. In Rajgrih, however, he approached the officer in charge of Kapyak's guest house and asked him to use his influence to arrange a meeting with the Vajji ambassador. The officer had instructions to make Kapyak feel warmly welcomed and keep him busy. He was only too happy to further Jayaraj's request along with dozens of others, especially as Jayaraj had asked both the usher and the merchant Sukhdas to put in kind words for him. Jayaraj took great precautions to ensure Abhaykumar never saw him with Kapyak. He worked diligently to get information on war production, procurement of horses, stockpiling of food and movements of armed forces units. He used his meetings with Kapyak to convey this information to him, always in verbal form, in great detail and without carrying a single piece of incriminating evidence.

His brief meeting with the usher's wife and his understanding of her point of view had created an interesting bond between them. They would sometimes meet – in Sukhdas's presence – and the woman would serve him the choicest food. She was protective of the sympathetic man who was a stranger in town. She became one of his best intelligence sources. She had deep insight into the latest talk in the Palace harem.

The peasant boy Dhvall also turned out to be a great asset. He adored Jayaraj and was out to do his best to make a good impression on his master. He had a large network of family and friends who knew a lot about prices, grain procurement and army movements in rural areas.

After two weeks of ceremonies and socialisation, a date was assigned for Kapyak's formal meeting with the emperor. Kapyak's credential papers had been sent to the emperor, and during the meeting, he was to pay his respects and hand over the State gifts he was carrying. Kapyak and Jayaraj conferred and agreed Jayaraj would act as Vaishali's representative in the meeting. The plan was fraught with danger but had been part of their joint brainstorming before they left on their different paths to Rajgrih. The idea was that Kapyak would enjoy diplomatic immunity, as he had followed proper protocol. Jayaraj would make himself scarce after the meeting.

CHAPTER 131

JAYARAJ AND HIS MESSAGE

Emperor Bimbisar had followed the tradition of lavishing the most generous hospitality on one's enemy before the war. The royal court was full of nobles dressed in their most resplendent. The emperor sat on his giant throne, wearing his ceremonial crown of gold and diamonds. All the military, religious and political powers of Magadha were represented. Ministers, priests and religious scholars sat in curving rows on either side of the hall. Behind them sat the Army chiefs Chandrabhadrik and Udayi and their officers. Troupes of singers, musicians and dancers stood ready to entertain the great gathering. Greek slaves lined the outer edges, fanning the inner circles with large feathered fans. The emperor's bodyguards and another unit of soldiers from the city garrison encircled the meeting.

The Licchavi representative had dressed for the occasion, and the Licchavi contingent spared no effort to display a dignified and impressive presence. The gifts they had brought included twenty all-white horses from the Indus Valley, five war elephants, a hundred jewel-inlaid swords and silk clothes from Kashi with gold threads woven into them.

Jayaraj had expected the Magadhan court to dazzle him and he was not disappointed. The court had a touch of opulence that the assembly of Vaishali lacked, and the dresses of the nobles glittered as if made of gold and silver. He walked slowly towards the emperor, bowed deeply and presented a letter from the Republic directly to the emperor, who accepted it with a gracious nod. Following the protocol, he said that he was honoured to be present as Vaishali's messenger to the great emperor.

The emperor spoke in his grave voice. 'Welcome to Magadha. Young man, I will read your letter separately. What may I do for the reputed eight clans of the Vajji Union?'

Jayaraj's heart had thudded as he neared the throne. He calmed himself with an effort. Now, it pleased him he could speak with betraying any fear. 'May I speak clearly, Your Majesty?'

'Why not, young man?' Bimbisar said. 'Say what needs to be said.'

'The Vajji Union requests you to reinstall Acharya Varshkar as the chief minister at Rajgrih.'

Bimbisar showed no sign the statement shocked him. 'That is for Magadha to decide. What role does the Vajji Union have in this matter? I have noted, incidentally, that the Vajji Union has granted asylum to him, and thus violated the terms of an existing treaty between Magadha and the Union. I place the responsibility for this violation on the Vajji Union, of course.'

'Your Majesty, on the contrary, the Vajji Union believes that the chief minister wages a silent war against it from its own heartland and that this happens with the emperor's consent.'

Again, Jayaraj was impressed by Bimbisar's stoic response. Neither he nor any of the nobles made any pretensions of shock or hurt. Bimbisar said, 'Is this…notion backed up by any proof?' His eyes bored into Jayaraj's. Jayaraj felt a bead of sweat drop from his elbow. He controlled the urge to twitch.

'Lord, the Vajji Union fully understands the value of the emperor's friendship. And it does not take any important steps without ascertaining the facts. I assure the emperor we have proof.'

'Young man, speak freely', Bimbisar said.

'Lord, the eight clans of the Vajji Union wish to establish a firm foundation for friendship.'

'What do they have in mind, Sir?' Bimbisar said.

'I am aware of the eight clans' views towards Magadha emperor, Your Majesty.'

'May I also know of their views?'

'Lord, the Vajji Union wants to become your followers. They wish to create a relationship such that they simply follow your wishes.'

'Then, I am keen to know how that stage may be reached.'

'You only need to speak your mind, lord.'

'That might not be prudent, your man.'

'Then may I speak out the Vajji Union's proposal in court, Your Majesty?'

'Yes. Please do so.'

'I will still have to ask the emperor's permission to speak without fear.'

'I grant it to you.'

'Lord, you know well that if you wish to marry a high-class Licchavi princess, you can easily do so.'

'The proposal is important. I am honoured.'

'On the other hand, emperor, the eight clans will also feel honoured. But there is a condition.'

'And what is that?'

'The Licchavi princess' son must be the future emperor.'

'I see. Is that all?'

'That is all, Majesty.'

'And young man, is there anything else you have to say?'

'Only a minor point, Majesty. It is this: Lady Ambapali, as you know, is the benefactress of the republic. The eight clans will not tolerate one man having rights over her. It would violate our code.'

'I understand that. What more do you have to say, gentleman?'

'Your Majesty, I have nothing more to say.'

'Nothing else?'

'Nothing, Lord.'

'Very well. I refuse to accept the proposal of the eight clans.'

Jayaraj felt as if a bucket of icy water had been poured over him. He stayed calm. 'Are you refusing to marry any of the eight clans' princesses, Your Majesty?'

'Well, the eight clans' offer pleases me, and I consider myself lucky to have it. However, I cannot accept it against the voice of my conscience. And as far as the matter of Lady Ambapali is concerned, I do believe that the law of the Vajji Union in this context has been called a cursed law by a person of eminence. I am confident that all Magadhans will take pride in using their swords to set right this grave injustice against the rights of women. Very well, young man, you must take leave now. Please do not forget to convey our gratitude to the eight clans for their kind offer.' The emperor's tone was friendly, as if he was explaining how things worked. There was no inflexion of threat, anger or sarcasm. But the words bit Jayaraj.

Jayaraj stood his ground. 'Lord, I fear this decision may have fearful consequences. It can damage the relations between the two states.'

'Young man, it is a matter of vision. Kings have their visions and emperors theirs. The emperor of Magadha must have his own vision, specific to his context. Perhaps my vision starts where yours and the eight clans' stops.'

'Shall I interpret that statement to mean the emperor is already committed to a war against the eight clans?' Jayaraj was amazed at his own effrontery.

'Is that why the eight clans have sent you here with a bribe?' Bimbisar's cold eyes again pierced Jayaraj's.

'The Vajji Union and the Licchavis are the centre of an alliance of thirty-six republics, Your Majesty. We are democratic, but it is known that we can wield our swords well.'

For the first time, the hint of a smile lit up Emperor Bimbisar's face. 'I am happy to hear that', he said. 'I will remember it.' The emperor flicked his right hand and seemed to see through Jayaraj.

Two tall ushers stepped up to him and bowed politely, blocking his view of the emperor. Jayaraj bowed and retreated from the audience, walking backwards. His head was lowered and his back stiff. His tightly clenched hands did not disguise it that he was quivering with rage.

CHAPTER 132

BEHIND CLOSED DOORS

Abhaykumar stood looking out of a chamber that had a small window overlooking an expanse of green. The light shone on his face. He was shaking his head and muttering to himself. It was a while before he realised that another person had entered the chamber and shut the door behind him. It was the emperor. Abhaykumar rubbed his face in his palms and took a deep breath as if he needed to steel himself for what was to follow. He said, 'Lord, we – I – have been cheated.'

'How so?' Bimbisar asked.

'The man who spoke to you was not the designated messenger who crossed the border openly. At the last minute, the Vajji Union slipped in one of their agents. I have asked for a report on who he was.'

The emperor raised an eyebrow. 'How did this happen, Sir?' he said.

'I still have to find out all about it, Your Majesty. The man who came into court was staying at an usher's place. He was an infrequent visitor to Kapyak's guest house. My men told me that much. We do not know more than that.'

Bimbisar said, 'Did the chief minister not send word on this?'

'He did send a message that Prabhanjan would get here with information on what the Vaishali war council is up to. But Prabhanjan seems to have disappeared.'

Bimbisar frowned. 'That is worrying.' He walked to the window and looked at the brightly lit garden for a while, apparently lost in thought. Then he turned to Abhaykumar, and said, 'Arrest that messenger.'

Abhaykumar lowered his head as he spoke. 'He has vanished from the city, Your Majesty.'

Bimbisar raised his voice enough to strike fear into Abhaykumar's heart. 'I want that man.' He leant forward and tapped Abhaykumar on the chest. 'I want him dead or alive. I will issue orders to the mayor and to the chief of Border Security. Send them to me now.'

Abhaykumar needed no more prodding. He saluted and dashed out of the chamber. Left to himself, Bimbisar paced up and down the chamber, stopping to gaze out of its small window at times. It was not long before he heard a flurry of footsteps followed by a knock on the door. Abhaykumar and the two officials entered the room and stood before him.

'Officers, what news do we have of Vaishali's messenger, who stood before me in court yesterday?' Bimbisar looked at each of his men in turn. His tone was menacing.

The mayor gulped and spoke first. 'Lord, he left the city two watches into the night. Since then, we have lost track of him.'

'Who let him enter the city?' Bimbisar asked, still keeping his voice low.

'Lord, we had no injunction against a single foreigner–'

'And Prabhanjan, our leading spy, was following an agent of Vaishali, I was told, when he infiltrated the border. What has happened of that agent?'

The chief of the border guards spoke this time. 'We do not know, Lord.'

'Is this how Magadha will be administered? By officers such as you?' Bimbisar finally exploded with fury. The chamber echoed from the shock. 'Get me that man! Dead or alive!'

Bimbisar turned his back to his men. They fled to obey his order.

CHAPTER 133

THE ESCAPE

Jayaraj and Kapyak had worked out their escape plans well in advance. Kapyak had left Rajgrih in disguise, carrying much valuable intelligence in the form of maps and written notes. Along his route, two of his toughest soldiers accompanied him. They travelled by well-chosen, lonely paths, and changed horses every eight hours. After his historic meeting with the emperor, Jayaraj slipped into an inn and left through the back door in a different guise. His pageboy, Dhvall, chose to go with him to Vaishali, and the two of them changed dresses at an abbey outside the city. From there, they followed a different route to flee to Vaishali well before the alert had been sounded for Jayaraj. In any case, no one would have recognised Jayaraj based on the royal pronouncement which spread outward slowly from Rajgrih.

Abhaykumar, unlike Jayaraj, was more of a soldier than a diplomat and spy. He was also a scion of a noble family who, unlike Jayaraj, owed his position to his lineage more than his skills. In any case, the emperor's extreme displeasure goaded him on to vow to bring the messenger from Vaishali back to Rajgrih, dead or alive. He left the city with a group of his elite guards, even as the chief of the border guards sent messages all the way to the border for his men to immediately detain Kapyak and Jayaraj.

The flight from Rajgrih turned out to be harder for Jayaraj, who had less of a start than Kapyak. He had tried to skirt the well-travelled routes but ended in skirmishes with the border guards on two occasions and chose to flee. He and Dhvall got away both times without injuries, but each time, it was a close call.

Jayaraj realised that the Magadhans had cast their nets well. There would be no easy escape for him.

CHAPTER 134

A FATAL DUEL

ayaraj knew that he was fated to duel to the death with Abhaykumar. He was not the type to flinch from such an encounter, but he did have strategic reasons to do his best to finish his mission fast, with or without the duel.

'Friend, this is the right time for us to put our horses to the test', he said to Dhvall.

'As you say!' Dhvall was his usual unquestioning and endearing self. They set off at a faster trot, kicking up the dust of the trail.

Jayaraj had decided not to stop until they reached a safe spot. He had not found time to pass on all the intelligence he had gathered to Kapyak. He carried a valuable map and important notes in a sheaf in his jacket. He had rolled them into a small iron cylinder stitched into the coat lining. Dhvall had a similar stack of papers.

As they rode along, challenging each other to ensure that their speed did not flag, Jayaraj sensed that Dhvall would love nothing more than to talk to him. Jayaraj, however, was burdened with serious thoughts that kept him occupied even as he rode his horse hard and scanned the horizon and the two sides of the path for any signs of danger. Jayaraj thought through the larger narrative that he had gathered during his mission and of the many smaller supporting pieces of intelligence. He tried to imagine the flow of his presentation to the War Council and thought about the possible weaknesses and fallacies in his intelligence gathering.

One thing was absolutely clear to him: Emperor Bimbisar was a formidable man, a vigorous enemy who was no fool. It was also clear that the rumours of his obsession with Ambapali had a foundation to them. War was inevitable. War clouds were on the horizon, and they were ready to burst. But the key to the matter was that the Palace of Seven Worlds was the centre from where they could win Magadha. Vaishali could overcome Arya Varshkar's warped and immensely energetic mind and Arya Bhadrik's muscle power with Ambapali at the centre of its strategy. Yes, Jayaraj thought, the Bimbisar, Varshkar and Bhadrik triumvirate was infallible unless Vaishali used the one weapon able to annihilate them.

It was clear to Jayaraj that Magadha was not straining under the burden of war. There were no signs in all of Magadha of the terror that was palpable in Vaishali. That was the thing that had disheartened him the most. The farmers of Magadha ploughed their fields as if there was nothing special this season. The lines of village belles carrying water in pitchers looked much the same as it would in any other year. The common men and women did not look harried or desperate. It was infuriating, but even the birds seem to be singing tunes of contentment.

Jayaraj had to acknowledge that this empire seemed better governed than the democratic Vajji Union. If the empire had not been about to launch a war against his homeland, Jayaraj would have publicly spoken to the assembly about his perception that the administrative capabilities of Magadha needed to be emulated by the Vajji Union, so that they could reach a more mature state of evolution. Even now, as he and Dhvall, rode furiously, their path was hemmed in by vast fields of golden wheat. The small villages they crossed had orchards around them. Healthy children played in groups in common areas. The villagers travelled mostly on healthy-looking mules.

He felt the need to talk to Dhvall. He slowed down his horse, and Dhvall, ever eager to talk, brought his horse alongside.

'Dhvall!' he shouted.

'Yes, master?' Dhvall leant forward.

'You know, I wonder how life would be…if our in-laws lived in one of these villages, our wives were two of those beauties…and we visited our in-laws as honoured guests! Just imagine how life would be!' Jayaraj smiled and winked at Dhvall.

Dhvall had been expecting serious talk. His face broke into a broad grin at this unexpected line of thought. 'Well, I have to say this is a coincidence, Master. One village on this route, not too far, is my wife's! I stayed there only a couple of times, and I was wondering…' He blushed.

'Aha! Wonders never cease!' Jayaraj chuckled. 'And your wife – is she there?'

'She is, indeed. I was not…' Dhvall did not finish.

'Well, well. You may not have been planning to tell me, but it is out now!' Jayaraj said. 'How far is it, do you think?'

'If we do not stop, Master, even for the night, we will be there by sunset.'

'And if we ride harder?'

'By afternoon, Master!'

'Hmm. But will your wife's family not imprison me?'

'Oh, no, Sir! I will tell them you are a prince dressed in simple clothes and returning from an audience with the emperor himself. They will treat you well! My brother-in-law is a good friend of mine.'

'I would like them to treat me well, indeed. I trust the treatment will include good food?'

'Oh, they are well-to-do villagers and very warm people, Sir. Don't even imagine anything will lack.'

'Well, friend, I was wondering how I could be sure of a safe harbour. And it happens you had the solution all along, but you kept it to yourself.' Jayaraj smiled.

Dhvall's face reddened with pleasure and excitement. He patted his horse, and the two of them accelerated.

Jayaraj had kept a vigil even as he had this friendly chat with Dhvall. He saw a thick wood ahead, along a bend in the path, a hill, and what looked like a deep valley next to it. The sun waned, and it would be dark soon. As he scouted the surroundings, he picked up the sound of horse's hoofs. Before long, he could discern mounted horsemen on the hilltop and counted thirteen of them. He saw the riders behind them were still far, the dust cloud of dust was in the distant horizon. But they would be there before long. Now the horsemen on the hilltop had started down the slope towards Jayaraj and Dhvall. The first of their arrows buried itself without force in the dust before them. It did not have much force yet.

'Well, here we are', Jayaraj said to Dhvall. 'Friend, you will have to be quick and brave, as usual. Cut across this forest to our right and be fast about it. Their arrows will be useless, and you will have a head start. You know this area well, I assume?'

Dhvall's eyes widened. 'But you, Sir? I will not –'

'Obey me', Jayaraj said. 'There is no other way. Our horses are tired, and we cannot go on and turn back. Run for it! Do not worry for me. Get to your wife's village. If you can get help from there, that will be well. But be aware it must be a large force, or there is no point.'

'I will do what I can, Master!' Dhvall said. 'My wife's family has many good warriors!'

Jayaraj waved Dhvall away, and he himself rode hard into the forest on the left. Quivers full of arrows had descended around the two of them by then, and they were lucky to get away unhurt. The enemy soldiers could make out Jayaraj's build and chose to hunt him down. They were close behind him now, but with the distance and the trees, they did not have a clear field of vision. Their arrows did thump into the trees just behind Jayaraj. He observed that they had fanned out in a circle. He slid down to the left side of the horse and kept his body out of the line of sight. Three soldiers surrounded his horse in a clearing.

'We got him!' one of them said.

'It would have been better to get him alive', another said.

They trotted over. Jayaraj said a silent prayer as he realised that these moments in a deserted forest might be the last of his life. He kept still and tightened his grip on his sword and dagger. He waited till the last moment before he sprang up with the suppleness of a gymnast. His right hand slit a throat with his dagger while his left stabbed a chest with his sword. The third soldier's horse bolted, and Jayaraj whispered into his own horse's ear and galloped away. The forest echoed with the cries of his pursuers.

The light was fading quickly now. Jayaraj realised that his pursuers were from a contingent of archers, led by a senior officer who shouted out commands in a voice that was familiar. If he let them use their arrows on him, he would surely die. He coaxed his horse to turn unpredictably, and twice, he attacked his nearest pursuer, taking him by surprise and killing him. The third man was more adept, and he carried a sword. When Jayaraj tried the same tactic with him, the man parried him with a stinging counter strike so hard that every nerve in Jayaraj's shoulder screeched in pain. It was his enemy Abhaykumar. Jayaraj manoeuvred his horse away and focused all his energies as he rode deeper into the forest. Abhaykumar was calling out to his men, and Jayaraj chose that moment to attack him with every iota of energy he could muster. It was almost pitch dark now, and Jayaraj was at an advantage because he had trained many hours for such situations. He came at Abhaykumar from the other side this time and got a blow in before his enemy could react. Abhaykumar fell off his horse, and Jayaraj thanked his stars as he heard the thud of the body falling on earth.

Now, there must be seven of them, Jayaraj thought. They were leaderless and had seen their comrades fall, so they must be dispirited. But they also knew that he was alone and wounded. He had felt a stickiness creeping up over his left shoulder. He knew that it was blood. The forest cleared, which was both a blessing and a curse. His horse galloped faster, but so would those of his tormentors. He came onto a wider, trodden forest path. Two men attacked him, one from each side. He feinted, swerved and decapitated one with a wide-arching sword movement. The other one flinched and reined his horse back, and Jayaraj was able to leave him behind. Now, finally, his horse started showing signs of utter exhaustion. The enemy soldiers were catching up with him. He looked up at the starry night and took in the desolate beauty of the silvery forest scape. This was as good a place as any to depart, he thought. Once again, he said his prayers and resolved to compel the men to kill him, rather than take him alive.

'Prince! Fear not! We are here!' an unknown, gruff voice echoed from ahead of him. A cloud of dust was approaching from a short distance away. Soon Dhvall's angelic voice called out, 'Master, we are here!'

Jayaraj's eyes were moist as he pondered at the improbability of this second deliverance. His pursuers and his rescuers were about equidistant from him. When the clash happened, there was a brief flurry of swords before Abhaykumar's men were cut down. Abhaykumar himself had recovered and led the pursuit again. Jayaraj ensured that his arch enemy was taken alive and trussed up. They rode to Dhvall's wife's village. Jayaraj's horse slowed them down, and it was past midnight when they reached.

'My Friends, you saved my life', Jayaraj said in a choking voice. 'I owe you, and I will repay this debt. But for now, I need another favour from you. Get me a good horse, please.'

'What, Sir? Will you not rest tonight?' Dhvall asked.

'No, my friend, I must go on', Jayaraj said. 'And you – you must also get to Vaishali tomorrow morning. Tell the head of the guards at the assembly your name, and he will send you to me. Take this.' He handed Dhvall a bag of coins.

'But you are injured, Sir!'

'Yes, yes…Give me a clean cloth for this', Jayaraj said. 'I must finish my work.' He smiled.

'I will come with you then.'

'No, you need to rest. But – remember this – make sure you come. What you carry is important to me!'

Dhvall opened the bag, and his eyes widened. 'These – they are gold!'

'Yes, they are.' Jayaraj grinned. 'Get your wife something. And buy yourself a horse.'

Dhvall's cousin led a powerful-looking stallion to Jayaraj, who stroked the horse's mane approvingly. He jumped on to it and grabbed the reins.

Dhvall's eyes were moist. 'Are you sure, Sir?'

'Yes.'

'And the prisoner? We do not know what to do with him.'

'He will recover soon. Free him tomorrow and give him a good horse and food to return to Rajgrih. Do not worry. He is a prince. He will not be vindictive towards your family aftcr you spare his life.'

'Very well, Sir.'

Jayaraj rode out into the dark night.

CHAPTER 135

CHANDRABHADRIK

Chandrabhadrik, commander-in-chief of Magadha's army, was a legend all over India. He was known to be far-sighted, fearless and patient. He had systematically reorganised the Magadhan armed forces since he had got the first signs that Vaishali was his next target. He drilled the lessons from the battles with Champa, Kosala and Mathura into his officers and their reports. Fresh recruits receiving sped up training made up for the men lost in those battles. He let talk of war spread so the populace would be ready for it when the time came. He ensured morale remained high. The people had almost forgotten the drastic upheaval of Acharya Varshkar's banishment.

Bimbisar had called Chandrabhadrik for a secret meeting. The emperor started, as usual, without preamble. 'Arya Bhadrik', he said, referring to the great commander by his shortened name. 'Perhaps you know why I troubled you. I believe you will agree with me when I say that if I do not soon win the title of Chakravarti, king of kings, I will not have done justice to my birth in the illustrious Shishunaga dynasty. Nor will you have done justice to your great position and your fame.'

Chandrabhadrik smiled. 'It is so, indeed, Majesty. The Chakravarti sphere extends from the Himalayas in the north to the ends of the land in the south, east and the west. Our geographers will have exact figures the dimensions of this varied land. I have travelled far and wide, as you have, Majesty, and we have seen some of the incredible diversity of the land. Forests, villages, ravines, mighty rivers, waterfalls, plateaus… All the features known to man are here. Now imagine you have a map of this land in front of you and let us dwell on what needs to be done. Our esteemed chief minister had planned that if we had to reach the southern shores, the path lay through the kingdoms of Avanti and Mathura. So also is it important for you to rule Roruk Sauvir.' He paused and closed his eyes as if searching for the right words to continue.

With his smile fixed, he said, 'Majesty, your eyes are trained on Vaishali, and ostensibly, the chief minister's effort is to support you in annexing it. Let us get this over with, but I must ask one question. If we are to annex Vaishali, we must also trounce their allies – the Malla, Shakya, Kosi-Kolon and the other republics. We must avoid making this a tactical move and instead wipe out the power of the republics. May I also venture to suggest, Emperor, that we prepare to transfer our capital from Rajgrih to Vaishali, to signal our intention for the next phase of our expansion? It could perhaps be Pataligram instead of Vaishali. But that is the move that will announce that we have destroyed the foundations of the central group of republics. It is not enough to win the war. We must make this war a stepping-stone on the path that you have charted out for the Shishunagas. We must change the thinking of the people who live there and root out their republican ideas.'

Bimbisar stood up, and Chandrabhadrik stopped talking. Bimbisar walked to a window and looked at the blue sky with his eyes closed, stroking his right bicep with his left hand. Then he turned to Chandrabhadrik and nodded.

Chandrabhadrik continued. 'This brings me to an important breach in Vaishali's defences. The Licchavis, Mallas, Shakyas and suchlike manage the republic. The Brahmans and Vaishyas do not command there the clout they have in our lands. Logically, these castes, particularly the merchant class among the Vaishyas, will not burn with the desire to help the forces of the republics in a war.'

Bimbisar's eyes gleamed. 'That is no ordinary breach, Commander! That may well win the war for us.'

'Indeed, Your Majesty. But as I said, the real war will be won after, as I have said, we have wiped out all semblance of republican thinking. And that will mean a relocation of the capital of the empire. That relocation will be a signal that we have a long-term view that spans many generations.'

'Yes, yes', Bimbisar said as if the point had been made too often. 'But let us still not lose track of the military imperatives. By making Champa ours, we have access to the eastern seas. But the path to the southern seas is still a long one. To start with, we need to annex Avanti. If only we had succeeded against Kosala, we would have extended our western domains all the way to Gandhar. I would have done much of the work that is needed in my lifetime. Now I will leave a large part of this task unfinished, for the next generation to accomplish. That slave's son, Vidudhab, rules Kosala with an iron hand, though he visibly owes a debt to Somprabh.'

'Well said, Your Majesty. He does state his indebtedness on every occasion. However, politics is politics, as you know well, Your Majesty. We cannot count on his gratitude. At present, given our trajectory, we must focus all our efforts on Vaishali. The chief minister has taken grave risks and continues to live a life of penury; Somprabh keeps waging his silent war. We invested in new forts and strengthened the old ones on the banks of the Son, Ganga and Bhagirathi rivers. And we also have a newly refurbished navy, which I described in detail to Your Majesty yesterday.'

'Yes, you have', Bimbisar said. He walked back to his ornate seat and motioned to Chandrabhadrik to take the seat next to it. He said, 'Tell me, Chandrabhadrik, what about the army itself?'

'Our army mainly keeps the akshauhini design, Your Majesty. We do not see a reason yet to change it. The divisional layout remains fixed at 21,870 chariots, 21,870 elephants, 65,610 horsemen and 109,350 infantrymen. The first division will guard the capital under Acharya Shambhavyakashyap. Apart from its guard duties, this division may also depute forces to make up for the losses of other divisions. This is our core force and is the key to our survival. It has our most committed and experienced men. I think you will agree with me when I say that no other military division comes close to it.'

Bimbisar nodded. Chandrabhadrik said, 'The second division is a professional fighting force of paid soldiers. This is again a key differentiator for us against Vaishali. Vaishali has no such force. This international division has been tested in many wars and never been found wanting. This division will be used in forward actions, and they can be counted on a highly professional fighting force.

'The third division is a volunteer division. It is no less formidable than the second division. What this division lacks in experience, they make up for through their commitment. These are men who have volunteered from our own populace and been trained thoroughly for two years. Vaishali also has such a force. These forces form the bulwark of our army, and theirs. They are equipped for both open war and stealth actions.

'Finally, Your Majesty, we have a mixed division of allied soldiers. These come to us from no less than twenty-seven kingdoms. We have the flexibility of keeping them in defensive positions on our lands or deploying them in Vaishali. Now there is not much ground to cover before open warfare starts. These forces are deployed near the border areas. I plan to use them for the first open conflicts, and only then use our own divisions.'

Bimbisar nodded and pointed a finger towards his commander as if to acknowledge a particularly good point.

Chandrabhadrik smiled. 'But besides these, we have a fifth division of defeated soldiers. As always, they will form the first line of attack against Vaishali. Just as the Chandal benefits irrespective of the victor in the fight between a dog and a pig, we benefit irrespective of the outcome of those first attacks.'

The emperor nodded his assent again with a thin smile. Then he frowned. He said, 'This is good, so far. I would like to see that the army is well equipped for actions in the forest as well.'

'Indeed, Your Majesty, we have taken action for that', Chandrabhadrik said. 'Our intelligence forces have fanned out to the forest swathes, and we have compiled the smallest details of forest features, caves, rivers and streams and defensive and ambush positions. Records are available of where to tap forest products and suitable stocking points for supplies. They have established ties and pacts with tribespeople. We are prepared to cut off the enemy's access to supplies that they think that they can count on. This includes materials such as fodder and firewood.'

'I am satisfied with this, Commander', Bimbisar said. He did not express any great delight, but that did not surprise Chandrabhadrik. 'Is there anything else you have to report?' Bimbisar asked.

'Well, just one more thing, Your Majesty. In addition to all that we have discussed so far, which is mostly conventional strategy, we have also invested in an informal army. The scale of this action is quite large. This force is essentially charged with robbing, looting and creating chaos. It is not bound by martial rules. We have a loose organisation in place for the force. One part of it is funded by us, and in addition, they keep their spoils. The other works for us as they are committed Magadhans.'

'Well done, Chandrabhadrik, well done!' Bimbisar spoke without smiling, but Chandrabhadrik knew that this was the highest praise he could expect. 'The plans seem fairly sound', Bimbisar said. 'Do you have a good grip on the economics of the campaign? As you know, that will make or break it.'

'Broadly speaking, yes, Your Majesty', Chandrabhadrik said. 'I have followed the precepts that I learnt from you and from the chief minister. We will time the offensive and the main actions to maximise the enemy's economic losses and not only their military ones. The idea will be to make the war unsustainable for them. I will follow the maxims that money begets money, and that only an elephant can catch an elephant.'

'Good. Then it is only a matter of my giving the orders?'

'Indeed, it is. We are ready, Your Majesty.'

CHAPTER 136

THE SECOND WAR COUNCIL

Supreme Commander Suman sat at the head of a large table in a brightly lit room. The war council of the Vajji Union was in progress. He listened without giving away any emotions as Jayaraj spoke. Jayaraj stood erect across the table, facing Sunand.

Jayaraj had recounted his experiences. He said, 'While it is true that the Emperor of Magadha does not have the best army command, or the best soldiers, and that their army has many drawbacks, we must acknowledge that Acharya Varshkar's war by subterfuge and Chandrabhadrik's plans for an overt war are unparalleled assets that Magadha has. We have little room for manoeuvre. The smallest lapse in our defensive actions will mean not only that we will be wiped out, but so also will the idea of republicanism, from the whole of these north-eastern parts. Clearly, these two Brahmans control the war efforts of Magadha, and that is no surprise, as that has been how the reactionary Aryan society operates. On the one hand, the Aryans had an elitist society in which the upper layers of Brahmans and Kshatriyas united to skim the cream of the economy, leaving the lower layers dispossessed. Now, the Shishunaga dynasty is not Aryan, and together these forces of new and old power bring greater dynamism to warring.'

'We are here to agree on how to win the war. We will not let the Aryans trounce us', Suman said in a matter-of-fact tone.

'Sir, we consistently rejected the Aryans' wishes for advancement in our lands. You could say that we suppressed their human rights', Singh said gravely. 'And we may have to pay for that now, in our time of trouble.'

'That historical perspective has merits, young man', Suman said, 'but we have a main topic of discussion today. Let us focus our thoughts on our two potential destroyers – Acharya Varshkar and Arya Chandrabhadrik.'

'But we should not forget a third destroyer, Sir!' Jayaraj said.

'Whom do you mean?' Sunand said.

'Somprabh. He is a master of war and strategy', Jayaraj said, and Singh nodded a vigorous assent. 'This man might be a bigger danger to us than the two stalwarts of whom we have heard for decades.'

'Tell me more about him', Sunand said.

'I cannot say anything about his origins', Jayaraj said. 'Perhaps only one person in this world can speak about them, but that person's lips are sealed on the topic.'

'And who is he?'

'She is Aryaa Matangi.'

Sunand stroked his chin. 'I see', he said. 'I see. And the emperor has given him such patronage, despite his lack of pedigree?'

'Yes, Sir', Jayaraj said. 'He performed extraordinary feats in the war on Champa and saved Chandrabhadrik's reputation from ruin.'

'Hmm. And he is formally a general of their army?' Sunand asked.

'No, the commander-in-chief is Chandrabhadrik. I am not even sure of Somprabh's formal title.'

'Well, I know all about Bhadrik, of course', Sunand said. 'We were classmates. He is a formidable man, no doubt…I am curious – what made you say that the Magadhan army's command is lacking?'

'Well, Sir, Chandrabhadrik himself is a legend, and for good reasons', Jayaraj said. 'And if he had been followed as he should have been, the enemy's army would have been invincible. What saves us from that situation is distrust in the Magadhan high command. I have got to know that Emperor Bimbisar fears assassination by Chandrabhadrik. He thinks that what happened in Avanti, where Pradyot usurped the throne after his father killed the king, could also happen in Rajgrih.'

'I see…And where is this man Somprabh?' Sunand asked.

'Well, Sir, people in Magadha say that he is on a study tour', Jayaraj said.

'Well, well. Do they? And what does Jayaraj say?' Sunand looked askance at Jayaraj, who flushed.

'I say that he is in Vaishali. He cannot be anywhere else', Jayaraj said softly.

Sunand sighed and locked his fingers behind his neck. Singh bolted up and said, 'What! Arya Jayaraj, are you sure? Somprabh is here, and we do not know about it?'

'Well, if I did not know about it, why would I say it?' Jayaraj said.

'Where is he?' Singh asked.

'In Madhuban forest. At this very moment, perhaps in a cave. The man we know as Balbhadra is none other than Somprabh.'

Swarnasen groaned, and an excited chatter broke out, only to be silenced at once by Sunand sweeping his hand and indicating a need for silence.

Singh said, 'I did suspect that. How many men does he have?'

'The estimates vary', Jayaraj said. 'It may be up to fifty thousand men, with ten thousand of them being horsemen. They are spread out over large tracts of the forest. You have been briefed earlier on the nature and the intent of their activities earlier. We now have reports that they have escalated their activities. They have built a system of small, hidden fortifications.'

Sunand grimaced, showing displeasure for the first time. 'So they are already at war with us. And when will Bimbisar launch an open war?'

'I still need to brief you on the enemy's state of readiness. Magadha has repaired all the existing forts on the Son, Ganga and Bagmati rivers. In addition, sixteen new forts have been built. Each fort is a base for three to seven thousand soldiers with all arms of the army being represented. A year's supply of food and water has been stockpiled in every one of the forts.'

Sunand murmured, 'Arya Bhadrik has certainly justified his reputation.'

Singh's face clouded. 'True enough. But go on, Arya Jayaraj.'

Jayaraj said, 'Your admiration for Arya Bhadrik is more than justified because he has also excelled in establishing a strong navy. The twenty thousand boats of the Magadhans are classified into different types. The deergha, a hundred feet long and thirty wide, transfers elephants, horses and chariots. It can, of course, also be used to transport infantry, fifty men apart from twenty boatmen. The chapla can travel very fast and is useful as an assault craft. It can carry twenty soldiers and eight boatmen. Arya Bhadrik plans that the navy will form the spearhead of the open war.'

Sunand drummed his fingers on the table. 'And what is the state of their finances?'

'That is a fundamental question, Sir', Jayaraj said. 'And the short answer is their finances are healthy. Very healthy. Their countryside shows no signs of shortages. People are cheerful, and morale is high. The treasury faced severe challenges two years ago. No longer. The Magadhan establishment has leant on the merchant class, who sent huge profits from the war. They have modern weapons, and in larger quantities than we do. Also, they have excellent intelligence on our preparations.'

'So their warring has not depleted their resources?' Sunand asked.

'No, indeed, Sir. They used their wars to buttress their resources, in fact, thanks largely to Arya Varshkar's stratagems. After the victory over Anga, they lavished land and titles on the local Brahman community to make them their staunch allies. In Champa, they have made the merchants their staunch supporters and borrowed heavily from them. The residents of Champa are generally happy with the administrative apparatus Arya Bhadrik put in place there. Their resentment at the sacking of the old kingdom has evaporated as they have better living standards now. Emperor Bimbisar has declared himself a devout follower of the Buddha. He took a large contingent, including all his officers and the headmen of his villages to proclaim their faith publicly. He has gifted his Venu-van garden complex to the Buddha as well. All this has helped him to ride on the great sage's popularity. He has projected himself as a model emperor, devoted to the welfare of the people and humble before the sages.'

Sunand stood up and stretched. The rest of the council stayed seated. Sunand sat down again with his arms folded across his chest. 'So, what is your advice, Arya Jayaraj? Is there no hope for us?'

'I would not say that', Jayaraj said. 'They are well prepared and powerful, and we would be fools to ignore that. But we must keep in mind we fight to defend our lives and independence on our land. The vast majority of their soldiers battle for money, for a salary. There is a difference.'

Singh clenched his fist and raised it to show his support of this statement.

'It is true they are flush with funds. They have a hundred and seventy million gold coins from the merchants of Champa, they have their loot from Anga. Their resources are vast. But so are their commitments. For example, the embers of war in Anga have not died out. Some of their forces are still tied down there. Also, they need to look over their shoulders at their perennial enemies, Avanti and Mathura. And most of all, their jewel, Arya Varshkar, is right here in our midst. We cannot take precipitate action because any harm to him will bring down the Magadhans in all their fury and desperation. But that does not alter the fact that he has placed himself at our mercy, in a way. Our republic lacks the wealth of the Magadhans, but our soldiers know that our rule is fundamentally better for them. We do not tax them too much, nor do we act capriciously with them. We do not abduct their women and force them into our palaces. Or take away their chariots or horses on our whims. We can still count on some goodwill from the leaders of the communities in the Vajji Union.'

Sunand joined his hands in a namaste. 'Arya Jayaraj, I congratulate you on your daring and your sagacity. If we survive this war, our future generations will be indebted to you.' He signalled with a gesture of his hand that Jayaraj should take his seat and then, called on Singh to rise.

'You have heard friend Jayaraj's statement. Now I will explain our readiness to you. For each fort that the Magadhans have on the rivers, we have two on our side. On the river Mihi, we have essentially fortified the whole of the riverbank through a series of forts. The land on the other side is of the Mallas, so we can cross over the Mihi to the far side. Incidentally, as you all know well, the Mihi flows very fast in these parts. Therefore, the Magadhans cannot attack us by sending their navy upriver. Our forts along the Mihi will be the nerve centre of our war efforts. Our main armouries and critical resources will be concentrated here. Are there any questions?' Singh looked around the room. There was complete silence. He had their attention.

'Further, we can use the Mihi to launch surprise attacks on the Magadhans downriver. We have built up a force of two thousand boats that are capable of carrying fifty thousand soldiers. We will have two hundred more war boats ready in the next two months. The Magadhans will have to cross large rivers to make good use of their navy, and we will need boats to stop them. The truth is that our naval skills will be crucial in this war. It is important to note that we have more skilled boatmen than the Magadhans. 'Historically, many boatmen left Magadha to settle our lands, drawn by better rights and freedom. You know well that they do not live as slaves here.

'We have taken our friend Kapyak's help to develop a small and versatile war boat. This is our best-kept secret, and when the time comes, we are sure that it will be of good use. Finally, on this topic, we have also invested in large boats for the transport of elephants and chariots, and we have invested in larger ports to streamline the movement of armed forces using the naval fleet.'

'Now let us turn to our southern and eastern borders. Here, our infantry is roughly as well organised as that of the Magadhans, and about equal in numbers as well. Further, we have invested in training them in modern methods of war learnt from our experiences in Gandhar. We do have fewer horses, chariots and elephants, but we should be too worried about this factor. In their campaigns in Mathura and Kosala, the vaunted chariots and elephants were often found to be lacking in flexibility and were easy to trap and finish off. Together with the Mallas and the Kosi-Kolon republics, we will have one and three-quarter akshauhini divisions deployed for war.'

Sunand said, 'Listening to you, Singh, gives me comfort. Things are not as dire as they seemed a few moments ago.' He turned to the chief of the navy, Syamantak. 'I now request the Arya Syamantak to brief us on the situation in the navy.'

Singh took his seat, and Syamantak rose and bowed. 'Friends, Singh has already touched on the key aspects of our naval strategy. We are better organised on this front than the Magadhans. We know that the outcome of war will depend on what happens in the south. I hope we can count on our friend Kapyak, and on his larger contingent, we are waiting for, to tilt the balance for us there. I am confident we will be able to launch attacks from our forts along the Mihi river. The Magadhans have many advantages, as we discussed, but they do not have any counter to those two thousand war boats we will deploy to attack them.'

Kapyak said, 'Sirs, the commander and my other friends will be happy to know the promised contingent of doctors and soldiers from Gandhar is about four days away. I would also like to take this opportunity to confirm an aspect of naval warfare based on my experience. The Mihi river meets the Ganga at

Didhivara, and the Magadhans army establishment is at Pataligram, downriver from this confluence. The lay of the land is a gift providing us with a means to launch a lightning strike at this Magadhan force major establishment.'

Singh said, 'Chief Sunand, Sir, I propose that the time has come for us to seize the initiative. We are as ready as we will be. We should not wait for Magadha to attack. We must attack first. Our attacks should be in waves, using the Mihi to our advantage, but holding the strongest forces in reserve for the last wave.'

Sunand spoke in a matter-of-fact tone. 'Go ahead, men. Singh, prepare the army. I will issue orders for the honourable Arya Varshkar and his associates to be arrested.'

CHAPTER 137

DRUMBEATS

The knives were out in Vaishali. The legendary Acharya Varshkar had been arrested. So also had Somil, Nandan, Kritpunya and their massive network of spies and assistants. Pundrik was under house arrest in Acharya Gaurpad's house, the acharya standing personal guarantee for him. The gates of the city were closed, and Royal Avenue was deserted. Entry to and exit from the city required letters of approval from the military command. The army also controlled and rationed all market supplies. They scanned all aliens, and the slightest suspicion provoked arrest. The army paid particular attention to patrolling all the water bodies and towers, but soldiers swarmed every corner of the city, anyway. Authorities announced a call to arms, and the army drafted all able-bodied men. For months, war production had been a priority, but now the war effort absorbed all production. Licchavi women joined the nursing services. Failure to obey the orders of the War Council and the military establishment meant the death penalty. While the people at large showed signs of strain, many young men took pride in burnishing and brandishing their weapons and in loud talk. The experienced soldiers were more stoic and reserved.

There was a ban on gatherings and celebrations, but stopping the heated discussions among civilians and soldiers proved impossible. Wherever men and women could gossip, they did. Some citizens still talked in hushed whispers of the bandit Balbhadra's ability to appear and vanish at will. They characterised Emperor Bimbisar as an ambitious and lustful man. Many people who had never entered the Palace of Seven Worlds commented the emperor's burning desire for Ambapali was the real motive for the war.

The Palace of Seven Worlds itself had lost its dazzle. Under wartime rules, merrymaking was forbidden, and excessive consumption of fuel and food was frowned upon. A tight security noose was cast around the Palace, and entry was heavily restricted. According to the plan, the War Council organised treasury and archives to be emptied, and all of Vaishali's wealth and important artefacts to be sent to designated underground vaults.

CHAPTER 138

THE MAGADHAN CAMP

A city had appeared almost overnight at the confluence of the Ganga and Mihi rivers, east of Pataligram. It was built under Chandrabhadrik's orders, with much of it being prefabricated. It was built as if it was meant to be a permanent establishment. Its layout was circular. A deep moat surrounded its wooden walls. At its centre was a royal house that was a hundred and fifty feet long and half as wide. A harem was built next to it. Right in front of the royal house was an annexe that was designed for the emperor to meet the army command and others he wanted to meet officially. Around this centre, there was a structured layout of all the facilities and establishments that were needed to keep the mammoth army funded, fed and fighting. These included the armoury, treasury, stores, medical facilities and the other arteries of supply, defence and maintenance.

Four protective enclosures surrounded the centre of the camp. The first was of thorny shrubs, the second of larger thorny trees, the third of wooden stakes and the fourth of bricks. Gaps of six hundred feet separating the enclosures held constructions for the different layers of society and supplies for storage. The first building housed the priests and ministers. It also contained the principal stores of food, water and the main armoury. The second had space for the army commanders and the elephants and chariots standing ready to deploy for war. The third housed the administrators and had room for more reserve war animals. The last enclosure sheltered the central corps of soldiers and merchants who kept the supplies going, the central market, and the prostitutes' quarter. All along the area outside, trained scouts blended into the landscape, ready to issue warnings at the first sight of approaching enemies. The path that led to the camp had been sabotaged well with camouflaged holes and deadly traps. These were laid according to a fixed design, and only a few chosen men knew how to navigate them.

The forces at the camp were divided into six units, each of them with three group leaders. There were eighteen operational units in the camp, and at any point of time, each of these units had at least half their strength on full alert. Thus, there was a multi-tiered and resilient system of defence without single points of failure. Access into the camp and exit into it were strictly controlled with passwords, and it was impossible for an impostor to penetrate the camp. Quick justice was dispensed to deserters.

A small group of intelligence officers continuously surveyed the situation with a vigilance bordering on paranoia. Their task was to protect the camp from insidious tactics like poisoning and arson.

CHAPTER 139

BIMBISAR MARCHES OUT

Bimbisar gave his priests all the time they needed to make their calculations. At the anointed time, when the morning sun was a pale red ball, he crossed the threshold of the inner sanctum of the Palace without fanfare.

A squadron of ten commanders led his army, an elite corps with cavalry, archers, elephants and chariots guarded the emperor and the harem, and a large elephant division brought up the rear. The procession that followed alternated between supply and military units, horsemen guarding the flanks always. Scouts rode ahead to make sure the path was free from danger.

The main army followed, divided into different formations: a crocodile formation in the front, a cart and diamond formation behind it, and soldiers circling them. Where the passage narrowed, the soldiers moved with discipline into lists, resuming their formations afterwards.

The giant army covered only eight miles a day for the first few days and then doubled its speed. They subdued the cities and villages on the way with a mix of the four traditional means – saama, daama, danda or bheda – request, bribery, punishment or deception. No human establishment had the means to stop this army.

Nor did nature. Streams and rivers crisscrossed the land, but the army's engineers made quick work of the crossings. Makeshift elephant bridges allowed crossing the shallow streams while building wooden bridges or joining hundreds of barges tamed the larger ones. Rivers were not the only barriers to the army. There were dense forests where the formations had to melt into thin marching lines. The march took them through slush, insect-infested undergrowth, thorny shrubs and dry patches. Thirst, fatigue and illness took a toll on marchers before they had set eyes on their main enemies.

The only way permitted to them was to march forward. The first men to reach the newly built camp sank to their knees and wept unashamedly with relief. More and more men streamed into the camp, filling it. Soon there were occupiers in the royal house, and the central block became functional. The path from Rajgrih to Vaishali remained full of marchers for many days as Magadha concentrated its might into the camp.

CHAPTER 140

THE VAJJI UNION PREPARES

'Then we leave for Ulkachal tomorrow', Singh said.

'Yes, we must. We need to inspect the stretch along the Ganga and the Mihi. Most importantly, we must test the new war boats. The eleven of us must go together so that we take decisions on the spot.' Kapyak said.

'Hmm, friend Kapyak, is there no risk someone will see us seen from the enemy's side on the Mihi?' Singh asked.

'It is not impossible', Kapyak said.

'So why not test the war boats on the Markat-Hrid lake where we are developing them? We could send them to the Mihi to ready them for action without risking someone seeing us there?' Singh said.

'That might work better. We can arrange the transport and test the boats without risking to compromise our stealth weapon', Kapyak said.

'But you and I must inspect the state of the fortifications, starting with Ulkachal, anyway', Singh said. 'Friend Kapyak, can you bring hand-picked men with you? It will be good if they help to inspect the fortifications and defences. I have sent a message to our man in charge of the Ulkachal fort. His name is Abheet. He is expecting us.'

'Very well, Arya Singh. We can ask the other group to get the war boats ready for action.' Kapyak said.

.

Riding with fifty Gandhar soldiers, Kapyak and Singh reached Ulkachal by noon the next day. To welcome them, Abheet stood at the entrance to the river fort. They entered his command room and started the review straightaway. Two maps with lamps placed below them hung along the wall of the room.

'Sirs, what you see here are maps of our forts and of the enemy's forts. We have the layouts, the exact numbers occupying the positions for our side, and our estimates for their side.'

'That is exactly what we are looking for', Singh said.

'Following your orders, Sir, we received reinforcements from the southern army. This has helped us greatly. After you have rested, we will present our detailed reports to you.'

Singh nodded his agreement. They reassembled in one hour, and Singh took briefings from each of the group leaders in the fort. He noted down their numbers, asked their concerns, checked about supplies and asked for suggestions, and wrote down detailed and meticulous notes. It was dark when he finished, and he and Kapyak reviewed the information they had received. They agreed on the letter to send back to Vaishali.

Abheet said, 'We are in the middle of the forts' inspections along the Ganga. If Arya Singh and Gandhar Kapyak do not mind sacrificing their rest, I can arrange a boat for the two of you.'

'Please do so right away, Arya Abheet. We do not need rest', Singh said.

It was a moonlit night. Singh, Kapyak and Abheet rode in a small boat. Its four boatmen steered it close to the riverbank. Across the vast expanse of the Ganga, they could see the Magadhan camp near Pataligram. Its lights were as impressive as those of a metropolis. They were visible for miles.

There were five Vajji forts between Ulkachal and Didhivara. Singh and Kapyak inspected each of them. At each fort, guards challenged them to state the password for the day or face death as they neared the landing. The three men dismounted at each fort, went up into the fortification and assessed the preparations. They issued orders on the spot to the commandants. Singh and Kapyak noted with satisfaction that the paths up to the forts were indirect, and traps made assaults impossible. Only a miracle would allow soldiers not knowing the lay of the land to survive a quick charge. The war boats that were ready were not visible even from the Vajji side of the river, let alone the enemy side. A meandering canal connected the Markat-Hrid lake to the Ganga, so the war ships could rapidly travel to the river. The inspectors did not find any cause for worry.

The boat approached Didhivara, the confluence of the Ganga and Mihi. Here, merchant ships of different sizes still docked at the jetties despite the war clouds. However, the war vessels and the fort were dark and still. Abheet whispered he had issued strict orders to this effect.

They reached Didhivara, the biggest of the five forts, just after midnight. The two leaders spent more time talking to the soldiers posted there and checking that spirits were high at this strategic and critical point.

By the time the three returned upriver to Ulkachal, the sky was lighter. They went ashore and walked up the path to the fort, having followed the protocol

and stated the password. Singh squeezed Abheet's shoulder and said, 'Commandant Abheet, friend Kapyak and I thank you. You have done all we could have
expected.' Abheet's teeth shone as he grinned.

They passed the first half of the next day listening to briefings from Jayaraj's
spies. The main news was that Bimbisar apparently waited for Chandrabhadrik.
He would not launch the main offensive without his commander-in-chief.

As soon as it was dark, Singh and Kapyak left for the next leg of their inspection. They travelled down the river, stopping at the forts after Didhivara.
On the second night, they reached the confluence of Ganga and Bagmati rivers.
The sight of the special forces units stationed at the main fort at this confluence
gratified them. They ordered some companies to travel upriver to Ulkachal and
train the soldiers there in the new river warfare techniques they had imported
from Gandhar.

Now it remained to check the string of forts along the Mahanadi river. Singh
and Kapyak returned by land to Ulkachal and caught up with the despatches
from Vaishali. They continued to receive intelligence briefings and respond to
them.

They launched the next leg of their inspection as soon as the moon rose.
Their boat rode the swift currents of the Mihi river to the confluence at Didhivara. There, they turned towards the east bank where they saw an endless
grassy plain where thousands of cows were grazing. Small huts dotted the plain.
The reports had told them both Licchavi and non-Licchavi groups occupied the
shelters.

They followed the Mahanadi river for four days. They had entrusted this belt
to an experienced commandant named Shantanu. Again, it pleased Singh and
Kapyak to see the men learning the new techniques of river war with skilled soldiers from Gandhar. At two forts, the duo joined the training sessions to reassure
themselves the preparation cut no corners.

At the end of this gruelling trip, they sent a joint communique to their
commander-in-chief and received an acknowledgement and reply within two
days. The state of readiness for naval warfare satisfied Sunand.

Next, Singh wrote to Jayaraj to increase his concentration of spies and report
every enemy move on the banks of the Son and Ganga rivers to the Vajji Union
command. He also enquired about the Magadhans' strategy to protect their capital from attack. Jayaraj had prepared his organisation for this last, decisive stage
of intelligence work. His force of spies, disguised as ascetics, monks, traders,
astrologers and prostitutes swung into action. The reports came in fast and in
large numbers. Chandrabhadrik had personally inspected the strengthening of
Rajgrih's fortifications. Check posts, ambush parties and traps dotted the land
from the banks of the Ganga to the Rajgrih. Chandrabhadrik had clearly spared

no effort to ensure the Vajji Union could not take the Magadhans by surprise with a lightning offensive against Rajgrih.

While the two armies swelled, manoeuvred and sharpened their weapons, Singh received and sent letters almost every moment that he was awake.

CHAPTER 141

THE MAGADHANS PLAN

Bimbisar and Chandrabhadrik were finally together in the Magadhan camp. The entire Magadhan command was in attendance, including Udayi, Somprabh and Minister Suneeth. Also present were the generals of the eight allied kings who had committed their support to Magadha.

Chandrabhadrik ensured they followed a strict agenda. They discussed every division and unit of the armed forces with its commanding officer. They repeated the entire chain of command, starting with Chandrabhadrik himself, to avoid doubt. They chose and confirmed the commandants of every important military institution, including the forts in the hills, the important river forts and the forest forts one by one, and assessed their readiness. The system of deputies – men who would over in case of key commanders' death or disability – was read out, and the commanders asked to memorise it. Somprabh was appointed commander of the southern army and had the eight allied commanders directly under his authority. The emperor himself had no direct involvement in the war's conduct.

Four men, who had trained for months, were now ordered to surface, each a perfect impostor of Bimbisar. This aimed to ensure the enemy would never have complete clarity in the emperor's whereabouts. Poets and musicians were ordered to launch their propaganda activities to boost the morale of the forces. Surgeons and doctors were given the best possible supplies and working conditions. The arrangements to hold enemy prisoners, and to raid the enemy's prisoner-of-war camps to release captured Magadhan forces, were reviewed. Special units had been created to help collect and organise Magadhan forces in case of a disorganised retreat, and to round up enemy soldiers cut off by Magadhan advances. The commander addressed the heads of these units and confirmed they wear clear about the command-and-control mechanisms they were to follow.

The elephant corps was to protect the front and rear of the main army, rapidly build and rebuilding works, firefight, destroy structures and transport loot under protection. The chariot corps had to check rapid advances of the enemy's forces, mount attacks to free up Magadhan captives and break the Vajji Union forces' morale with lightning strikes. The supply corps was to play its usual critical role of readying camps, paths, bridges and wells and maintain weapons, arms, ammunition and armour. The commanders of these corps received their initial orders and answered probing questions testing their complete readiness.

Chandrabhadrik praised Somprabh's bravery, acumen and hard work at length. He ended the session with a directive to all officers to follow the traditional discipline of the Magadhan army.

CHAPTER 142

OPEN WAR

A large Vajji camp stood across the Mihi river, and forts dotted the river-bank. A temporary bridge of boats spanned the river at the point closest to the camp. Kapyak's special forces guarded the bridge. The Vajji Union had put into practice its strategy of making this territory the nerve centre of their war effort. The forts had ample stocks of weaponry and hosted a large reserve of soldiers. The swift current of the Mihi made river-borne attacks by the Magadhans very difficult.

The nearest Magadhan centre was Pataligram, a town Varshkar had set up many years before with his typical foresight, intending to make it a base for war against the Vajjis. It was still a small town, lacking the grandeur of cities like Rajgrih or Vaishali. There were no signs yet of the megapolis from where dynasties like the Mauryas and Guptas would rule a significant part of India. Its houses were few and its streets usually deserted. The Magadhans periodically sent a regiment to occupy the town. They camped there for a month or so, and the city showed signs of thriving life. After they left, the Licchavis crossed the border and harassed the remaining residents, and it became a ghost town again. The Magadhans came back, and the cycle continued.

The Magadhan commandant of the town was a white-haired veteran heading a unit of twenty men. With this limited force, he could not hope to keep Magadhan control over the city permanently. The constant shifting of authority between Magadhans and Licchavis made life in the town harsh for the few brave inhabitants of the Pataligram. This inhibited the growth of the town.

.

The eastern side of Pataligram was under the Licchavis and the western side under the Magadhans. The commoners had fled, and their houses had been requisitioned by the armies. The soldiers on both sides lived in constant fear of bearing the brunt of the enemy's first assault. Somprabh had established his base on a level field more than half a mile to the south of Pataligram. He laid out this establishment in a circular formation. The formation was divided into four quadrants with appointed chiefs. Somprabh set up camp at the centre of the formation.

The forces were grouped into circular formations that were laid out with precision. Infantrymen, cavalrymen, chariots and elephants stood at defined intervals. The archers were placed in a central group. The entire formation was laid out in three concentric circles. Every horseman had three infantrymen in front of him, and every chariot and elephant had fifteen infantry and three horsemen before them. In addition, five men brought up the rear of each of the chariots and elephants. These circular formations were grouped into synchronised units that consisted of forty-five chariots, two hundred horsemen and six hundred and seventy-five infantry. The Magadhans had arrived at this formation as an ideally dimensioned one that could be augmented with more chariots if the need arose.

The Licchavis were well prepared but on less scientific lines. Singh had organised the Licchavi army into three independent divisions. The wing-attacking division comprised elephants at the flanks, elite horsemen in the rear and charioteers in the core. The Malla King Saubhadra headed this division. The second division was to lead frontal attacks with cavalry in the rear, elephants in the centre and cavalry in the front. The Licchavi chief Vajranabhi headed this division. A third division, intended for mixed use, had chariots in front, followed by cavalry and elephants. Its layout was close to that of the Magadhans. The Gandhar Kapish led this division.

Outside these divisions, Singh had created an elephant corps and kept it under his control. This corps consisted of the three thousand most highly trained elephants that had proven themselves to be stable in earlier conflicts. Singh had stationed himself in the rear of the Licchavi army with his elephant corps. Further, the Licchavi general Mahabal headed a cavalry corps of twenty thousand fully armoured horses. In the centre of the army stood a reserve corps of infantrymen and archers for the Licchavi forces' heads to summon as circumstances demanded.

•

One watch of the day had passed. The sun had risen to its zenith and had started its descent. The two armies finally stood against each other, in the open. The endless arrays of weapons and armour shone in the bright light, as far as the eye could see. The two chiefs had completed their tours of inspection.

Somprabh was dressed in a white silk robe under his steel armour. He rode out ahead of his army and halted his horse Dhumraketu about sixty feet ahead of his army. His face bore no signs of emotion. From his ranks, the sound of a conch blared across the hum of the two armies. The Magadhan ranks erupted with war cries.

Singh rode to the space between the two armies, equally impassive. His dress was ochre coloured. The Licchavis's conches drowned out the cries of the Magadhans, and the Licchavi broke into their war chants.

As if by synchronisation, Singh and Somprabh unsheathed their swords at the same time. They saluted each other by touching their glinting swords to their helmets. An arrow whizzed down from the sky and landed only a few fingers away from Singh's horse.

War had begun.

The two chiefs melted into their ranks. Singh saw the Magadhan army moving forward with drilled precision. He issued his last orders to his front line. Even as he rode hard for his command centre, he dictated despatches to be sent back to Vaishali.

Two thousand chosen cavalrymen, brandishing swords and spears, led the Magadhan attack. Following Singh's orders, his chief Mahabal took his two thousand cavalry and led them at a deliberately slow pace, in a curved formation, avoiding a head-on approach. Mahabal's men advanced silently until the shortest distance between the combating troops had narrowed to thirty feet. Then Mahabal shouted an order and his men rode hard to the right. The Magadhan cavalry turned to pursue the seemingly retreating Licchavis. Now, Singh ordered his second division, under Vajranabhi, to launch an all-out attack.

In no time, the engineered precision of the Magadhans fell apart before the onslaught of the Licchavis. The Magadhan troops leading the attack were enveloped on three sides by the enemy. Somprabh took stock of the situation. He issued orders to one of his chiefs to attack from their flanks with elephants and chariots, while three others formed a circular front to attack the Licchavis with freshly regrouped formations. The fighting had now spread over a field of sixty miles.

Now Singh saw his forces under these twin attacks and sent word to his troops to fall back in an orderly manner. As this manoeuvre was completed, he ordered his elephant core to be pushed forward through channels that had been kept strategically reserved for them. The earth rumbled as dozens of elephants, with iron chains on their trunks, charged forwarded into the Magadhan ranks. The Magadhans were trampled as the skies echoed with the din of the trumpeting elephants and the cries of their victims. The Licchavis had skilled archers on the elephants, and they inflicted heavy casualties on the Magadhans. Somprabh saw his army reeling and ordered in his special forces. These were men who had been trained for this particular occasion. They were short, agile and acrobatic. Protected by thin but strong armour, they darted between the elephants and inflicted injuries on them. The elephants went berserk, and the Licchavi elephant corps lost control of them. In no time, the rout of the Magadhans was reversed, as the crazed elephants crushed all who were near them, with the Licchavis bearing the brunt of the casualties. The earth turned red with blood.

Singh surveyed the scene of the disaster with equanimity. He pressed eight thousand cavalry to encircle the field and attack it from all sides. Somprabh saw his men wilting under this attack. He put together a unit of his chosen men, and flanked by chariots with elephants in the front and rear, led a strike right into the core of the Licchavi army. The surprise incision completely disrupted the Licchavi chain of command. The Magadhans' morale surged, and their formations fell back into their accustomed precision. Their advance became steady and determined. Heaps of corpses piled up as the battle raged on. The hoarse shrieks of men merged with the plaintive cries of wounded animals. The electrifying war cries gave way to grunts and oaths as weapons clanged. The Magadhan ascendancy lasted for a short while. Singh managed to unify his forces by pulling back from the ground where his elephants had been rampaging and mounting chariot attacks against the Magadhans to link up his divided forces. Now the battle raged with fury, both sides seeming to sense that victory was almost theirs. But victory eluded them both.

•

Emperor Bimbisar surveyed the bloody battle from a distance of about five hundred feet. He was mounted on his elephant, the legendary Malayagiri, and had occupied a hillock together with his personal bodyguards. A stream of messages was fed to him. He sent back missives to Somprabh and his field commanders. IIe had watched the Licchavis take on the fabled might of his best forces and beat them back.

Now, as he watched on, Singh ordered two fresh infantry units to form into staff formations and attack the core of the Magadhan army. They had sliced through several layers of the Magadhan formations before they were stopped by the special forces that Somprabh pressed in to attack them and beat them back. Not to be deterred, Singh led a cavalry charge with ten thousand horsemen.

The waves of attack, repulsion and counter-attack roared and ebbed. The sun had become a dull orb in the western sky, and screams of pain drowned out the cries of vigour. Corpses, carrion and broken chariots littered the battlefield. While the more battle-hardened troops used elephants' bodies as cover for archery, many of the younger soldiers baulked and fled the ground. They had to be pushed back into action on pain of death. Some young soldiers were shocked beyond redemption.

As the sun drew towards the horizon, the ardour of battle dimmed as well. The two sides blew conches that signalled the cessation of war and the commencement of rescue and relief operations. The soldiers who returned to their camps were pale, haunted shadows of the swaggering men who had marched out into battle.

CHAPTER 143

A SHORT CONSULTATION

Singh lost no time in carrying out a thorough inspection of his encampment as soon as he returned from the battlefront. He reviewed the arrangements for the dead and the wounded, and for prisoners of war. Next, he turned to writing down despatches for Chief Suman. Finally, he summoned his direct reports and carried out a quick discussion with them, giving them his assessment of the day and taking in their views as well. They deliberated on plans for the next day. A major topic of discussion was the replacement of dead or wounded officers with reserves and men who had demonstrated bravery worthy of promotion. The group agreed to reinforce security around the camp perimeter.

After his men had left, Singh continued to pore over maps and plans. Then he took a quick bath and a meal and lay down on his mat for a short rest. He was woken up by a guard who announced that Kapyak had reported to see him.

Singh sat slumped for a while as Kapyak stood at attention. Then he stood wearily and washed his face with water from a basin. He gave Kapyak a brief hug, and they sat down at the table that had the maps.

Singh was pensive. 'Friend Kapyak, Chief Somprabh is a good general.'

'Indeed, he is!' Kapyak said. 'He is Acharya Bahulashavya's closest disciple and confidant. He could not but be among the best in the world.'

Singh stretched his arms and locked them behind his head. His muscles bulged. 'They have suffered today, but our losses were not light either.'

'Has General Singh, who has just shattered the pride of a mighty empire, himself succumbed to dejection?' Kapyak asked, smiling.

'No, no. I am not shaken easily. But I am practical. I suspect they will not go for a repeat of today's open battle and its slaughter. I think they will cross the Ganga at Pataligram and go straight for our jugular. They will attack Vaishali.'

Kapyak nodded. 'I see. But friend, they will not find it easy to cross the Ganga.' He smiled.

Singh gripped Kapyak's shoulder and looked deep into his eyes. 'You stand between them and Vaishali! Vaishali's honour will be in your hands.'

Kapyak's eyes twinkled. 'I do. And I assure you, friend, they can launch from their side of the Ganga, but they will not touch our side.'

The lines on Singh's forehead melted. He smiled. 'Is there anything I can do for you?'

'Nothing except one favour. I want you to rest.'

'I feel rested. Friend Kapyak, remember one thing – the Magadhans will never attempt a daylight crossing.'

'Even better. Our plans will work better by dark.'

Singh nodded. 'I will rest now.'

'Be at peace, General.'

Kapyak saluted and left.

CHAPTER 144

AN EVENTFUL NIGHT

After the stormy day of battle, an eerie hush prevailed all night and the next day. Through the night, and all day, both sides tended to the wounded, rites for the dead and the exchange of prisoners. At sunset, Singh received the first missive about military activity. The Magadhans had amassed war elephants on the banks of the Ganga. The intelligence wing's assessment was that an attempted crossing was in the offing. Singh did not need to think for long before he jotted down his message on a parchment, affixed his seal and sent his first message to Kapyak, who was stationed at the confluence of the Ganga and the Mihi. His second message was a joint one to Chief Suman and Chief Minister Sunand. He warned them that the war could singe them directly, and soon.

Kapyak was prepared for the moment. Singh's message triggered the execution of his plans. It was the fourteenth night of the waning moon – a pitch-dark night. As Kapyak surveyed the river, he took in the familiar sight of the stars shimmering on its rippled surface. Across the vast expanse of the river, he could see a few lights flickering in the Magadhan camps. The bank of the river on the Licchavi side was thickly forested.

Kapyak had stationed his elite archers in the cover of the forest. Some of them were positioned on treetops. His assistant Priyavarman was in charge of the unit. Another unit of battle-hardened infantry lay waiting behind camouflage nets, on the sandbanks. They were armed with swords and spears, but they kept their weapons immersed in the sand so that their reflections would not give their presence away. These infantrymen were led by assistant-chief Pushpamitra. The third, and the largest, unit was stationed in war boats that dotted the whole of the bank of the river. Each boat had fifty soldiers. Kapyak personally led this unit. The boats were invisible to the naked eye, and they stretched in long lines from Markathand to the confluence, leaving no part of the riverbank unprotected.

The night was inky black, and the only sound that permeated it was that of the gentle flow of the river and the lapping of its waves. Every once in a while, the cry of a bird penetrated the silence. Kapyak signalled to an oarsman, who summoned one of the soldiers on his boat. The soldier stepped forward and saluted.

'What is your name, young man?' Kapyak asked.

'I am Shuk, General, Sir', the man replied.

'And how courageous are you?'

'Very, Sir', came the unflinching reply.

'Really?' Kapyak grinned.

The man smiled, and his teeth showed in the dark. Kapyak pressed the man's blank shoulder. 'Young man, I need you to do the most important task. Will you do it?'

'Yes, I will, General, Sir!'

'Even if it means danger to your life?'

'I do not care as long as the danger comes after I have finished what you want, Sir!'

'What if danger comes before?'

'That will not happen, Sir!'

'I thought as much. I was a young man like you once. Very well. It is time for you to execute your task then. Can you swim to the other side?'

'Of course, Sir.'

'You must stay hidden on their side.'

'I know a hundred ways of staying hidden, Sir.'

'Yes, I expect so. But be aware that they are no fools. They are also hardened soldiers, and they will have their men keeping watch.'

'Yes, indeed, they are, Sir. But I am Shuk.' His teeth showed again, and Kapyak laughed. 'I will go underwater and stick to one of their boats. I will enjoy it, Sir!'

'Yes, yes. But you must do more. You must signal to us when their boats launch.'

'As we discussed earlier, Sir?'

'Yes, friend, as we discussed earlier. Show me now', Kapyak said.

Shuk put two fingers in his mouth and made the sound of a tern bird. Kapyak knew that this was not the season for the terns, and he had assumed that the Magadhans would not know that.

Kapyak patted his arm. He said, 'Go now, young man. Our lives depend on you.'

Shuk saluted and turned without a word. His dive was almost soundless.

Kapyak walked to the stern of the boat and jumped overboard in a fluid move. A few strokes took him too close to the bank, and he waded over to the forest area. He knew this area like the palm of his hand by then. He entered the forest at a point marked by a large stone. Two soldiers appeared from the dark to greet him. At his signal, they lit a hooded lamp and produced a parchment for him to write on. He wrote at a furious speed, rolled and sealed the parchment, and ordered it sent to General Singh. When the messenger had left, he conferred with the soldiers in whispers. When he was satisfied that they were ready for the night that lay ahead, he said a few words of encouragement to them.

Even as he spoke, his subconscious mind had been tensely tuned to receiving Shuk's cry. When it came, he almost felt a sense of relief. After a few moments, the cry sounded again, travelling easily over the water. Kapyak called out a coded alert to be relayed to Priyavarman, who was not far away. Kapyak was pleased to see the morphing of shadows as the archers readied their arrows. He sensed that he could hear the quickening of his men's breath. Kapyak moved to the riverbank and concealed himself behind a thick tree.

Now the silence was pierced by the gentle sound of splashing oars. The riverbed sloped gently in this part, and the water was shallow. The sounds had come from close by. The sounds of the oars drew nearer. Kapyak felt his heart thudding but restrained himself from taking action. He deepened his breath to calm himself.

He felt a lightness in his heart as Priyavarman shouted an order. The silence was shattered by the twanging of bowstrings and the hissing of arrows. Then, screams rent the air from the middle of the river. Almost immediately, the splashing sound of the oars receded. Kapyak sensed the elation of his men.

Silence descended over the dark battleground. Shuk's cry sounded again. Kapyak abandoned caution and whispered, 'They are returning! There will be more of them!' His whisper was picked up and passed on.

The dark waters of the river became frothy now, and the sounds of oars were loud, distinct and spread far and wide. The enemy oarsmen were rowing fast and hard. Their boats were in the hundreds. 'Fire away!' Priyavarman's command rang out. The hissing of arrows did not drown out the advancing splashes of the oars this time. The cries were loud as the arrows found targets, but the Magadhans advanced with speed. The shapes of their boats were now distinct, and some of them had reached the Licchavi bank. Priyavarman shouted an order, and the bank was lit by torches that blinded both attackers and defenders for a few moments. The scale of the attack was mind-numbing. The enemy boats and men almost formed a bridge across the huge span of the Ganga.

The Licchavis's arrows flew fast and furious and inflicted heavy damage on the Magadhans. Guided by the dazzling torches, Priyavarman's war boats swung into action, attacking the Magadhan boats and cutting down the Magadhan attackers who were still wading on to the shore. The riverbank became a seething battleground as some Magadhan soldiers survived the Licchavi defences and reached within arm's length of the defenders.

Now Priyavarman's war boats had gathered in strength. They had iron buttresses that pierced the Magadhan boats and sank them. The night exploded into a fury of fire and noise. Kapyak's eyes scanned the chaos of war and locked on one strong Magadhan boat, where a short, well-built man in shining armour stood with his hand on his hip, calmly directing the attackers. Kapyak saw arrows bouncing off his armour as he ignored them with studied calm. Kapyak looked for Priyavarman but could not see him. He ran to the clearing behind him and grabbed a mace. Taking care to stay behind his men for as long as he could, he waded into the water and then dove inside. He swam to the Magadhan officer's boat. When he surfaced, he waited till he had gathered his breath. He manoeuvred himself to the stern, careful not to announce his presence. He was not surrounded by the Magadhan boats. Then, using all his might, he pulled himself up and sprinted to where the enemy officer stood. He brought down the mace in a fluid mace on the officer's head. The officer collapsed and toppled overboard. Kapyak saw the soldiers around him swing into action, and he jumped after the Magadhan. Another Magadhan boat drew alongside. Kapyak said his prayers as the Magadhans threw spears at him. He held on to the enemy officer and was saved because the soldier did not dare to risk hurting their own officer. Now he heard many splashes as the enemy soldiers jumped into the water. He held on to his quarry and drew his dagger. He fought off the first two attackers but felt clutched from behind by an iron grip almost at the same time as a spear grazed his tight, and the darkness descended on him.

The last thing he remembered was the tight grip on his neck loosening, and an external force guiding both him and the unconscious officer towards his own men and away from the enemy, even as a Licchavi war boat rammed the Magadhan boats.

While the fighting raged fiercely at the vortex of the Magadhan attack, two men surfaced after what seemed to be a very long time under the water, in a quiet spot near the Licchavi bank. They gasped for breath for a long time and then struggled to the bank where they lay spent, breathing hoarsely. One of them got to his feet first and motioned the other to follow him. They wrapped their dishevelled and wet black clothes around them and drew their swords. They exchanged looks and nodded. Not a word was spoken. They could not be seen even from a few feet away; such was the darkness there. One of them pointed to a clearing, which led to a path towards Vaishali. They sprinted towards the path.

CHAPTER 145

THE RENDEZVOUS

It was two watches into the night. Royal Avenue was deserted. The spectre of war had put paid to the city's revels. The only signs of human presence in the windswept night were the ghostly pairs of guards who paraded the length of the avenue, all the way to the city's walls.

The outer wall of Vaishali had one, and only one, secret door. Its presence was hidden behind dense undergrowth, and it was used for matters of great delicacy. Only a select group of people knew its password at any point in time – Chief Minister Sunand, Chief Suman, Singh…and Ambapali. Two men strode up to this door, and one of them knocked loudly on it.

Torches appeared in the windows, and arrowheads glinted in the slits in the wall above. 'The sign?' a voice rasped.

The man who had knocked said, 'Ganga'. He spoke without raising his voice, with confidence. Pulleys and hinges screeched as the door swung open. The two men strode walked calmly in. They were dressed in the style of the elite of Vaishali, except that their clothes were all black and a bit bedraggled. They did not pause to look at the contingent of guards, and the guards did not interfere with their progress. Any visitor through the secret gate must have a business that had to do with the war. The two men walked without pause. They skirted Royal Avenue but stayed parallel to it.

At one crossing, a shadow emerged from a corner and motioned to them. From then on, the shadow flittered across the lit portions of the streets and lingered in the dark when guards were within visible range. The two men skilfully followed the shadow. In a short while, they were at the main gate of the Palace of Seven Worlds. The gate was open, and the squad of guards stationed there stood motionless as the three men strolled in. The gates rumbled and closed as soon as the men had passed them.

The Palace of Seven Worlds looked as grand as ever, but it displayed a stony silence. The nights of magic, lights, music, wine, song and dance had long stopped. The three men walked fast. When they crossed the seventh compound wall, another figure stood waiting for them.

'This way, Sirs', a woman's voice said. The man who had guided them thus far stopped. The woman who took them onwards was covered in black. She led the two visitors at a stately pace through a maze of rooms, steps, corridors and halls. They descended a flight of stairs and saw a silver gate with a highly ornate latticework at the end of the steps. The delicate light that strained through the silver work was composed of multiple hues.

Their navigator opened the door, and the two men stepped into a room that took their breath away. It was a hall that was relatively smaller than the one used to welcome citizens in the inner compound, but it was large enough, and it out-shone the public hall in grandeur. It seemed as if there were countless lamps in that hall, even in these times of austerity. The oils in the lamps gave off a pleasant and heady mix of scents. It was mostly covered with marble and granite, and gold was used to accentuate its opulence. Strategically placed octagonal crystal pillars created infinite reflections between them. It was a while before the two visitors noticed that the carpets that they stood on was soft and jewelled. At the centre of the hall stood a sixteen-sided golden seat, covered with peacock feathers and an ornate canopy that shone with inlaid gems. A golden stool next to the seat bore three crystal bowls and an emerald pitcher that seemed to promise a large reserve of wine.

A curtain parted, and a presence filled the room. It was Ambapali. One of the visitors drew his breath sharply and closed his eyes as if to calm himself. The other bowed and swiftly retreated from the hall. Ambapali stepped forward. She wore a thin waistcloth that was almost completely transparent in that dazzling light. She wore nothing above the waist.

Her visitor stood dumbstruck. He looked at the waves of her hair descending to her shoulders. A single ornament decorated her forehead and a chain of gems as large as grapes graced her neck. He knew she had not bothered to put on any make-up.

He had had eyes only for Ambapali. As she drew near, he saw that she was followed by sixteen chosen maids, each of them a beauty in her own right. One of them carried a flat vessel, and others carried water and oils.

Ambapali greeted Bimbisar by prostrating herself, and her maids followed suit. Bimbisar gulped and extended his hand to lift Ambapali.

She said, 'Please take your seat.' Her eyes were moist.

Bimbisar had not uttered a word. He removed his shabby cloak and sat down. Ambapali sat on the floor. In an instant, the vessel had been filled with warm water and scented oils. Ambapali washed Bimbisar's feet. Bimbisar shut his eyes as he trembled with emotion. When he opened them, he looked into her eyes and felt his heart flutter.

'Lord, you have been foolhardy!' She smiled, and her eyes twinkled. 'What a task you set for yourself!'

'I had to do it. I could not hold back', Bimbisar said.

'I know.'

'You know of my mind's weakness?' It was his turn to smile.

'Indeed', she said with a laugh. 'I was waiting as well.'

'I thought, perhaps it is now or never. Who knows this demon of a war…who knows if it will consume this Bimbisar? And what if I am denied all that I want now?'

'Lord! Do not say that!'

'I already feel I am in paradise', he said, taking her wet hand in his.

'I was worried for your life, my love', Ambapali said. 'I wanted to see you, but I do not think you did right to come into your enemy's den.'

'Oh, I did right. How blissful I feel. Being with you, here and now, is an elixir. It has made my life meaningful.'

'And I am delighted, lord', Ambapali said. She filled a bowl with wine and handed it to the emperor. His gaze drew her closer. She sat next to him.

He held the bowl to her lips. 'Make it sweeter', he said. His voice was a hoarse whisper.

She took a sip, then drained the bowl and leant back as the wine warmed him.

The maids seemed to hear a command from Ambapali, though she had eyes only for Bimbisar. They withdrew to a corner of the hall, leaving the enamoured couple in the centre. Soon, gentle strains of music enhanced the intoxication of the lovers.

CHAPTER 146

THE WAR RAGES ON

The Magadhan forces had suffered heavy losses by the time they retreated that night. The Emperor himself, and Chief Udayi, were not to be found. This was the most shattering news in that hour of darkness. Rumours flew fast. Had they been taken captive by the enemy's special forces? One soldier stated that he had seen Chief Udayi being taken prisoner. Of the emperor, there was no news.

Somprabh saw it as his duty to preserve his men's flagging morale. But he could not help feeling despondent at the reversals in battle and even more at the inexplicable absence of the two leaders of the Empire's war machine. He despatched a note to Chief Chandrabhadrik. When he stepped into the forward zone for a reconnaissance, it was all he could do to maintain a stoic look and an erect bearing. The men who stepped forward to brief him looked haggard and defeated. The casualties had been heavy.

Somprabh took some decisions on the spot. He issued orders that no talk must be indulged in on the subject of the disappearance of the emperor and Chief Udayi. Reinforcements were pressed into the evacuation and care of the wounded. When Somprabh returned to his tent, he was gratified to see Chief Chandrabhadrik reach there at a full gallop, kicking up a cloud of dust. The two men waited till they were inside the tent before they spoke.

'Chief, I am sure you understand how things are', Somprabh said.

'Is the emperor hurt, in your view?'

'No, that does not seem to be the case.'

'And Udayi? It is true…'

'It does seem to be. There is at least one witness.'

'Who was shadowing the emperor?'

'Arya Gopal. He is missing as well. I did not mention him in my despatch.'

'Has anyone seen him, dead or alive?'

'No, Sir.'

'Have you pressed the top spies into service?'

'Yes, I have, Sir.'

'This is highly suspicious, though. How could both the emperor and Arya Gopal disappear together?'

'I agree with you, Sir.'

'So it is confirmed, and triple checked – none of the soldiers saw them?'

'That is correct, Sir.'

'And they themselves did not enter the front, as per our plans?'

Somprabh nodded, frowning. 'Is there more to this than meets the eye? Some strategy?'

'A strategy that you and I do not know of – that is the most frightful thought.'

Chandrabhadrik cleared his throat and swallowed. 'What of our navy?'

'It is no longer fit for war', Somprabh said simply. 'The enemy was prepared. Their defence was fearsome.'

'Somprabh, how did you allow that campaign to be mounted?' Chandrabhadrik asked.

'The emperor himself insisted on it, Chief.'

'I see…And what if he joined the attack in his impetuosity? And was hurt?'

Somprabh lowered his head. He whispered, 'I do not know…It will be a catastrophe.'

'Yes, it will, for all of India. The eastern empire will break down…And if he has been captured…' Chandrabhadrik shuddered. 'Enough of this. We must fight on.' He drew himself up to his full height and looked into Somprabh's eyes.

Somprabh saluted him. 'I will do my best. I will do all that is humanly possible.' He gritted his teeth.

'Very good. That is what we need. Now we must divide the forces into two and lead them from the front. You will attack the city of Vaishali directly. I will engage with their armed forces and cut them off from their central command. I will make every one of those Licchavi soldiers fear for his life.'

'And I will raze the city to the ground', Somprabh said. 'There will be a level field where that city of sin stands today. Donkeys will plough it.'

'And then it will not matter whether the emperor is dead or alive. As long as the Brahman is alive, the empire will go on.'

The two men summoned their direct reports. When they addressed them, they were calm, composed, and their words were full of fire. They breathed new vigour into the Magadhan war machine.

CHAPTER 147

A DIVIDED RULE

The Magadhans controlled the eastern side of Pataligram and the Licchavis the western side. Archers from both sides inflicted heavy damage on enemy quarters. The city now resembled a bleak hell. Order and sanitation had broken down. It had become impossible to dispose of dead bodies properly. Vultures and pigs feasted on the mangled remains of corpses. The air was smoky and rancid.

The Magadhans had fought off a Licchavi attack. A horse-mounted Magadhan officer galloped around a central square that had just been cleared of the enemy. His platoon guarded him. 'Citizens! Pataligram is now firmly under Magadha! We shall behead anyone found sheltering Licchavis! The emperor grants you immunity for having done so in the past! Step out, step forward!' The howling of dogs greeted his words. A roof that been smouldering collapsed with a soft implosion, creating a maelstrom of dust. From next to it, the Magadhans made out a form emerging with slow, unsteady steps. It was an old man walking with a pronounced limp.

The old man walked up to the officer and greeted him with a namaste. His hands were trembling. 'Sir, I am a Magadhan. I would like immunity, and I will pay tax.'

'As I said, immunity is yours', the officer said softly. 'Have no fear! Now tell me, who else is here?'

'No one alive!' the old man said. His eyes grew moist.

'They are – all dead?' the officer asked.

'Yes, all dead. Or fled.'

'And you? Why did you not go?'

'I could not. I am too old.'

'Hmm. Well, you say you are a Magadhan, and you will pay taxes?'

'Indeed, I am, and I will.'

'Very well –'

The sky darkened with arrows. The old man ran back into the ruin, with a nimbleness surprising for one who had been limping a few moments ago. Half the Magadhan soldiers collapsed. The officer was struck by an arrow in his shoulder. He muttered an oath and pulled it out. He turned his horse eastward, and the Magadhan platoon beat a hasty retreat, carrying their wounded with some difficulty and leaving behind a dozen dead men.

Now the Licchavis charged into the square. They were all infantrymen, one of them carried a large drum. He used it to good effect, drowning out the war cries and the screams of the wounded.

'Citizens! Listen!' the Licchavi commander shouted after he had signalled the enthusiastic drummer to stop. 'Pataligram is ours. It belongs to the Licchavi Republic. We shall execute any citizens guilty of harbouring Magadhans! Step out and swear allegiance to the republic! You shall be spared!'

The old man's head appeared first from behind a heap of rubble. Then he limped to the commander. 'Sir, I salute you!' he said and joined his hands in a fervent namaste.

'Greetings!' the commander said. 'Where are the others?'

'The ones who were alive ran away. Now I have only corpses for company.' The old man lowered his head to weep and blew his nose.

The commander's tone softened. 'You did not flee?'

'I am too old, Sir', the man said.

'So there is no one else here? No one at all?'

'None living, Sir.'

'I see. Well, it is simple – you are a subject of the republic. Is that clear?'

'Yes, Sir, of course.'

'You will pay taxes to the republic. Is that clear?'

'Of course, it is, Sir. Of course, I will. It is as clear as day.'

If the commander had any doubts about the clarity of the day, he left them unsaid. 'Hmm. Very well. And you do understand there is a death penalty for harbouring the enemy?'

'Indeed, I do, Sir! Very clearly!'

'Good.' The commander was satisfied with his conquest. He turned, and his men staked out their defensive positions. The old man disappeared.

CHAPTER 148

A NEW KIND OF CHARIOT

Somprabh summoned one of his aides, a man named Saambh. He said, 'Saambh, I am trusting you with a message that I do not want to write. Take it to King Vidudhab. Say this to him, word for word. "This is Somprabh's communique. Pull out all your reserves and move towards Vaishali. Move with deliberation. I had named three abbeys earlier. Destroy them. Raze all fields and buildings in the way and leave no doubt in the enemy's mind about their fate. Strike fear deep into their hearts. Advance on Vaishali's south-west and a force of fifty thousand of the toughest Magadhan soldiers will join you as you near the city. Together, launch an all-out attack on the fortifications. They cannot withstand our attack. Tomorrow, you and I will wash our swords in their famed Holy Pond." Go now, and come back before sunset. Tell me his reply wherever I am and in whatever state. Is that clear?'

Saambh listened gravely, bowed and left at a trot.

Now Somprabh turned his attention to his great weapon, his group of great chariots. These four iron chariots had no visible charioteer and were made entirely of iron. It was a concept unheard of till then and one that had been perfected with years of painstaking effort and trial and error from Acharya Shambhavyakashyap and his pupils. No known weapons could do more than scratch those chariots, and the fiercest war elephants were useless in front of them. Somprabh satisfied himself that his men had memorised the system of communication with flags.

Next, he sent a despatch to Chief Chandrabhadrik and then ordered his second-line officers to crank up the attack formation that had been decided. It took a whole watch to organise the formation, which had twelve thousand war elephants, sixty thousand horsemen, eight thousand regular chariots and two hundred thousand infantry. The four great iron chariots were kept in the centre so that they would not be visible to the enemy at the start of the engagement.

Then Somprabh sent word to his men they should rest till the signal was given. He also sent word that he would be in the attacking force himself, and this time it was a matter of his life and death.

When Saambh returned in the evening, sweaty and breathless, he found Somprabh seated calmly at his desk, meditating. The news was good. King Vidudhab had organised his forces in a crescent formation and had reached the outskirts of Vaishali. When three watches of the night had passed, Somprabh gave the order for an all-out attack. This time there was no effort at deception. All the resources and all the might of Magadha were pressed into the river crossing.

Kapyak and his men had seen the warning signals. The Licchavis fought hard and used every last defence that they had. But the sheer numbers were in the Magadhans' favour. Even with heavy losses, they established three bridge-heads of boats across the Ganga and defended them successfully. The battle had already passed into the hands of the Magadhans before the great chariots had crossed the river. Once that was accomplished, the Licchavi defences crumbled in the face of the fearsome iron contraptions that the Magadhan's had unleashed. As dawn broke, the Magadha had seized the day.

The Licchavi officers and their men did not lack resourcefulness or brav-ery, but they had no answer to the great chariots. These deadly machines broke through ranks of elephants and cavalry, and through fortifications like knives cutting banana leaves. The Licchavis's last-ditch efforts to throw groups of hun-dred men against the great chariots came to no avail. The Licchavi army reeled and retreated in disarray.

While the great chariots created mayhem, the Magadhans' conventional weapons multiplied it manifold. The Magadhans reached Vaishali walls and began bombarding the city with huge projectiles. As they had planned, several city dams and water reservoirs collapsed, and both fire and water started gnaw-ing at the great city's innards.

Somprabh had steeled himself to be utterly ruthless in this attack. Now that victory was within sight, he issued orders to fire arrows tipped with chemicals, explosives and smoke emitters. The Licchavis had realised by then it was time for them to sell their lives dearly and fought with the quiet desperation of men who were cornered. This latest attack broke their fighting spirit. Many Licchavi sol-diers and their animals became blind and deaf. The losses of the Licchavis would remain in oral histories for centuries to come.

With four watches of the day remaining, Somprabh's forces reached Vaishali's inner wall. They were greeted by the sight of clouds of dust being kicked up at the horizon by King Vidudhab's army. The encirclement of Vaishali was com-plete. The invaders mounted assaults on the walls of Vaishali. Ropes and ladders snaked up along the besieged walls. Even as Chief Suman calmly directed the defences of the city, he ordered women, children and the scions of the assembly members to be evacuated to hidden safe houses. By the time these plans were executed, the city was already burning, and the remaining defenders at its main gate knew that time was fast running out for them.

Somprabh galloped along the lines of his attacking men, bloodied sword in hand, calling out to some of them by name and exhorting them onwards. On both sides of the wall, the warring men knew that Vaishali would fall soon.

CHAPTER 149

THE LULL

omprabh heard a shout above the commotion of war. He saw a man charging towards him, brandishing a bloodied sword and shouting at the soldiers to get out of the way. It was Gopal Bhatt, a senior officer, calling out to him. 'General Sir! An order from the emperor!'

'The emperor?' Somprabh said.

'Yes, Sir!'

'Praise the gods! Then he is alive! Where is he?'

Gopal Bhatt drew his horse nearer and whispered, 'In Lady Ambapali's palace.'

Somprabh's mind reeled. He felt as if the great tumult of war had suddenly turned into a dreamy silence. He gulped, and said, 'What? Where did you say?'

'In Lady Ambapali's palace, General, Sir!'

'You mean…He is there and not taken prisoner?'

'No, General, he went there on his own accord.'

'On his own?' Somprabh steadied his breath with an effort.

'Indeed, Sir.'

'And what is his command?' Somprabh asked.

'It is to protect her palace. The Licchavis might attack it.'

'The Licchavis attack it?' Somprabh raised his voice. 'With what objective?'

'To take the emperor captive.'

Somprabh took in the scenes of the desperate battle ahead of him. His lips formed a thin smile. 'I see', he said. Without a word more to Gopal Bhatt, he charged to the top of a hillock. There, he turned his horse around to face the enemy walls. He drew a trumpet from his side and filled his lungs with air. The urgent blasts of the trumpet seemed to cast a spell on the seething, seemingly infinite mass of soldiers. They turned towards the source of the sound to see

Somprabh holding his sword, high with a large white cloth covering its point. A tense silence came over the battleground, before the moans and cries of the wounded, much more muted than the clashing and clanging of metal, stone and wood, filled the air. The Magadhan forces retreated, and the ladders and ropes fell away from the walls of Vaishali.

CHAPTER 150

THE LICCHAVI WEAPON OF DESTRUCTION

ven as the Magadhan iron chariots were smashing the Licchavi forces, the Licchavis's own weapon of destruction was inflicting heavy losses on the Magadhans in the southern theatre. This weapon was a mobile cannon that could compact hurl out any material fed into it, whether stones, metal pellets or lumps of wood, at such a high velocity that it fatally pierced or impacted all forms of life that came in its way.

General Chandrabhadrik had organised his forces into a complex formation with elephants on the fringes, cavalry in the inner ring and chariots in the core. As Somprabh led the attack on the eastern side, Chandrabhadrik launched his on the southern front, as per the Magadhan plan. As fortune would have it, the Magadhan iron chariots trampled the Licchavi forces on the eastern front, but Chandrabhadrik's forces ran into the Licchavi super cannons on the southern front. The Licchavis under Singh were also better prepared for defensive action, having had a day of rest.

The Licchavi cannons made mincemeat of the advancing Magadhan army. General Chandrabhadrik was directing its advance from the inner core. The collapse of his elephant units created havoc in the Magadhan forces, as the elephants stampeded away. It was all Chandrabhadrik could do to save his own life, gather his charioteers and archers into a rectangular formation and himself retreat to a point three hundred feet in the rear, with a reserve of cavalrymen surrounding him. He issued a despatch to Somprabh to send him reinforcements. His messenger broke through, but within a few hours, Chandrabhadrik's position had been cut off on all sides by the Licchavi forces and their allies.

As Chandrabhadrik sensed the battle slipping out of his hands, he issued orders for a last stand from the top of a hill. By now, his men were demoralised. They knew well that the tide was against them. Singh chose this point in time to launch a charge with his best cavalry and chariot units. The Licchavi offensive punctured the Magadhan lines like a needle through cloth. This was the final blow. The Magadhan forces were in complete disarray and reeling before the enemy.

The sun had become pale. As Chandrabhadrik maintained a stoic face and issued quick orders to his men, his moustaches shone like silver. His word betrayed no sign of despondence, but the august warrior could not hide the lines of worry on his forehead. His men's and his own fate now depended on reinforcements from Somprabh. The allied Kosala army had fifty thousand men hidden in the adjoining forest areas. They were best suited to step in and turn the balance in the Magadhan's favour. Unfortunately for Chandrabhadrik, in the chaos of war, this much-needed support did not materialise. Now, he heard from one of his men that Somprabh had declared a ceasefire just as the Magadhans were on the verge of taking Vaishali. He prepared to go down fighting with the last of his men.

Singh seemed to have heard the news of the ceasefire as well. He needed to confer with his colleagues. He realised that Vaishali had survived by a miracle. Here, he knew that the battle was won. He gave ordered to his second line to press on and finish the task ahead of them.

CHAPTER 151

THE BREAKING OF THE CROWN

Emperor Bimbisar lay sprawled on the bed. He wore loose silk clothes, and his untied thick locks of hair reached his shoulders. His eyes presented the bleary redness that comes from staying up all night and consuming too much wine at the same time. His gaze was vacant. He definitely had no thought for the commotion of many urgent voices coming from outside. He was thinking of the joy of union with Ambapali, an ecstasy even gods may not have experienced. He thought the meaning of the empire's might, and the value of his own life paled before this exquisite pleasure.

The noises travelling from outside became more strident. The swords clashing and horses whinnying intruded on the emperor's senses. He stretched and let out a yawn. He picked up a cup and an emerald pitcher. When he tilted the pitcher, seeing it contained not a drop of wine disappointed him. He sighed, dropped both the cup and the pitcher, and looked around him. There was no one in sight. He reached for the silver gong and rang it. To his surprise, it was Ambapali herself, and not Madlekha. Her face was pale, her eyes wide and her clothes dishevelled.

Bimbisar guessed that something must be very wrong. He tried to sit erect. 'What is the matter, Lady Ambapali?' he asked.

'The palace is under attack, lord!' Ambapali said. 'The soldiers of the Republic are attacking us!'

'Why?' The emperor put his feet on the ground.

'To capture you.'

'I see', Bimbisar said. He drew himself up to his full height and locked his fingers behind his head. Then he smiled languidly at Ambapali. 'Why are you afraid, Ambapali? Do you not see that I have my sword with me?' He pointed to his bejewelled sword.

'Lord, I have something disturbing to tell you', Ambapali said.

'Disturbing news? Well, there is a war on. There will be some disturbing news. Tell me.'

'General Udayi has been killed.'

Bimbisar swallowed and nodded. His face became grave.

'And Arya Chandrabhadrik is surrounded by the Licchavis. He must surrender or die soon.'

Bimbisar sighed. 'Then Somprabh and my elephant corps will save the day', he said.

Ambapali spoke in a whisper. 'Somprabh has declared a ceasefire.'

'A ceasefire?' Bimbisar exclaimed. 'By whose orders?'

'His own, it appears, lord.' Ambapali's voice broke.

A vein in Bimbisar's forehead throbbed. He strode to the peg that held his sheathed sword and picked the sword up. 'This is Bimbisar's holy sword, washed in the oceans on both sides of India. And I swear by this sword that I will lope of that degraded cheat's head before the day has ended.' He sounded the gong again, and when Madlekha appeared, he summoned his aide, Singhnad. He ordered Singhnad to prepare to take him out through the secret passage.

His appearance was calmer, and his breath less ragged now. He turned to Ambapali. 'Lady, do not fear. I will not be gone for long. I must administer justice to that upstart Somprabh, and then I shall return in force. I believe that your men will be able to hold out till then.'

Ambapali trembled but held back her words. As the emperor and Singhnad were leaving, Singhnad came to her and whispered urgently in her ear. 'Lady, the way things stand, either Somprabh or the emperor must die soon. Only you can stop a calamity. Please think about what you can do.'

'Singhnad!' the emperor bellowed impatiently.

'Your Majesty!' Singhnad replied and ran ahead. He drew his sword and motioned for the emperor to follow him.

They walked in silence through long corridors that were musty and dimly lit. At several points, they climbed down flights of crudely hewn steps. After about an hour, Singhnad signalled the emperor to stop.

'What now?' Bimbisar asked.

'We are at the Ganga already. I will have to see if the boat is ready to take us over', Singhnad said.

'What do you mean? Are our men not in command on this side?' Bimbisar asked.

'They have retreated, Your Majesty. There are elephants still on this side, but they will cross over soon. I am not sure – they may already have gone.'

Bimbisar shivered with rage. Singhnad lowered his gaze, bowed and moved towards a small hole in the tunnel.

He was back very soon. 'All is well, Your Majesty', he said. 'Please follow me.'

They slithered past the hole and crawled to a pit. An unpretentious boat was moored in the water. They lowered themselves on to the boat, and Singhnad rowed them away gently. They joined the large procession of boats that the Magadhan elephants were being ferried on. The boatmen and soldiers knew Singhnad, and they seemed to guess who his passenger was.

Chaos reigned on the opposite bank. This was no orderly retreat. The emperor's nostrils flared with rage. He jumped off the boat before Singhnad could tie it and help him descend. He marched on with his sword unsheathed. Many soldiers considered challenging this unkempt but imposing man, but sense prevailed as Singhnad frantically gestured to them and they understood whom this furious man was. Gradually a small procession formed around the emperor.

Soon, Bimbisar was at the entrance to Somprabh's camp. Six guards armed with tridents stood guard there. They made as if to stop the large man who walked with a heavy step, but once again, Singhnad and the others managed to convey that they should just step aside.

As Bimbisar strode into Somprabh's tent, he saw that Somprabh and his officers stood in a semicircle. Somprabh had a lectern in front of him was writing something with concentration. The men looked grave.

An officer saw Bimbisar, saluted and said, 'Victory to His Majesty!'

Others joined the chorus of greetings. Somprabh looked up.

'Som!' Bimbisar bellowed. 'Did you – did you declare a ceasefire?'

'Yes', Somprabh said in a cold voice. He did not bother to greet the emperor. Some of the other men turned pale.

'With whose authority?' The emperor trembled with rage now, his biceps clenched as if he could hurl himself on Somprabh.

'My own.'

'And who gave you that authority?' The emperor's nostrils twitched.

'It is vested in me. I am the commander of the forces', Somprabh replied, showing no emotion.

'Why did you not consult me?'

'It was unnecessary.'

Bimbisar rolled his head and seemed to calm himself. He nodded. 'I see', he said. 'And why was the fighting stopped?'

'I saw it as a futile war. A war with a worthless aim.'

'Of what aim are you aware?'

'I have now become aware that a womanising, wayward emperor, violating the traditions he was sworn to, started the war to make an empress out of a courtesan.' There were muffled gasps and exclamations in the tent.

'And you, who stand there lecturing me, do you know what your duty is?'

'Indeed, I do. I have not studied at Takshila for nothing. It is my understanding that an empire's army must be used to advance the empire. Not to fulfil the emperor's lusts.'

'Do you know you are talking to the head of the empire? Does the empire mean more than me?'

'Indeed, it does!'

The emperor's eyes blazed, but his words were slow, soft and deliberate. 'I declare that I shall anoint Lady Ambapali as my empress. She will reside at the Royal Palace. If this means killing all the Licchavis and razing the Vajji Union, I shall do it. If it means burning Vaishali to rubble, I shall do it. I order the war to commence right away.'

'I disregard this order. Not a drop of Magadhan blood will be shed towards this objective. Ambapali will not become empress.'

'And if she does?'

'One of us must die for this question to receive a definite answer.'

Bimbisar snorted and raised his sword.

Somprabh spoke to the men around them. 'Gentlemen, this a duel between an emperor who is in clear violation of his duty to his empire and an appointed commander who is only concerned for his duty to the same empire. Please stand back and let us settle this matter between the two of us.'

'Duty!' Bimbisar screamed. 'You, who do not know your lineage, dare to talk about duty! Ungrateful wretch!'

It was impossible to say who made the first move. The swords clanged, and then the two men were locked in a test of strength. Somprabh danced away and thrust again, only to be parried away. Bimbisar pressed in an almost got the better of Somprabh. He used his bulk and pressed down with all his might. The edge of his sword was very close to Somprabh's neck. Somprabh jerked his knee up, caught Bimbisar close to his groin and rolled away. The battle continued with both men using every bit of swordplay, strength and acrobatic skill that they could muster. The whirring of their swords and the clashing of steel sped and slowed in an irregular rhythm.

Without warning, Bimbisar's sword broke in two. He swayed to protect himself from being stabbed in the chest and slipped and fell. Somprabh pounced on him, pinning the emperor's chest down with his foot as he held his sword's edge against the emperor's throat.

Somprabh panted as he spoke. 'Now the time has come for me to execute your death warrant! I take it that you have no fear?'

Bimbisar looked Somprabh in the eye and smiled.

A scream erupted from behind Somprabh. 'No!' it was a woman's voice. Somprabh looked over his shoulder to see a vision he had not expected. Ambapali was running towards him, covered in dirt. Her clothes had lost all their finery, her face was anguished, and her hair bedraggled – but her lustre still shone. She ran to him with her arms outstretched in a gesture of supplication. 'Som! Dear Som! Spare the emperor! I vow that I will not become his chief queen.'

Somprabh heard this declaration without betraying any sign of emotion. He kept his foot firmly on Bimbisar's chest, and his sword pinned the emperor. Ambapali reached him and fell at his feet. She gathered her breath before speaking. 'Do not kill him, Som. I shall never meet him. Unfortunate that I am, I will tear off the part of my heart that I had given to him. Spare his life! He remains a great emperor, though he lies helpless! Take my life instead! This life which you yourself saved!'

Ambapali lay spent, unable to speak any more.

Somprabh raised his eyes skyward. The moon glimmered in the east, and the sun was a dull sliver in the west. The assembly was hushed. Somprabh's shoulder twitched. He closed his eyes and took a deep breath. Then he removed his sword from Bimbisar's throat and took his foot off the fallen emperor's chest.

'Imprison the emperor. I grant him his life. However, he must answer to the charge of dereliction of duty before a military court. Take Lady Ambapali back to Chief Suman. Treat her as a State guest.' He walked slowly out of the tent, without a glance at anyone, sheathing his sword.

It was dark outside. The sun had set.

CHAPTER 152

SURRENDER

Singh had left the command of the southern theatre to Kapyak. He withdrew to Ulkachal, in the centre. He spent his first hours there sending despatches through his entire chain of command. At the end of the flurry of messaging, he summoned his deputy chief, Abheet.

As Abheet stood at attention, Singh said, 'Not much time is left before sunset. We should hear from Kapyak soon. I am surprised we have not.' He stopped to write a few lines and hand over a scroll to Abheet. 'Friend, send this to Priyavarman. And ask Pushpamitra if the boats with supplies have been sent to Pataligram. Oh, and do ask Shuk to send some pork and sweets. If the meat can be warm, that would be great. The last meal I had was of cold meat, and I have forgotten when I ate it.'

Abheet smiled. 'Anything else, Chief?'

'Show me that map!' Singh jumped up to his feet. Abheet brought it over. Singh pored over it and frowned. 'So, here we have…' He shook his head. 'Any minute now. It should be any time now. Chandrabhadrik is a great warrior, but he does not stand a chance.'

Abheet had left the tent. When he re-entered, he asked, 'So this will be the end for Chandrabhadrik?'

'Yes. It will be. I do not see what else…'

Abheet said, 'Chief, the boats for Pataligram have left.'

Singh was reading a despatch. He stroked his chin. 'Arya Abheet?' he said. 'The weapons confiscated from the Magadhans? Make sure they stay here. Do not send them towards Vaishali.'

A guard burst into the tent and saluted the two men. 'Chief Commander Suman is here, Sirs!' he said.

Singh stood up to greet the chief commander. Abheet saluted him as well. 'Chief Commander! I had no idea you would be here!' Singh said.

'Young man, I could not sit still after receiving your exciting message!' Suman said. 'Is this true? Have we snatched victory from the jaws of defeat?'

'We have indeed, Sir! Like men, nations have their fates.' Singh smiled.

Suman took a seat and motioned the other two to sit. Suman said, 'Do you know this? Somprabh has taken the emperor prisoner! And his soldiers have handed Lady Ambapali over to me.'

'Was she captured by the Magadhans?' Singh asked.

'No. She – she went to the Magadhan camp to ask them to spare the emperor's life.' Suman shook his head.

'I see. And does she have anything to say now?'

'No. She has been unconscious since then. As a precaution, I left her in Acharya Agnivesh's custody. He is treating her.'

'I hope she is not in mortal danger?'

'I do not think so, not with the acharya doing his best for her…But Singh, what do you say of Somprabh's sense of duty?'

'He is a great man, Sir. He is worthy of respect, indeed.'

'I have a sense that all this, which was unimaginable, will become immortal in recorded history.'

'Kapyak's last message was that Arya Chandrabhadrik should capitulate any time now. He received no support from the rest of the Magadhan army, but held our forces off for all night and all day.'

'He cannot last long', Suman said.

'I have been waiting for Kapyak's final message', Singh said.

'We can afford to wait. Chandrabhadrik may be able to fight on tonight, but no longer.'

A messenger came running into the room and saluted the men. He was panting. 'Sir', he said to Singh, 'you have been waiting for this message!'

Singh fumbled with the seal and broke it. He heaved a sigh, and his shoulders relaxed as he read it. 'General Sir, Arya Chandrabhadrik has surrendered. He heads this way.'

Suman nodded, while Abheet raised his arms in exultation.

'Treat him well. He is a good man', Suman said.

'I will do so, Sir', Singh said. He handed over a scroll to Suman. 'These are the rules for a temporary treaty', he said.

Suman read the scroll very quickly. 'That is all right', he said. 'I will leave this to you.'

'But will you not welcome him?'

'No, no. I will head back. I will leave this to you. And I trust you will be diplomatic and far-sighted. Is there anything else?'

'No, Sir.'

'Very well. I shall leave.'

'At this very instant?'

'Yes, young man. I told you I could not stay once I had read your message. There is much to do there as well.'

Chief Commander Suman acknowledged the salutes of his men and strode out of the tent. Soon, they heard the sound of the hoofs fading into the distance.

A large boat docked at the steps on the riverbank. Three soldiers jumped off it and ran to the tent. The leader greeted Singh and said, 'Greetings to the Chief. Arya Kapyak has brought Arya Chandrabhadrik here.'

Singh rose. His eyes were shining.

In a few moments, Chandrabhadrik entered the tent followed by Kapyak, who had his sword drawn. Chandrabhadrik's bearing was erect, but his eyes were lifeless.

Singh took a step forward and touched his turban with the tip of his sword. 'I, Licchavi commander Singh, greet you with respect, Chief Chandrabhadrik! I have the highest respect for you.'

'Young man, I congratulate you on your victory', Chandrabhadrik said. His demeanour remained calm, but his eyes took on a defiant look. 'I salute the gentlemanly conduct of your officers.'

'I take pride in your praise, Sir', Singh said.

'However, as you know, I fought until the end. I face defeat now. May I know –'

'The terms of the temporary peace, Sir? Here they are. I trust you will find them reasonable', Singh said. He handed over a written scroll to Chandrabhadrik.

Chandrabhadrik took the scroll, unrolled it and read it without betraying any emotion. When he was done, he nodded. 'Young man, you are reasonable, indeed. I do have a request, though.'

'Please speak freely, Sir', Singh said. 'I will do what I can.'

'We urgently need to consult Chief Minister Arya Varshkar. We cannot take the next steps without his counsel.'

'We fully understand that', Singh said.

'Then, there is one more thing. This is just a confirmation – I trust you will return the captured soldiers with their weapons and horses, following our traditions.'

'They will', Singh said.

'I am grateful to you, young man', Chandrabhadrik said. He sighed and took out his sword, careful to keep his movements slow and deliberate. Holding his sword horizontally with both hands, he presented it to Singh. 'I have never done this before, but I have no hesitation today. Here is my sword.'

'No, no, Sir! Your sword was where it belongs. Please let it stay there', Singh said with a bow.

Chandrabhadrik lowered his head. He did not say a word, but his gratitude was clear. He sheathed his sword and added a note to the treaty to mark his acceptance of it, along with his two requests. Singh further wrote a line after taking the scroll and sealed it. No sooner was this done than a messenger stepped forward to take it and carry it to Vaishali.

CHAPTER 153

THE INSPECTION

Singh was at Pataligram within a few hours to inspect the state of its affairs. He saw that most of its houses were damaged and its streets deserted. Some of the houses had been reduced to ashes and rubble. When he looked for the large mansions that he was familiar with, he was greeted by their skeletal remains. Royal Avenue was dotted with garbage and refuse. The fields on the outskirts of the city had been trampled and would not yield a harvest that season.

The riverbank had become a quagmire of slush, swamp and rotting animal bodies. From one end of the horizon to the other, the bank was a scene of the apocalypse. Inland, the Magadhans had not been able to attend to their wounded. The sights in their camp made even the battle-hardened Singh cringe.

When Singh turned to the battlefield, the sights that greeted him were even worse. The administrators on both sides had done what they could, but the scale of war had been such that it was beyond human capacity to erase its horrors. He was pained to see that among the dead and dying, there were still some Magadhan soldiers who showed signs of life. He issued orders for them to be tended to, and sent a written note to Acharya Agnivesh, asking for urgent medical help to be despatched to Pataligram. He ordered Kapyak to speed up the task of requisitioning vacant houses in the city for temporary use. The wounded were to be shifted there while help arrived.

As news of Singh's inspection and his quick administrative orders spread, many of the city's dwellers started trickling back into the city, carrying their belongings with them. Singh sought out the elders among them and introduced himself to them. He spoke to them in simple and clear terms and urged them to get on with the task of restoring their lives. He asked them to help his men in their work and to let them know what help they wanted in turn.

As the day drew to an end, Singh conferred in private with Kapyak. He told Kapyak that he would leave immediately to tend to the closure of the terms of the treaty. He discussed the plans to handle the enemy prisoners of war, who were still trickling in. They were to be treated well and released with their weapons, but in small groups. The whole exercise was to be conducted in a way that they did not pose any threat to the victors.

CHAPTER 154

THE TREATY

Vaishali's assembly hall buzzed with an excitement that it had not witnessed for a long time. The defeat of the Magadhans was a momentous event. The days of war had drained the Licchavis of their colour, and the vast scale of loss and suffering brought about by the war were still fresh in their minds. Each of the Licchavis had reasons to grieve. Even in that heavy and depressed atmosphere, the signing of the treaty brought a sense of purpose and cheer to the Licchavis. Representatives of the thirty-six kingdoms and the eight clans were in the assembly hall. Chief Minister Sunand and Commander Suman had taken their seats.

General Singh was one of the last men to enter the hall. He was greeted by a roar of applause. Commander Suman rose to his feet and waited for the greetings to die down. Then he spoke. 'Gentlemen, fortune has favoured us with the victory. The enemy wants peace. We are gathered here to approve the terms of peace.'

The representative of the Mallas and Kolas was on his feet. Suman nodded to him.

'We do not want peace!' He spoke in an inflamed voice. 'We want to finish the Magadhan Empire. It has always been a thorn in our flesh. I propose that we use this opportunity to finish them off. We establish republican rule not only in Magadha but also in their conquered territories.'

'But, Sir, Magadha and their dependencies like Anga do not have the eight clans or their equivalents', Suman said. 'They do not have established traditions of republicanism. They do not have any significant numbers of your communities. At best, we can rule them the way we rule the non-Licchavis within the Vajji Union.'

Chief Minister Sunand raised his hand, and Suman bowed to him. Sunand said, 'Gentlemen of the assembly, this young man's proposal is to set up an independent republic in Magadha. Republicanism implies rule by the representatives of the people. It is not a question of administration, which empires also have, but a question of governance. The absence of hereditary kingship is a key element here. There is no question of a ruler and ruled. The people rule the people. The council – such as this one – represents the people. Within the Vajji Union and its eight principal clans, we have Licchavis, but we also have slaves and non-Licchavis. We have newcomers. We try to rule these others kindly, but they do not, in fact, influence our way of governing. Now consider the immense diversity among those non-Licchavis. They include, for example, merchants who live within our borders and live by the rules we settle. Their influence ranges from Greece to the eastern islands. Then there are the sculptors and artisans, much less influential and wealthy, but no less a part of our society. Their work surrounds us at this very moment.

'Gentlemen, think through the difficulties we have had in integrating these diverse groups into our social fabric. Now, imagine the complexity we will deal with if we take on the task of setting up similar regimes to govern Magadha and its annexed territories. They will overwhelm us. I do not see any other result. What shall we do? If we send a Licchavi to Magadha, he will be an outsider to their system and ways of working. If we send a non-Licchavi, we may create the ground to replace the current hostile regime with another one. Recall that for a short while at least, that person will have an absolute power I do not have here. Imagine the consequences if things do not turn out as we want them.'

The hall was silent as the assembly digested the elder's words. Then a Malla chief said, 'But shall we just forget this invasion by concluding this peace treaty? What then? We cannot bear their attacks forever, for sure?'

Suman said, 'There is one more thing – if ever the Magadhans win, they will swallow us up. It is a simple matter for them to make this another division of their empire. They will draw on the support of the non-Licchavis. This is the bitter truth: they only need to win once to finish us, while even in our hour of victory, we cannot finish them.'

Sunand nodded. He said, 'That is true.'

'And does that not mean we should uproot them when we can?' the Malla asked.

'But how?' Suman said. 'Once again, think about the steps that it requires. It has taken all our strength to resist the invasion led by Bimbisar and Acharya Varshkar. And what if we create an enemy empire led by a Licchavi? What chance would we have against them?'

'Why not make Magadha and Anga independent republics?' the Malla chief said.

'That is the core problem', Sunand replied. 'We don't have the power to create republics there. Their imperialist traditions are too strong, and they are too large. They can swallow us, but we cannot swallow them. Establishing new kingdoms is possible there, but establishing new republics is not.'

'But why not, Chief Minister, Sir?' another member of the assembly interjected.

'Because it requires a feeling of a single and unified society, a sense of unity. This is just not possible in Magadha or in Anga with their vast scale and their deeply entrenched social distinctions and castes. There is no concept of nationhood and equality as we know it. The very idea of equality and the ideals of rule by the people are anathema to them…. Let me call on the man of the hour, Commander Singh, to provide his view on this complex topic.'

Singh stood up, and the hall fell silent. 'Chief of the Republic, Sir and Members, we must remember that royal clans have life spans, like the human body. The youth of a powerful dynasty can be a terrifying thing for those that come in its way, but the old age carries less terror. This stage of Magadha's Shishunaga dynasty, Gentlemen, is its advanced old age. Let there be no illusions on that. And even then, our victory has not come easily. I do not need to remind you that it was not a foregone conclusion, and I do not need to tell you how we are completely spent in this war. Yes, we have saved ourselves and our prestige, but it has by no means been easy. Now, what if we leave the wolf's cave to enter a lion's cave through our miscalculations? What if we try complex political manoeuvres and end up creating an empire that has the size of Magadha and combines it with fresh dynamism? And perhaps we should also consider how many years, perhaps decades, we will need to recover our losses?'

He paused and waited for his words to sink in. He looked around at the assembly. No one raised a hand to speak.

Singh continued. 'Now, Gentlemen, let me remind you of another factor. Our armed forces are stretched from here to the Ganga, and they are struggling to manage the complex logistics of victory. But there is land beyond the Ganga. The Magadhans have many forts that remain untouched by this war. And most of all their capital Rajgrih remains untouched! And remember, Gentlemen, that this fortress city has excellent natural barriers and has never been taken by an enemy. Never! Those of us who have studied military science know that a fortress cannot be conquered by brute force. It has its own supplies of water and food. We have lost more than a million men in this war. Do we have another million to lose, even assuming we have the stomach to take on this huge task?'

Singh bowed and sat down. His eloquent speech provoked a buzz of discussion, but no one stepped forward to speak.

Chief Minister Sunand rose to his feet. 'Gentlemen of the assembly, you have heard Commander Singh speak. I think the message he wants to convey is very clear. First, let us secure our position. Let us not entertain grand dreams that have no basis in reality. So, the question is: should we sign this treaty with the enemy, or not?'

Multiple answers were heard, but the consensus was firm: sign when the enemy was on their knees, and when the terms were dictated by the Vajji Union.

'Then we have to consider three things. First, we must weaken the enemy such that they do not raise arms against us for a long, long time.'

'Why not forever?' the Malla chief asked.

'Because that is not within human powers. Second, we must take sufficient compensation for our losses. Third, the far-east shores should be open to us for trade and commerce. We should ratify the temporary treaty and agree to permanent peace on these terms.'

The motion was put to the vote and passed with unanimous approval. Singh was appointed the negotiator on behalf of the republic.

·

The official signing of the treaty with the Magadhans marked a day of rejoicing for Vaishali. The atmosphere of austerity and fear lifted, and colours and festivity brightened the city. The evening was lit up by thousands of lamps. After many nights of fear and ghostly silence, strains of music and sounds of dancing were heard in some mansions.

The Palace of Seven Worlds remained unlit, undecorated and silent.

CHAPTER 155

A WEALTH OF TEARS

It was midnight. The sky was overcast; not a single star was visible. The clouds seemed unable to make up their minds. Once in a while, a tentative, barely perceptible drizzle descended on the earth, making the fires crackle. The air remained heavy and oppressive. Thousands of pyres burned in the war zone. Their ghastly smoke made the air acrid. They dotted the flat land on either side, as far as the eye could see. The fires were consuming the dead bodies of the casualties of war. They hissed and crackled as they devoured flesh. Their colours sometimes change from yellow to blue and red. An army of men carried the bodies of their fallen comrades into the fires. There was no time for ceremonies. Great warriors who had made the earth tremble before them were now no more than corpses strewn in the bloodied mud. Few of them had died with their heads and limbs intact. In this hell on earth, the fallen men had finally achieved equality. There was no distinction between king and pauper. Crowns lay strewn in the melee of bodies and limbs, and none could tell whether a crown belonged to the head nearest it. The soldiers carrying the dead to the fires had their heads wrapped in whatever cloth they had mustered. Many of them had collapsed in exhaustion and shock in the first few moments of performing their duties. The ones who had persevered looked like an army of faceless ghosts.

Somprabh sat in a meditative posture under an enormous tree. His dishevelled look showed that he had not thought about his appearance for many days. He had matted and dirty hair; sweat and dirt streaked his face. His eyes showed no sign of emotion as he surveyed the infernal scene before him.

Often, the cries of owls and jackals pierced the fierce buzzing and crackling of the fires. They startled the men at work and visibly perturbed Somprabh. But he quickly returned to his meditative state.

He thought about his life and all its twists and turns. He thought about his days as a student in Takshila when the future had seemed so bright and full of possibilities, and his mind and body knew virtually no bounds. His thoughts wandered to the princess of Champa and her tear-streaked face in the soft moonlight. He relived the heightened ecstasy of his senses as his fingers created music, and he saw Ambapali dancing to it. His hands trembled and lined appeared on his forehead as he thought of Emperor Bimbisar lying, defeated, on the ground, and of Ambapali's despair scream. He thought about how meaningless and lonely his life was. And he realised that more terrible than this night would be the days following it.

An unexpected sound impinged on his train of thought. Soft footsteps that he had barely heard had not stopped, and they were now very close. His hand reached for the hilt of his sword by reflex. He had ordered his men not to approach him under any circumstances. He made out the silhouette of a woman.

It took a while before the faint light playing on her face revealed her identity to Somprabh in his despondent state. He was on his feet in an instant. 'You!' he said. He cleared his throat.

'Yes, it is I.' His visitor drew even nearer. 'I wanted to see you in this state and in this place. I lived a hard life...I stayed alive to see you here. It is said that a woman's life has sixteen phases. Today, my being a woman and a mother have meaning. My life, unfortunate as it was, has attained its goals.'

Somprabh stood speechless. The faint, flickering light of the flames showed the lady's austere and dignified demeanour. The lines of her face spoke of the hardships she had endured.

Somprabh lowered his head. In the next instant, he had fallen at her feet. The lady gently sat down and lifted his head into her lap. No one else was nearby. Somprabh felt as if a cloud had burst. He did not know what was happening, and it took him a while to realise he was crying his heart out, sobbing as uncontrollable tears streaked his cheeks. He felt a calmness descend on him as his tears ran dry, and his face felt the caresses of her warm hands.

'Mother, what brought you here?' he asked.

'My son, it has been many, many days since I cried with you', she said. 'In the prime of my life, darkness overwhelmed me. I cried, and I cried. I spent all my tears. For forty years, my eyes have been dry. There were times when I sought deliverance in tears, but they did not come to my aid. Tonight, I thought the time had come to meet you, to embrace you and to weep. The almighty will see that this woman, who had no tears to spare for forty years, has a small bounty of tears to share with her only son tonight.'

Somprabh sat upright. 'Mother', he said, 'take me across that pool. Take me to your hut. Give me shelter!'

'Son, there is an important task to accomplish before that.'

'A task? What is that, Mother?'

'Your father's freedom.'

'My father…Where is he?'

'He is captive.'

Somprabh's nostrils flared. He picked up his sword. 'I will make short work of his captors wherever they are.'

Lady Matangi's lips trembled. She looked straight into Somprabh's eyes. 'You are the one. You made him captive. Now free him', she murmured.

Somprabh drew himself up to his full height. His muscles were taut; his eyes closed. He rolled his head backwards. When he looked at his mother again, his eyes were red. 'Is the emperor…'

'Yes, Son. Do not dishonour me further.'

Somprabh collapsed to the ground. His elderly mother could barely slow down his fall.

After that, she stood at that spot, shivering. Her face was blanched. Sweat broke out on her forehead.

When Somprabh recovered from his faint, he saw that a shadow had come over his mother. 'Mother! Are you all right?' He shook her gently. 'I will never forgive myself…'

'You are blameless', Lady Matangi said. She lowered her head. Her hands were trembling now. She made a supreme effort to look at her son again with pleading eyes. 'Ambapali is your sister. But her father is Varshkar.'

She swooned into the thunderstruck Somprabh's arms and never awakened.

CHAPTER 156

FATHER AND SON

he guards at the prison stood at attention. Their stiff bearing and wide eyes showed that they were thunderstruck to see the general, alone, at the gate.

'Is he asleep?' Somprabh asked.

'No, Sir, he is awake', one of them said.

Somprabh nodded. 'All right. Open the door.'

Somprabh walked in to see the emperor calmly pacing the cell.

The emperor paused mid-stride and turned to face Somprabh. He showed no reaction. He sighed and said, 'Young man, have you come to kill me? I am ready.'

Somprabh stood silent, stunned.

Bimbisar continued: 'But I do have a last wish. It is this – if Ambapali has a son, he should be the emperor. It was my promise to her, the promise of the emperor of Magadha.'

Somprabh gulped, and said, 'I promise, Your Majesty.'

'By your sword?'

'By my sword.'

'Very well… Young man, you are young, energetic and a good swordsman. I trust… that you will make sure you behead me in a clean stroke. I have become an old man in these last hours, and I do not wish to tolerate pain. You could say that I have become a coward. Of course, I would say that this is not how I was…'

Somprabh felt the ground shifting below his feet. A film of sweat covered his face, and his tears mingled with his sweat. Words failed him. As Bimbisar stood nonplussed, Somprabh fell on his knees.

'Forgive me', Somprabh said. 'Forgive me, Father!'

Bimbisar's face crinkled with puzzlement. He leant forward. 'What? What is that you said?'

Somprabh's head lolled to the ground near Bimbisar's feet.

Bimbisar gingerly lowered himself on to his knees. He grunted as he lifted Somprabh and held him in an embrace. 'What did you say?' he asked again.

Somprabh looked into Bimbisar's eyes for the first time. 'Father,' he said in a hoarse voice.

Bimbisar said, 'I had never thought I would hear this word…Is it…Am I dreaming? Have I lost my mind out of fear of death? Tell me. Why are you here, and why do you…'

'Yes, Lord, you are this man's father.'

'Do you…? Say that again!'

'I am your son, Your Majesty.'

Bimbisar's held his son in a tight embrace. The two men heard each other's heartbeats. 'Say that again!' Bimbisar demanded.

'I am your son. I greet you, Father! Your son greets you', Somprabh said.

Bimbisar was crying like a child now. 'Live for a hundred years, Son. A thousand years!' he said.

'An important task remains, Father', Somprabh said.

'What is it?'

'To honour Mother.'

'Is Lady Matangi here?'

'She has left us.'

'Left? And I could not see her?'

'Father, now you can only see her body.'

Bimbisar recoiled and lowered his head. 'I see…Then…' He paced the cell a few times, walking listlessly and with a limp.

'She left behind a wealth of tears and two messages', Somprabh said.

Bimbisar sighed. 'I envy you your last meeting, Son. So there were two messages?'

'Yes, I have conveyed one to you.'

'And it is worth more than an empire. What is the other?'

'Lady Ambapali is my sister.'

Bimbisar collapsed in a heap.

Somprabh said, 'There is more, lord.'

'There is nothing more I want to hear. Kill me. Now!' Bimbisar's eyes betrayed deep grief.

'Lord, Lady Ambapali's father is Acharya Varshkar.'

Bimbisar clutched his heart, and his shoulders sank as he heaved a deep sigh of relief. He stood up and held Somprabh again.

'Father, come now. We must attend to Mother', Somprabh said.

They walked the long path to the funeral ground, the son leading the father. They bathed lady Matangi in the water of the Ganga, and Bimbisar took off his threadbare robe and covered her with it. Somprabh scoured the ground for dry wood and created a pyre. Father and son performed the last rites for the woman who had united them in her death. The air was heavy and humid, but the clouds held back their rain.

They sat under the tree below which Somprabh had surveyed the ground in what now seemed to be a different epoch. They sat silent till the funeral pyre was reduced to embers and ashes. There may have been much to talk about, but as they dwelt on the tangled threads of their fates, both men seemed to prefer the solace of silence.

Much later, Somprabh stood up, raised his sword to his turban and then placed it at Bimbisar's feet. Then he walked around his father. 'I will go now. Farewell, respected Father.'

Bimbisar staggered to his feet. 'Son, do not be…It is my time to go. This empire is yours!'

Somprabh said, 'This empire will be the inheritance of Lady Ambapali's son. A promise was made, and it must be kept.' He turned quickly and walked away.

Bimbisar called out to him, but Somprabh's figure had soon disappeared into the impenetrable darkness that surrounded the ground.

EPILOGUE

1

A year passed. Vaishali had won the war but lost the battle to recover its glory. The ten-day war had cost about a million lives. Many of those who had fought were maimed, and they lived miserable lives in the densely populated inner city. The major cities of the eight clans had been attacked as well, but the city of Vaishali had borne the brunt of the Magadhan war machine. Vaishali's grandeur was a thing of the past. The reminders of the ravages of war remained all over the city – half-burned mansions, dilapidated palaces and crumbling roads. Many citizens had fled. The city's markets no longer drew foreign merchants. The scions of its business families had sunk into lethargy. The masons and artisans saw no takers for their skills. In the aftermath of the war, famine and epidemic had taken a heavy toll on the children and the elderly. From one dawn to another, the city that had resounded with music, dance steps and laughter was reminded of its misery by the sounds of the angry, the dispossessed and the deprived. Cries of fury and arguments were heard most often.

The administrative machinery was broken. The assembly meetings ground to a halt after the last few meetings broke down in acrimony. The erstwhile elders who had run the government had retired and a new group of inexperienced administrators had not been able to fill their shoes. Most telling of all, the Holy Pond had dried up, and the Blue Lotus Palace had crumbled. People would often openly accost the governing officials. It was a sad departure from the times when the officials had been answerable to the public but commanded respect. There had been a spate in violent crime.

Many women were forced to prostitute themselves. Often, such women openly declared that Ambapali was their role model. They said that they would rule over the men who grovelled before them the way Ambapali did.

There was no respite for those who left the city. In the outskirts and villages, robbers were a menace. The fields were barren and untended. Villages were full of people whose skeletal frame and haggard faces told of starvation and misery.

The idyllic days of bonds within families and villages were gone. The sorrow of war weighed heavily on Vaishali.

·

The doors to the Palace of Seven Worlds were never opened. There was no sign that it was lit at night. No garlands or flowers bedecked the gates. The throngs of young men had, of course, stopped. People looked at the edifice and curse the palace and Lady Ambapali. A small part of the palace had collapsed. Ambapali did not care to get it renovated. The unthinkable happened slowly, but steadily: cracks appeared and then widened in the walls, creepers took hold and flourished in the neglect, and spiders, pigeons and bats claimed their territories.

Many of Ambapali's admirers were dead. She rebuffed those who survived. The unthinkable happened: The Palace of Seven Worlds was closed to all men. The hundreds of servants, clerks, guards and followers were dismissed. Only two faithful servants remained from the old days: the venerable Lallbhatt and Madlekha. Lallbhatt was that small establishment's connection to the outside world.

Naturally, only these two knew of Ambapali's son. When the time came, Lallbhatt carried him to the emperor of Magadha.

2

Acharya Varshkar ran the empire. Emperor Bimbisar became a recluse, spending months without leaving his palace, and showed signs of total eccentricity. He did not hold court, and the servants reported he had taken to walking the palace corridors half-dressed, brandishing his sword and muttering. The staff feared his moods and approached him with apprehension.

On one of those occasions when the emperor was indulging in his new habit, he was startled to see a man built as heavily as himself, carrying a staff and a bundle wrapped in a spotless white cloth. He raised his sword and growled, 'Who are you? What business do you have?'

A lesser man would have quailed. Lallbhatt deftly used his staff hand to draw a gold coin and show it to Bimbisar. The emperor gulped and drew closer. Lallbhatt gently placed his staff on the ground and uncovered the top of the bundle to reveal the beatific face of a sleeping baby.

The sight of the coin had calmed Bimbisar. It told him who had sent this unexpected visitor and explained how he had gained access to this part of the palace. The emperor could not take his eyes off the baby. His gaze was soft and loving. 'What is this, friend?'

'I believe he is the future emperor of Magadha, Your Majesty. I am Lady Ambapali's servant. She requests you to accept her gift.'

Bimbisar's lips moved, but he seemed to change his mind about speaking. He stretched his arms and took the baby. Nodding to Lallbhatt to follow him, he turned and walked along a dimly lit hallway until they were in a grand hall. Here, he placed the baby on the throne with a tenderness unimaginable only a short while ago. When he turned to Lallbhatt, the old faithful was wiping his tears. Emperor Bimbisar walked to a gong and rang it thrice. The baby slept through the commotion that followed. In no time, the emperor's bodyguards and the other palace staff had assembled. Some servants, rubbing their eyes, rushed to light up the hall.

The emperor was now laughing like a man possessed. 'Pay your respects! Celebrate this moment!' he shouted like a madman. 'Victory to the future emperor of Magadha!'

When his words sank in, the gathering broke into a tumult that woke up the baby. Lallbhatt took him in his lap, and the baby boy relaxed. From that epicentre, the good news spread to all parts of the palace. The lights came on. A new era had dawned.

Later, Bimbisar gave his sword to Lallbhatt and asked him to take it to Lady Ambapali. He also slipped a small object into Lallbhatt's palm. He made sure that no one saw what it was.

3

Another ten years passed. Some, who thought they were young, aged, some of the old died, and children became adults. Ambapali became a character from the past. Stories about her and the war became part of the folklore that the elders recited. As with any folklore, those stories contained elements of the bare truth, some embellishments and some flights of fancy. The new generation of youth grew up having heard of Ambapali and perhaps having glimpsed her in their childhood. The run-down Palace of Seven Worlds, with its crumbling walls and its aura of a magnificent past, its doors perennially closed, became an object of fascination for them. The legend of Ambapali, Bride of the city when the city was a centre of the world, gripped their minds. Now that neither man, nor God, nor elf could see her, her cult grew even stronger, fuelled by myth and speculation.

Gautam Buddha visited Vaishali after many years. His visit brought a dramatic turn of events. The main gate of the Palace of Seven Worlds was thrown open after more than a decade. Its giant hinges creaked, and the noise brought a frenzy on the city of Vaishali. The news that Ambapali would appear in public for her meeting with the Buddha spread across the city. A horde of young men – and women – flocked through the open gate to see Ambapali, the lady who had made emperors and kings grovel before her. In a pale imitation of the grandeur of early times, once again, elephants, palanquins, chariots and horses once again made their way to the Palace of Seven Worlds.

In the first compound, a woman dressed in an austere white robe sat atop an elegant chariot. The woman sat with her head bowed, ignoring the milling crowd which had been struck into silence as soon as they saw her. She wore not a single piece of jewellery, there was no touch of adornment on her. And yet, she exuded a radiance that struck awe into the onlookers, both men and women. A few maids stood behind her. They were flanked by horsemen, servants who carried incense and offerings for the Buddha.

Across Royal Avenue, on a platform under the large tree, sat the great sage. He was eighty years old, and his hair had turned white. He had a lined face, but his charisma had magnified over the decades. His ochre robed, lean and clean-shaved disciples sat in rows below the platform.

Lady Ambapali's chariot stopped some distance from him, and she dismounted with Lallbhatt's help. She proceeded on foot towards the sage, who sat in the Lotus position, his eyes closed and his visage serene.

'Lord, Lady Ambapali is here', the Buddha's disciple Anand said to him.

The Buddha opened his eyes, and his smile captivated all who stood before him. Ambapali prostrated herself before him and offered him incense. She placed a garland at his feet. With her hands folded, she said, 'Lord, I request you to grace my home with the monks of your order, and to accept lunch from me.' The Buddha smiled. Elated at this sign of acceptance, Ambapali performed a circumambulation around him, bowed again and left.

Now a commotion rose from the ranks of the other visitors. 'What has happened, Anand?' the Buddha asked.

Anand said, 'The leaders of the eight clans are arriving shortly to seek your blessings.'

The Buddha sighed. 'See, Anand, how times change. This may be my last visit to Vaishali. Recall our earlier times, when I told you and the others that Vaishali was a city that seemed blessed with divine powers. See how this city of gold, towers, unearthly gardens and learning has withered to a shadow of its past. See how hubris and decadence take their toll on the vigour of a nation.'

As Ambapali returned to the Palace of Seven Worlds, driven by Lallbhatt, her chariot's wheel collided with that of the chariot leading the procession of nobles of the eight clans. The arrogant noble shouted at Ambapali. 'Courtesan! Do you not see that you are in the way of the nobles? Move aside! Give way to your superiors!'

The crowd recoiled at this low and mean behaviour.

Ambapali, who had kept her head bowed all along, now raised her eyes and fixed her gaze on the noble before her. He flinched and looked towards the others for support.

'Move aside', Ambapali said. 'I am in a hurry to reach home. The Buddha will visit my abode for lunch tomorrow, and I cannot waste a single moment.'

Another noble signalled to the one in front to be quiet. 'Lady Ambapali, we will give you a hundred thousand gold coins. Let us host this lunch. It is very important for us.'

Ambapali looked straight ahead. 'It is not a thing to trade. And even if you gave me all of Vaishali, my answer would be – no. Now do not embarrass yourselves any further. Stand aside!'

Lallbhatt cracked his whip, and Ambapali's chariot surged forward, blowing dust into the air. The nobles were crestfallen.

Now the leaders of the eight clans greeted the Buddha and his Sangha and prostrated themselves before him. They announced their names one by one. They sat on the ground and asked the Buddha to preach to them.

The great sage spoke with simplicity and touched them with his uplifting sermon. The chief minister bowed before the Buddha and said, 'Lord, we trust you and the entire Sangha will bless us with your presence and have lunch with us tomorrow?'

The Buddha smiled at Anand, who said, 'The Lord has already accepted Lady Ambapali's invitation.'

The nobles were disappointed, but there was nothing they could do. They performed their obeisance to the Buddha and his followers and left.

4

The next day, the Buddha and his monk followers marched to the Palace of Seven Worlds. They wore their traditional ochre attire and carried their begging bowls. As the procession wound its way along Royal Avenue, with their heads down, drawing the admiration of the city's people, Ambapali was supervising the finishing touches to the preparations and elegant but bright decorations that an army of newly recruited staff had worked on overnight. The Palace of Seven Worlds looked vibrant and alive. Its walls and corners had been dusted. Simple banners, bunting and flowers added colour to the whole complex. Meanwhile, on Royal Avenue, the legendary sage and his followers were given tokens of love and adulation from the throngs on either side. Many merchants and their families stepped forward to lay their best clothes on the path so that the holy procession would walk on them. The sage and his followers were showered with flower petals. They were greeted with cries of welcome and admiration at every step.

Ambapali stood at the outer doorway of the Palace of Seven Worlds. She prostrated herself before the Buddha. 'Lord, I am blessed forever. Thank you for this honour. Please come in.'

The Buddha and his Sangha walked across the compounds of the Palace of Seven Worlds. They crossed the seven walls and reached the inner compound, where Ambapali had made arrangements for the Buddha and the twelve hundred monks to eat. The monks took their seats with their usual discipline.

Immediately, Ambapali and her maids started serving them the simple but delicious fare. The monks thanked their hostess and ate their fill. When the Buddha signalled that the meal was over, Ambapali first supervised the clearing of the leaves and then sat on a mat before the Buddha.

The Buddha then gave a short sermon. Ambapali listened to him with rapt attention. He then asked her, 'Ambapali, what do you desire?'

'Lord, I do have one wish that I want to beg for', Ambapali said.

'And what is that?'

'I would like one of your monks to gift me his upper robe.'

The Buddha smiled and looked at Anand. Anand immediately took off his upper and handed it to Ambapali. Ambapali bowed and took her leave. She returned in a few moments, dressed in the robe. She had removed her simple silken clothes and the little jewellery that she had worn. As she approached the Buddha, she trembled and fell at his feet.

The Buddha touched her shoulder and gently directed her to sit before him. 'Rise, Benefactress', he said. 'What do you want?'

'Lord, how can I describe the irony of my impure life? I was forced to live a life in which my magnificent body dictated my destiny, and I never had the opportunity to pursue piety. Lord, I have wealth…much wealth, and it is the accumulation of my impure austerities. I am restless and empty-hearted. I cannot describe how I have survived until now. Two days in my life have a special significance for me. On the first, I became the mother of Magadha's future emperor. But because of what fate has gifted me today, I have the temerity to want more.'

The Buddha smiled and nodded to her to proceed.

'Lord, now that you have blessed this abode, how can it be allowed to signify lust and sin? Even a trace of its past must not be allowed to remain…Lord, I would like to submit all of this – the buildings and the land, the chariots, the elephants, the treasury and the stores – everything that I have to the Sangha. As for myself, this robe is enough to protect my modesty. Lord Tathagat, give me shelter. I will honour the gift of this robe.'

She fell sobbing at the Buddha's feet. The Buddha placed his hand on her head and beckoned her to sit before him. As Ambapali calmed down, a new radiance emanated from her.

The Buddha turned to Anand. 'Young man, this palace will be converted into our foremost monastery. I wish this Palace of Seven Worlds to become an establishment for the search of truth and for the education of monks.'

The onlookers who witnessed this great event passed on the word to others. Soon the whole city knew of Ambapali's astonishing sacrifice. Cries of 'Long live Ambapali!' echoed in the city and wafted through to the newly incarnated monastery.

5

The great sage sat on a thin mat atop a flat rock in the Palace of Seven Worlds. He seemed rested after his days of travel, and this enhanced his usual radiance.

Ambapali entered her former domain in a completely new persona. Her head was shaved, and her body draped in a shapeless ochre garment. Her feet were bare and bleeding, and her eyes swollen. Her closest attendants had accompanied her when she left the Palace of Seven Worlds, and now her following had increased manifold.

Anand greeted the procession with joined palms and spoke with reverence. 'Lady Ambapali, are you all right? May I help you?'

'Sir, I wish to ask the Lord to initiate me into monkhood', Ambapali said.

Anand stood silent for a few moments. Then he bowed and said, 'Very well, Lady, I shall convey your request to the lord.'

He walked to the spot where Buddha sat. The sage sensed his presence and opened his eyes.

Anand spoke in a whisper. 'Lord, Lady Ambapali is at the door. She is caked in mud, and her eyes are red. She looks very tired. She asks to be initiated.'

The Buddha said, 'Is she to become a monk out of compulsion? Because she has given away all that she has? Or because she sees the purity in our ways? What do you think?'

'Lord, can women who have adopted our ways follow our eightfold path?'

'Yes, they can', Gautam Buddha said in a resolute tone.

'Lord, if women who have no refuge seek it in the Sangha, and if we choose to grant it to them and they can achieve our goals, then Ambapali can surely be accepted among us.'

'Very well', the Buddha said. 'It is decided then. Ambapali is to be welcomed into the Sangha on the strength of her purity; not in return for her generosity, and not because she needs shelter.'

Anand went swiftly to Ambapali and conveyed this decision to her. Ambapali's eyes moistened. She said, 'Sir, as in an earlier life I took a dip in a holy pond and wore a new garb that marked a new phase of my being, so today your acceptance marks a new phase of my existence. I accept the eightfold path.'

Anand returned to the Buddha with this news. The great sage said, 'Now listen to me, Anand. Had we not admitted women in our midst, this faith would have lasted a thousand years. Today's decision means that it will last in this form for five hundred years. Just as fertile fields of paddy and of sugarcane are laid to waste by insects, so will the faith be eaten by some of our future adherents. But just as the farmer builds mud walls and uses herbs to protect his life-sustaining field, I must build a system of checks and balances to allow nuns into our order. Ask Ambapali to come here.'

Ambapali and her followers performed their obeisance to the Buddha by walking around him and prostrating themselves. They chanted the eternal lines.

Buddham saranam gacchami – I seek refuge in the Buddha

Sangham saranam gacchami – I seek refuge in the Sangha

Dhammam saranam gacchami – I seek refuge in the faith

The Buddha addressed Ambapali. 'Blessed Ambapali, hear me! The faith that you knew until now had at its core attachment and not detachment, union and not separation, multiplying the desires and not decimating them, living in dissatisfaction and not finding solace, seeking the crowd and not finding oneself. Know that your future will take you away from ease and towards difficulty, but it will lead you on a path that will be the opposite to your earlier path.' The sage was silent for some time. Then he smiled and spoke again. 'Go now, Ambapali. Today you have earned a wealth that is beyond compare. Now you must use this wealth for your own good and for the good of the world.' He raised his voice so that his words rang loud and clear in the whole garden. 'Monks, today we welcome the great and the pure nun Ambapali among us.'

The garden echoed with cheers and victory slogans. The monks and the commoners knew that they had witnessed a moment of great historical importance. Ambapali made her way through the throng of men who looked at her with pure adoration. She felt a lightness in her heart. As she paused to wipe her tears of happiness, she noticed a monk who looked familiar. He had followed her for a while.

'Who are you?' she asked.

'I am Somprabh, Lady', he said.

Ambapali did not speak. Her steps did not falter. A smile played on her face as she kept walking. The setting sun painted the landscape in a saffron hue. One seeing Ambapali from a distance may have been forgiven for imagining the parting of her hair was filled with sindoor, the vermillion powder that is the mark of a bride.

AFTERWORD

BRIDE OF THE CITY: A POPULAR INDIAN NOVEL

Acharya Chatursen wrote twenty-eight novels (including *Hriday Ki Parakh, Somnath, Vayam Rakshamah, Sona Aur Khoon, Vaishali Ki Nagarvadhu* and *Aalamgir*), about four hundred and fifty short stories and many essays on history, religion, politics, society and health. *Vaishali Ki Nagarvadhu* (literally, *The Bride of the City of Vaishali*) is by far his most popular creation. It is popular in the sense that it employs popular elements in its narrative structure. Founded on history and mythology, this is a work that presents social, political, and cultural transformations and conflicts that occurred in the times when Buddhism and Jainism took birth.

Bride of the City was published in Hindi over 1948 and 1949, but as the author informs us in his preface to the novel, it was researched and written over the period 1939–1947. This was a crucial period in Indian history. As the end of colonial rule neared, the possible forms of the emerging free Indian nation occupied the thoughts not only of political leaders but also of the public at large. On the one hand, there was the dimension of republicanism versus imperialism[1], and on the other hand, the vexing issue of how different identity groups would share the assets and responsibilities of the new nation. The debates, machinations and conflicts of those years have no obvious connection with the context of *Bride of the City*. Although the story takes place around 500 BCE[2], it addresses themes of republicanism versus imperialism, national interest, women's rights and the status of mixed races that have very visible echoes and grave consequences in the times in which the book was conceived, researched and published.

Rajendra Yadav[3] juxtaposed the constructs of a popular novel set in the past and the challenges of the times in which the novel was composed in his

---

1 The British Raj included 565 'Princely States' that were vassals of the Raj.

2 No dates are mentioned in the novel.

3 Rajendra Yadav (1929–2013) was a Hindi Fiction writer. He was a pioneer of the *Nayi Kahani* (New Story) movement and editor of *Hans* literary magazine, which he revived in 1986. A film based on his novel *Sara Akash* (*The Infinite Cosmos*) was one of the early films in Indian 'parallel cinema', or cinema that was not bound by the conventions of 'Bollywood'.

analysis of Devaki Nandan Khatri's *Chandrakanta* (1888). Yadav's was the first such analysis in Hindi literature, and he criticised the absence of such studies in the field. He wrote:

> 'The criminal negligence shown by Hindi literary critics towards this aspect of criticism has long niggled at me. It finally drove me to my resolve to pierce the haze of sorcery that is Chandrakanta. After all, every generation explored the ruins of the past and peered into magical wells to understand their predecessors' lives and times. Assessing the path to their present has energised them and shown them the way to the future.'[4]

A book's popularity has two sides – economic and cultural. The marketplace settles economic success, while cultural recognition depends on the work's content, its structure and their bearing on society. In *Bride of the City*, Acharya Chatursen showed readers aspects of the past that had a grave bearing on their present. As he explains in his preface:

> 'It is true that this is a novel. But it is even more true that this is a serious enquiry seeking to peer through the haze of two millennia that has shrouded the ebb and tide of religion, literature, politics and culture, and that historians have chosen to ignore.'

Clearly, Chatursen blended mythology with in-depth historical research to produce this epic. The Gandharvs and Jarasandh hark back to mythology, and the snake woman Kundani, with her magical powers, is one of many episodes adding elements of fantasy to enrich the narrative. Nationalists often pass off mythology as history, and this has its dangers. A novelist has the license to mix history and mythology, and a great novelist has the ability to blur the borders between opinion, history and mythology into a single compelling narrative. Despite Chatursen's dexterity, *Bride of the City* is not a historical novel. The narrative includes many supernatural and sensational turns of events that are neither historical nor logical. These elements do add to the novel's cultural popularity.

The novel starts with an introduction to the geography, politics and society of Vaishali. An abandoned girl child is discovered in a mango orchard. This girl grows into the fabled Ambapali, whose revenge on the Republic of Vaishali gives the novel its overriding story arch. On the long journey of revenge, the narrative takes us through subplots of deception, intrigue, politics, State expansionism, love, lust, conspiracies, fights and open warfare, to end with the rejection of the materialistic life. Ambapali and many other characters take refuge in Buddhism

4 Rajendra Yadav (2014). *Atharah Upanyaas*, ('Eighteen Novels'), p. 19. Delhi: Radhakrisha Prakashan.

to find meaning in their lives. Many kingdoms and republics – including Sravasti, Kaushambhi, Videha, Anga, Kalinga, Gandhar – are part of the setting at various times. However, Vaishali and Magadha dominate the story, and it is their conflict that sucks in the others.

The conflict between Vaishali and Magadha is not a simple matter of boundaries and assets. It is about the clashing forces of republicanism and imperialism and of Aryans and mixed races and the establishments that support these contending forces in their desire to accumulate greater power and status. King Prasenjit's son, Vidudhab, details the process by which mixed breeds have been segregated and had their rights usurped:

> 'This is the mean Aryan tradition: to collect a bevy of women to fulfil your desires, to buy them, win them over with deceit, to use force where needed. To abduct weeping maidens, to rob unconscious, intoxicated virgins of their innocence. And there is no bar to having them without marrying them. You so-called brave Kshatriyas collect beauties by fighting, winning, bribing…and these so-called Brahmans, those cowards, conduct yagyas for you and grovel before you to collect the slave girls that your unions produce. [...] You Aryans are wicked beyond belief! The king of Videha called a council. One old Brahman received thousands of cows with gold coins tied to their horns and two hundred slave women wearing golden ornaments. It makes me sick! The Brahman sold the cows and took the gold and the women home. If those women have children, you will gleefully declare them mixed breeds.'

The vexed question of rights and powers is related to the social transitions of the period. Different identity groups coexisted, and power struggles were frequent. The measure of power was the ability to influence political and social decision-making. For an extended period, the Brahmans had absolute power in such matters. The emergence of the ascetic orders of Buddhism and Jainism brought a new protocol for social engagement – one in which different races and groups treated each other as equals. Brahmanism had nourished imperialism; the new faiths catalysed social democracy. The Buddha's effort was to dismantle the distinctions between 'high' and 'low' in the Brahman-established worldview. He emphasised self-searching and introspection over-elaborate and expensive rituals. He freed many communities from the oppression of the Brahmans and initiated young Brahmans into monkhood, directing them towards celibacy and austerity. Many wealthy scions gave up their luxuries to join his order. The Brahmans reacted to these sweeping changes by advocating that the path to giving up worldly pleasures should be taken after one had established a family and grown into old age. The new faiths of Buddhism and Jainism shattered the old order.

Prasenjit's mixed-breed son usurps the throne from his father and takes power in Kosala. His anguish comes through in his questions to his father: 'Why did you produce me with a slave? And does my life become less valuable because you did? Do I not deserve a place in society?' The churning of social and class barriers defined new political equations, and conflict became a means of resolving these new equations.

In the novel, Bimbisar's ambitions for his empire and his desire for Ambapali lead to a terrifying war between Magadha and Vaishali. The two warring sides are stretched to their limits in this war. While the Magadhans seek to expand their empire, for Vaishali, it is a question of survival of its republican system. The leaders of Vaishali believe in the inherent superiority of their ways. They see their organisation as one driven by duties and not by rights. They are governed by a group and not by an individual; this group is elected by citizens. But the system in Vaishali has its flaws. Many of its inhabitants are non-Licchavis, who do not have voting rights. In this supposedly ideal system, discrimination based on gender, race and caste exists. The prevailing law is that the most beautiful young woman may not pursue her own aspirations. She must be the property of the nation – the Bride of the city. The establishment of Vaishali uses this law to devour Ambapali. Chief Minister Sunand goes down on his knees to get Ambapali to acquiesce to the 'cursed law':

'Lady Ambapali, I need not look deep inside you to understand that you are burning with fury. All I can say is this: save us. If you do not, the city will be aflame, and our enemies will fan the fires. These fires will consume many people you know and love. I beg you to give yourself to Vaishali, on your own terms.'

The oppression of women is common to the republican and imperial systems. Princess Kalingasena is compelled to renounce her love and give herself to the ageing King Prasenjit, whose wife Nandini tells her that in their present situation, 'The man has total rights over his women's body and soul.'

In the novel, Kalingasena submits to Prasenjit's machinations but does not accept an erasure of her identity. 'I will fight this, Lady Nandini', she says. 'I have given myself to King Prasenjit, but I have not given up my right to think, to have opinions and to state them. I will claim my rights.' Queen Nandini replies, 'I understand you, Sister. But I do not see what you can do, and I do not wish you to come to grief. Here we use the word pati, master, for husband.' Kalingasena says, 'I will change this, Lady!'

In Chapter 60, 'The Panchala Council', Chatursen dwells at length on the process by which women's rights were usurped. The members of the council abandon Vedic traditions to institutionalise new marriage laws. Whether in this council or the assembly of Vaishali, policies were designed and decisions made by men. In the Panchala Council, one member clearly states women had rights under the Vedic traditions that are to be taken away.

It is interesting, therefore, that most well-developed and powerful characters in *Bride of the City* are women. Ambapali accepts the 'cursed law' but does so on her terms. These terms take her to dizzying heights of wealth and power, from where she can get her revenge on Vaishali. Between the ravages and savagery of war and intrigue, words of humanity emerge, coming from women such as Kalingasena or Rohini. Seeing slavery on her arrival in Vaishali shocks the newlywed. She asks in anguish, 'How can people buy and sell humans like sheep and goats? And how can you have unlimited rights over them?' The princess of Champa also stands for human dignity.

Among the men, it is Somprabh who displays humanitarian concerns and principles. His bravery and his strategic manoeuvres take the Magadhans to the cusp of victory in a bitter and bloody war. However, he is fundamentally opposed to a war waged for the emperor's personal benefit. He calls for a ceasefire even as his forces are within sight of victory. He does not hesitate to take on the emperor. Before duelling with the emperor, he says, 'I have not studied at Takshila for nothing. It is my understanding that an empire's army must be used to advance the empire. Not to fulfil the emperor's lusts.'

The horrors of war and the feelings expressed by characters such as Somprabh, Kalingasena, Rohini and others are pointers to Chatursen's hopes for a future less riven with conflict and inhumanity for his country. The recurring references to the plight of the mixed races reflect his hope that the emerging nation would provide equal opportunities to the marginalised. More than the recurring themes of war and violence, decadence and lust, racism and prejudice, it is the egalitarianism of the Buddha's preaching that is the central theme of this huge work. Acharya Chatursen used the canvas of this novel to depict the possibility of a future nation in which there was no place for oppression based on gender, race and caste.

Dr Ram Manohar Lohia[5] is said to have speculated on what might have gone through the Buddha's mind when he met Ambapali, or the Christ's when he met Mary Magdalene. It is natural for a grand encounter between persons who represent the sacred and the profane to arouse curiosity in popular culture. The meeting of the Buddha and Ambapali, recorded in Buddhist texts, has become a part of Indian folklore. Dan Brown wrote his bestseller *The Da Vinci Code* based on stories and unofficial statements. *Bride of the City* is a similar creation on a grander scale. Its author may have spent a decade researching and writing it, but

---

5 Dr Ram Manohar Lohia (1910–1976) was a socialist thinker and political leader, known for his progressive views on abolition of caste and protection of civil liberties.

the reader unfamiliar with its context is free to just enjoy it as a great read – and perhaps find shades of *The Da Vinci Code, Lord of the Rings* or *Game of Thrones* in it.

Balwant Kaur

Assistant Professor, Department of Hindi
Miranda House
The University of Delhi
Delhi, India
June 2020

GLOSSARY

Acharya – A highly learned person

Arya – Used in this text as an honourable prefix for a male. Pronounced aar-yuh.

Aryaa – Feminine equivalent of Arya (see above). Pronounced aar-yaa.

Ajivika – An ascetic sect that emerged in India about the same time as Buddhism and Jainism.

Akshauhini – A battle formation of 218,700 warriors.

Asur – Traditionally, demons who fought against the Devs or gods. In this work, the term should be interpreted as a tribe of aboriginal people.

Ashwamedha Yagya – Sacred ceremony demonstrating sovereign power. It ended with the sacrifice of a horse.

Bhoj – Feast.

Brahma – The creator, in the Hindu Trinity.

Brahman – The caste of priests.

Bhagwat Gita – Hindu religious and philosophical text.

Chakra – In traditional Indian medicine, one of seven centres of energy along the spinal column.

Chandal – A 'lower' caste, responsible for disposing of corpses.

Charvaka – Ancient philosophical school emphasising materialism and rejecting ritualism.

Dasyu – Aboriginal people, hostile to the main characters of the novel.

Dharma – The rightful path

Gandharv – Heavenly being. Also used for skilled singers.

Havi Yagya – A type of yagya. Yagya is a ritual done in front of a sacred fire, often with mantras.

Jiva – A living being

Kshatriya – The warrior caste.

Madhvik – A type of wine.

Maharaja – Great king.

Maireya – A type of wine.

Manav – Literally, human. Used in this work as a term for the Asur Aboriginals to refer to non-Aboriginals.

Mantra – Sacred verse.

Moksha – Salvation.

Namaste – Greeting in which the two palms are joined in front of the chest.

Nirukta – The science of etymology.

Raja – King.

Rajsuya Yagya – A grand and sacred ceremony that established the consecration of a king.

Havi Yagya – A ritual, part of the Rajsuya Yagya.

Ratna Yagna – A ritual, part of the Rajsuya Yagya.

Samadhi – A state of meditative consciousness.

Samrat – Emperor.

Sangha – Literally an association or community; the organisation led by the Buddha.

Shudra – The lowest caste

Siddha – The perfect one.

Sutra – Literally a thread, but generally used to mean a related collection of tales or texts.

Vaishya – Caste of traders, merchants and professionals.

Vihara – Monastery.

Vratya – Wandering ascetic.

Veena – Ancient Indian plucked-string musical instrument.

Yagya – Sacred ceremony.

Bodhi tree – The tree under which the Buddha attained enlightenment.